T0129825

CHESAPEAKE CHAOS

MALEVOLENCE AND BETRAYAL IN COLONIAL MARYLAND

A LUKE TREMAYNE ADVENTURE

Geoff Quaife

Order this book online at www.trafford.com/
or email orders@trafford.com

Most Trafford titles are also available at major online book retailers.

Note for Librarians: A cataloguing record for this book is available from Library
and Archives Canada at www.collectionscanada.ca/amicus/index-e.html

Printed in Victoria, BC, Canada.

ISBN: 978-1-4269-0673-2 (soft)
ISBN: 978-1-4269-0674-9 (ebook)

*Our mission is to efficiently provide the world's finest, most comprehensive
book publishing service, enabling every author to experience success.
To find out how to publish your book, your way, and have it available
worldwide, visit us online at www.trafford.com*

Trafford rev. 8/3/2009

www.trafford.com

North America & international
toll-free: 1 888 232 4444 (USA & Canada)
phone: 250 383 6864 ♦ fax: 812 355 4082

CHESAPEAKE CHAOS

Geoff Quaife

Trafford
PUBLISHING

LEADING CHARACTERS

Cromwell's Men

Luke Tremayne	Cromwell's agent, and cavalry colonel
Andrew Ford	Luke's senior sergeant
John Halliwell	Luke's sergeant

The Browne Plantation and Neighbours

Robert Browne	Maryland gentleman planter
Elizabeth Browne	His wife
James Browne	His son
Thomas Browne	His son
Priscilla Browne	His daughter
Lucy Browne	His daughter
Humphrey Norton	His servant
Abigail Hicks	His servant
Rachel O'Brien	His servant
Timothy Lipton	His overseer
Matthew Sherman	His gentleman tenant, and physician
Richard Goodwin	His gentleman tenant

The Severn Puritan Settlement

Harry Lloyd	Nephew of Edward Lloyd

The Amerindians

Tamuagh	Susquehanna war chief
Black Cougar	Mysterious Susquehanna warrior
Straight Arrow	Local Nanticoke leader

White Deer	*His son*
One Ear	*Renegade Nanticoke*

The Jesuits And The French

Father Renaud	*French Jesuit envoy*
Father Austin	*Head, English mission*
Jean de Liette	*Captain, French marines*

Real Historical Characters

Lord Baltimore	*Catholic Proprietor of Maryland*
William Stone	*Protestant Governor of Maryland*
Sir William Berkeley	*Anglican Royalist Governor of Virginia*
Oliver Cromwell	*Commander of the armies of the English Republic*
Edward Lloyd	*Commandant of the Severn Puritan settlement*

PLACES AND NATIONS MENTIONED IN THE TEXT

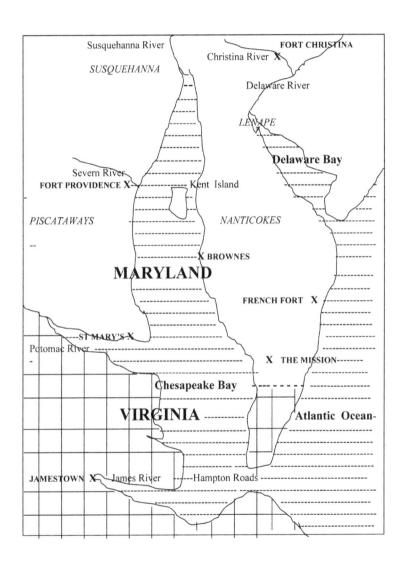

THE BROWNE PLANTATION

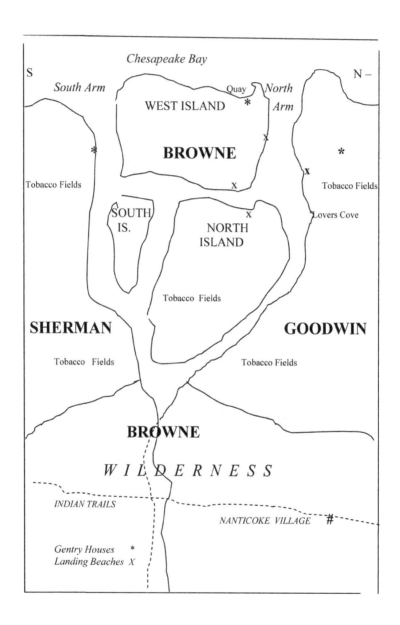

1

Early January 1650, Dublin Castle

LUKE TREMAYNE WAS TALL AND WELL BUILT WITH SPARKLING blue eyes. Formally, this thirty year old Cornish born Lieutenant Colonel commanded the cavalry regiments attached to Dublin Castle. He was responsible for maintaining local law and order, while Oliver Cromwell led the army of the new English Republic in the conquest of Ireland. Tremayne's secret role was as special agent for Cromwell, who as the effective leader of the army had a powerful influence on the struggling English government. Luke worried that the politicians would call Cromwell back to England to confront a renewed threat from a Scotland, now aligned with the new King, Charles II, before Irish resistance was broken. Luke detested politicians and Catholics.

Cromwell was reluctantly resident in Dublin Castle recuperating from an illness that had slowed his campaign to capture the inland towns. He was impatient to return to the field and complete his God given task. Therefore Luke was apprehensive when summoned to attend the ailing general on a drizzling winter morning. The general's chamber was cold, and his demeanour abrupt, 'Bored are we, Tremayne. Wearied by patrol after patrol in areas already pacified?'

Cromwell's next remark was unexpected, 'What do you know about the Province of Maryland?'

'It's a colony next to Virginia, created as a haven for English and Irish Catholics by Lord Baltimore, to whom the late King gave absolute power,' replied a disconcerted Luke.

'Yes, but it is in chaos. The situation is more complex than this Irish fiasco. There is a peculiar malevolence at work in the province, and I have been asked to help.'

'Why would a Catholic colony which has remained Royalist throughout our civil conflict seek help from yourself, the scourge of the Papists; and even more incredible, why would you accede to such a strange request?' asked an incredulous Luke.

'Lord Baltimore is anxious to recruit settlers for Maryland as he believed many displaced local gentry would be anxious to find a new home away from the troubles of Ireland. At the same time he emphasized that in the changing political circumstances he has a number of Protestant settlers, and had recently encouraged a group of Puritans expelled from Virginia by its Anglican governor, to resettle in his province.'

'But how does any of this interest you?' probed the bemused Luke.

Cromwell responded, 'Lord Baltimore has stressed his loyalty to the new English government, and as a measure of his good faith has promulgated a law for Maryland that encourages Anglican, Puritan and Catholic to put aside their religious differences, and tolerate each other. But there is a personal factor. Some years ago Baltimore recruited a Royalist officer of considerable wealth to settle in Maryland, and to monitor the situation for him. This man is known to both of us. In the early days of the Civil War he was one of the most brilliant Royalist officers, and my direct opponent. Our patrols clashed on many occasions, and on one of these you were captured. Even though you were the most junior of officers you negotiated a remarkable release.'

Luke had tried to forget the rash decisions of his youth. As a young cornet he led his troop into an ambush, and spent three days negotiating their release. The Royalist commander was impressed by his behaviour, and let him and his men return to their company. Luke thought for a while and tentatively exclaimed, 'Robert Browne!'

'Yes, after he played a major role in 1642, Browne inherited his family estates and retired to civilian life, but almost immediately migrated to Maryland. There were rumours that his men had participated in a massacre, and that the King to avoid embarrassment, encouraged his emigration.'

'So, what's the problem with Browne today which involves us?' Luke asked.

'Browne wrote regularly informing Baltimore of the countless plots against his authority by Puritans, Catholics, his own administration and neighbouring Virginia. His last letter hinted at malevolent forces at work, after which no more letters were received. Baltimore contacted his Governor, William Stone, who reported that Browne was still on his estate. His Lordship suspects that Browne is still writing, and his letters are being intercepted. I think Browne may have turned against Baltimore. I am interested to discover the nature of the malevolent forces, as they may endanger the new English government's attempt to bring the American colonies under its control. We need to know what we are getting involved in,' replied Cromwell.

'Where do I fit in?' asked Luke, fearful of the answer.

'As Baltimore cannot trust anyone, and Browne may be in serious trouble, you will go to Maryland and find out what is going on. You will have authority from both Lord Baltimore, and from the English government to act as you see fit. You do not need to use subterfuge. I doubt whether you or your men would make good settlers. You will take twenty or more troopers with you and openly present yourself as a military mission on a fact finding enterprise for Lord Baltimore, or where it is more appropriate for the English Government, or even myself. Use your discretion as to whom you claim to represent. You may need to be all things to all men.'

'Are there any specific objectives?'

'Yes, Lord Baltimore's attempt to stay on side with the current Puritan government in England is being undermined from within the Catholic camp by renegade laity, and the behaviour of the Jesuit fathers. Despite the orders of their Provincial to submit to Baltimore, not all have done so. There are rumours that they have links with the French Jesuit missionaries working out of Canada. To both Lord Baltimore and the English government French involvement in the Chesapeake is completely unacceptable. Be ready to depart on the next ship leaving for Barbados, from where you will sail to Virginia, and then make your way to Maryland.'

'It will be a change from patrolling the wintry Irish countryside,' Luke muttered almost sarcastically.

'More than you think. It will be very, very different. There are no horses in Maryland. You will leave your mounts behind. Your troop will have to adapt to being infantrymen. As there are no horses there is no need for pikes. Tremayne, you are now colonel of a special force of musketeers. Against regulations arm your officers and men alike with pistols, muskets, swords and daggers.'

Four Months Later, Jamestown, Virginia

Luke's departure was delayed for a week during which time he met Lord Baltimore in Bristol and received a satchel of further authorizations for any activity he thought necessary, and letters for numerous persons along the Chesapeake. It was not easy for the twenty five soldiers of the English Republic to gain passage through the still Royalist colony of Barbados. Local authorities were alert to imminent attack from forces of the English Republic, and suspected any newcomers as har-

4

bingers of that invasion. A large purse, and a mission for a royalist peer removed some suspicion. Virginia might prove more difficult.

Luke and his men disembarked from a sea going merchantman at Jamestown and immediately set about organizing their progress up Chesapeake Bay to Browne's plantation, which was located across several islands scattered along its north eastern shore. With two of his men guarding their possessions which had been dumped at the quayside, the others found lodgings at a waterside tavern, The Porpoise. The men had trouble settling in, delayed by a suspicious landlord who was unhappy about such a large group of armed strangers seeking hospitality. Payment in advance, and in English coins, rather than in tobacco, overcame his hesitation. Luke had hardly completed negotiations when an affray occurred on the quayside opposite the tavern. He emerged into the daylight to see his two men being attacked, and dragged away from their possessions by five or six armed locals. Their leader was a pimply faced, smiling youth whose nondescript uniform indicated some local authority.

Luke, followed by the rest of his irate soldiers, approached the locals and asked quietly, 'Sir, why are my men being harassed?'

The callow youth asked impertinently, 'These scum belong to you?'

Luke ignored the insult. 'By whose authority do you detain the servants of an English gentleman on a mission for Lord Baltimore?'

'Scum of all sort try to enter the colony. I maintain law and order in these waterside precincts. Your men refused to identify themselves, and resisted my attempts to search their possessions for contraband. Do you have any proof of who you are, or any authority for entering this colony?' demanded the novice soldier.

Luke by habit preferred to be the hammer rather than the anvil. He turned on the nasty young man, 'Cuds-me boy! I show my authorization to someone of equal status. Take me to the Governor!'

'The Governor is up river, but I will take your documents to the local magistrate.'

'No, you will not. Send the magistrate to me, release my men and return the goods you purloined, or I will charge all of you with theft. Identify yourself you pockfredden turd!'

Luke's men surrounded the smaller local group. Their pompous leader suddenly realised he was outnumbered, and tried to push his way through Luke's encirclement. The English soldiers held their ground. The youth whispered that he was Cadet Lieutenant John Castle. He turned in fear to face a coldly furious Luke who with two hands lifted the puny knave by his doublet and berated him, 'You need a lesson cowbaby. Remember your scriptures about a haughty spirit coming before a fall?' With that Luke lifted the lad almost above his head and threw him into a large muddy puddle. The youth got to his feet spitting mud and venom amidst the laughter and catcalls of Luke's men, and even some of Castle's own gang . He ran away shouting profanities, and threatening to return with the magistrate, and a body of men to wipe the smile from Luke's face.

Andrew, Luke's long standing and experienced sergeant, was not impressed with his Colonel. 'Jehu, Luke! We are not even in Maryland, and you have provoked an argument with the local authorities. So much for a diplomatic mission!'

Luke ignored the criticism and his party re-entered the inn. After a meal of a corn pancake filled with chicken pieces they heard the beat of a single drum and the plod of many feet. Through a bay window in the front chamber of the tavern Luke saw a large company of armed men approaching The Porpoise, led by a well dressed civilian on horse back, and a leering Castle.

2

LUKE CURSED THAT CROMWELL HAD MISLED HIM. THERE WAS at least one horse on the Chesapeake. Luke was about to prepare for an onslaught on the tavern when the civilian whom Luke assumed was the magistrate, ordered the men to stand down, and entered the establishment on his own. Luke approached the magistrate and introduced himself as a Cornish gentleman, who disgusted with the execution of the late King, had offered his services to Lord Baltimore. He handed over his authorization from the lord, and waved another letter from Baltimore for the Governor of Virginia. The magistrate who identified himself as Charles Atkinson read Baltimore's authorization, but he was more impressed by the sealed letter to the Governor. He ushered Luke towards a bench in the far corner of the tavern's large chamber, and ordered a jug of Dutch beer.

'I'll pass on the letter to the Governor. He and Lord Baltimore have worked together for many years, and we harboured his brother Leonard, the then Governor of Maryland when the unruly settlers on Kent Island revolted against Baltimore's authority. Unfortunately that co-operation may not last much longer.'

'Why?' asked an interested Luke.

'According to our Governor, Sir William Berkeley, the new King has withdrawn Baltimore's charter, and turned Maryland into a royal province.'

'Strange! Baltimore knows nothing of this?' exclaimed Luke.

'A new royal governor, the poet Sir William Davenant has been appointed, and has already left Jersey to take up his position,' continued Atkinson.

'Why would the King do such a thing? Baltimore has been a loyal Royalist throughout the Civil War.'

'The King, apparently anxious about the imminent English Republican attack on his loyal American colonies felt that Baltimore's toleration of Puritans was unacceptable. In addition there are many Royalists, within and outside Maryland, that resent Baltimore's absolute power. What they accept from a King, they resent in an absent lord.'

'That I hear goes for many Virginians?'

'Many Royalist Virginians cannot see the point of two separate colonies on Chesapeake Bay, and resent the interfering nature of Baltimore especially his restrictive Indian and trading policies. Consequently Tremayne, your paper support from Baltimore will be of little value in the anarchy that has enveloped Maryland for a decade. Your soldiers are your real authority.'

'What do you mean?'

'Law and order is only rarely enforced by Baltimore's representatives. Each planter is an independent authority relying on the firepower of his men to maintain his position. There is absolutely no sense of community. There are no real towns, and most public events are held in the manor houses of the leading gentry. Governor William Stone has effective control only in the south around St Mary's; the Puritan republicans dominate along the Severn River, while Kent Island off the Eastern shore contains troublemakers of various kinds. The only constant is Baltimore's legal authority, which if it continues to be ignored may force Virginia to intervene.'

'Not a pretty picture. The sooner we reach Browne the better. How do we get there?'

'You can only go by sea. Purchase or hire a couple of six oared shallops! On the other hand you could take passage on a supply sloop that visits all the settlements along the Bay on a regular schedule. It's a bit slow this time of year, as the ship has to confront strong north westerlies. Sorry for the behaviour of young Castle, but our best people are too busy making money to provide any sort of community service. The planters reluctantly provide the harbour side militia, and therefore insist on making the appointments. I'm afraid it is somewhat corrupt. As soon as he has the resources the Governor will abolish it and appoint his own force.'

At that moment, John Halliwell, Luke's other sergeant, returned to the inn with the two soldiers - the defenders of the group's possessions - who had been beaten by Castle's cronies. John interrupted Luke's discussion with Atkinson and firmly asked the magistrate to punish the locals for their assault and theft. Atkinson was happy to comply. He went outside and questioned Castle and some of the local militia who all claimed had done nothing. An annoyed Atkinson ordered Castle to send the entire contingent home. As Castle left the area he turned towards Luke with a contemptuous leer, and a hand gesture that was anything but friendly. Luke had created a vindictive enemy who would waste no time in exacting his revenge.

Luke's attempt to obtain two shallops for their journey up the Bay failed. He could hardly believe his bad luck. He could see several unused shallops beached along the riverbank. Luke's interpretation of his failure quickly changed from accepting their unavailability to anger at what eventually emerged as deliberate obstruction by the boat owners. This conspiracy theory was confirmed when John Halliwell saw young Castle talking to one of the owners prior to Luke's approach. Luke was forced to seek passage on the next sloop heading north. Half expecting a similar boycott Luke was pleasantly surprised when the landlord of The Porpoise recommended a friend, Captain Murchison, a Scot with a decade's experience on the Chesapeake, who regularly supplied the planters along its shores. His sloop, *The Mary Jane*, was due to leave the next morning, and could accommodate the soldiers and their supplies. Luke sent Andrew to negotiate the details.

Later that day, as Luke stood in the entrance of the tavern he saw magistrate Atkinson, and a man of military bearing riding towards him on a fine white stallion. 'It's the Governor,' whispered the landlord. Luke had heard nothing but praise for Sir William Berkeley who on the outbreak of the Civil War returned to England to fight for the old King, but with his defeat returned to his post in Virginia, which he kept resolutely Royalist. The Governor introduced himself and did not waste time, 'Tremayne, I gather from Atkinson, and from the letter he passed on to me that you are a confidante of Lord Baltimore. I understand you are sailing north as soon as you can. Would you take a letter to Governor Stone? He has been a loyal servant of Lord Baltimore, and deserves to know that the King has revoked his Lordship's charter, and appointed a royal governor to succeed him. We do not expect Davenant for twelve weeks, that is if he can break through the English Republic's blockade. Stone will have plenty of time to prepare his handover.'

Luke invited the two gentlemen to drink with him. The landlord was delighted to have such powerful customers, and his servants were falling over each other to see that the Governor was a contented guest. The conversation turned to current developments in England, and the late civil wars. Luke admitted that he had served in the New Model army reaching the rank of Lieutenant Colonel, but then untruthfully proclaimed that the purge of Parliament by the army and the subsequent execution of the King had sickened him, and provoked his desire to assist Lord Baltimore.

Luke's relaxed social discourse with the cultivated and popular governor whose political and military prowess was widely appreciated was suddenly ended. The Governor turned on Luke, 'Boddikins man! You must take me for a fool. Our discussion, and the demeanour of your men confirm that you are soldiers on a mission, openly for Lord Baltimore, or is that only a cover for the new nefarious government in England. I would very much like to know. I am not happy with twenty five well trained and heavily armed troops, only recently removed from Cromwell's army marching around my colony. If you stayed in Virginia I would disarm you and restrict your activities. But Baltimore and Governor Stone need all the help they can get – even if it is from pulpit thumping rebels.'

'Perceptive, Sir William. We are a New Model military unit, but on a fact-finding mission for Baltimore, without any military objective. His Lordship is not sure that Governor Stone knows what is going on, and one of Baltimore's most trusted informants has suddenly stopped sending reports.'

'Robert Browne?'

'You are well informed,' commented an impressed Luke.

'Not really, Stone has told me that Browne is the only planter outside the St Mary's area that supports Baltimore. At our last meeting several months ago he hinted that Baltimore's enemies might, for that very reason, strike against Browne. When you deliver my letter to Stone inform him of your real mission in detail. It will lift his spirits.'

The Governor indicated that he was about to leave, and by the time he had reached the door two of the landlord's servants had his horse ready for mounting. As he turned away to mount his steed he whispered to Luke, 'Take this uniquely clipped Spanish doubloon. If you need help get it back to me.'

Luke joked as he stroked and patted the Governor's fine white stallion, 'What I want is a horse. We are a cavalry troop, but I understand horses are useless in Maryland.'

'Not useless, but unnecessary and costly. The preferred method of travel is by water; and tobacco cultivation needs humans with a hoe, not horses with a plough.'

Next morning Luke and his men boarded *The Mary Jane*. There was a considerable delay. Captain Murchison and most of the crew did not appear. After half an hour a man came aboard accompanied by half a dozen others. He introduced himself as Murchison's boatswain, and apologised that the captain and several of his crew had overindulged. He would be acting master of the ship on its current voyage to deliver goods at St Mary's, unload the passengers on Robert Browne's island and deliver supplies to the planters in the northern Chesapeake. The ship took some time to leave the James River and turn north along the western shore of the Bay.

After some time Andrew urgently motioned John and Luke to join him at the stern of the sloop, well away from the crew. Andrew was agitated, 'There is something amiss. I spoke to Murchison yesterday and was surprised to find that for a sea-faring man he treated strong drink as the Devil's brew. And I have been watching these sailors. When I served the King of Sweden I was seconded to the navy for a whole year. These men know nothing about sailing. They are landlubbers, not seamen. And they seem extremely nervous. They are up to no good, and I suspect we are about to become their victims.'

3

'Rubbish Andrew! You are unusually edgy. Many a God fearing sailor relapses into a drinking binge, and as for the crew the boatswain probably had to make up the numbers at short notice. Verily, if it came to a fight we outnumber them four to one. No wonder they are nervous. It is not us that have to worry. We could easily take over this ship,' replied Luke.

But John supported Andrew, 'Luke, we only have our swords and pistols. If the crew emerged with muskets we could be in trouble.'

Luke, with good humour capitulated to his sergeants' joint concern, 'Our muskets and ammunition are in the two large black chests on the deck. Tell the men to gather around the box, and arm themselves before the crew can see what is happening.' Luke's men assembled around the chest, and sang bawdy songs while Luke, Andrew and John diverted the attention of the crew. So engrossed were Luke and his men in these activities they did not appreciate that the sloop had left the Bay, and was sailing up a small tidal river. Finally alerted to the situation Luke asked the boatswain why they had diverted up an ever narrowing river. 'No problem, sir. I am about to anchor the ship, and deliver some goods to a settler whose quay you can see on the port side.'

The crew lowered the pinnace, and rowed towards the wharf. Andrew was alarmed, 'God's mercy Luke! When does it take the whole crew to unload a few chests? When do real sailors leave their ship in the hands of their passengers?' Before Luke could reply John pointed up river. Two boats with a dozen men in each were rowing towards them. The boats were quickly positioned on each side of the *Mary Jane*. Its deserting crew reversed their direction and placed themselves off the bow of the ship. Volleys of musket fire from all three boats were now directed at Luke's men on the deck of the *Mary Jane*. The pirates were preparing to board.

Their leader shouted, 'You tickle brained varlet! Surrender the *Mary Jane* and you can leave unmolested.'

Luke yelled back, 'No way. You swag-bellied maggot!' With plenty of ammunition, Luke's men returned fire in such rapid succession that the attackers were taken aback.

Their leader repeated his demands, 'Give us the ship. Your lives don't interest us. Why die for nothing?' replied the pirate.

'You flybitten churl! You have blundered. It is not us who are about to die. You don't have the firepower to dislodge us, but a few more volleys of sustained musket fire from us, and your boats will sink. You have, to your loss, pitted yourself against a troop of professional soldiers.'

'Perhaps soldier, but you cannot flee. You do not have the ability to move the sloop downriver and escape into the Bay,' replied the pirate leader.

'Now you take me for the fool. These are tidal rivers. In a few hours the currents will take us back into the Bay where our plight is more likely to be noticed,' countered Luke. His bravado was shaken when he noticed that the crowd that had gathered on the quay were stabilising a small cannon. Luke shouted at the pirates. 'You scut brained toads. Happy to destroy half your profit by damaging the sloop.' He whispered to his sergeant, 'Can that cannon harm us?'

'Time will tell,' Andrew answered laconically.

Luke had no idea how long the tide would continue surging upriver. It could be as little as under an hour, or just short of six. The crew had lowered the sails before they disembarked, and tossed over a large anchor. If he were to benefit from a changing tide and the prevailing winds he would only need to raise the anchor, and unfurl the sails. Luke countered the cannon with a burst of musket fire into the throng on the quay. A few men remained, but most ran. They managed to get one shot away that fell so far short of the ship, that Luke relaxed. When he refocussed on the pirate boats, he was surprised to find they had turned around and their occupants were rowing upriver away from the *Mary Jane* as fast as they could. John directed Luke's attention down river towards the Bay. A frigate had anchored, its draft too deep for the shallow river. Four or five boats filled with armed men were lowered from its sides and headed for The *Mary Jane* and the pirates.

In the leading pinnace were Charles Atkinson, and a man that Andrew recognized as Captain Murchison. While the other boats slowly gained on the fleeing pirates the leading pinnace drew alongside the *Mary Jane*. Atkinson, Murchison and six men who were clearly veteran sailors boarded the ship.'

'Glad to see you Mr Atkinson,' Luke said.

'It did not take you long to get into trouble Tremayne. The pirates did not know what they were taking on. We could hear your firepower when we were still out in the Bay. This is Captain Murchison, and the real crew of the *Mary Jane*. They were drugged and when they came to, Murchison was distressed to find his ship missing. Its cargo is valuable.'

'Is this a run of the mill pirate operation, irrelevant to our specific mission?' asked Luke.

'Probably. The supplies for many settlers, and your own possessions, especially your arsenal would have been ample reward. In addition the boat itself is most valuable. This would have been a most profitable raid. No one in Jamestown other than the Governor and myself know the nature of your enterprise. On the other hand you did humiliate John Castle.'

'Is that relevant?'

'Possibly. These tidal pirates are part time. Most are indentured servants of the local planters who take a cut of the takings. Some of the more successful have graduated into fulltime ocean going pirates who continue to shelter in the Bay. The real criminals in these enterprises are those inhabitants of Jamestown, often in high places, who inform the pirates of suitable pickings.'

'You know who they are?'

'The man behind this attack is a small time planter, Nicholas Castle, John's uncle, who paid a number of his colleagues to appoint his nephew to command the harbour side police - an ideal position to reconnoitre the rich pickings moored in our harbour. Young Castle took an immediate dislike to you, Tremayne. This could be a boyish act of vengeance.'

Captain Murchison turned the sloop and as it passed the frigate, Charles Atkinson, was transferred to the larger ship. The *Mary Jane* sailed out into the Bay and headed north. Some time later Captain Murchison alerted Luke that he was entering the Potomac River and would soon land at St Mary's. As they came closer to the quay the captain commented, 'You're in luck Colonel. Normally the Governor sends a servant to receive the mail but I see him on the wharf.'

Luke disembarked, and with Captain Murchison approached the Governor. The sailor introduced Luke as an agent from Lord Baltimore, who also had a message from Governor Berkeley. Luke handed Governor Stone a number of letters. Stone asked, 'Are there any I should read in your presence?'

'No,' replied Luke. 'However I alert you to two issues that the letters confirm. They affect your position. The King has revoked Lord Baltimore's charter, and appointed your successor. This royal governor has already left Europe. Secondly while initially I intend to investigate Robert Browne's circumstances, my remit from his Lordship is to assess the general situation and report back. While in the colony I am to aid you against the enemies of Lord Baltimore.'

Governor Stone was taken aback at the news from Berkeley. 'I expected the attack on Lord Baltimore to come from the new government in England, supported by those malcontents on the Severn, not from the new King.'

'Have you recent news of Browne?'

'No, I have not heard from Browne in months,' Stone coldly replied.

Murchison put an end to further conversation, 'Your Excellency, I must take advantage of the tides and leave immediately.'

Luke farewelled the Governor who appeared traumatised by the news he had received. As the *Mary Jane* sailed east north east across the Chesapeake, zigzagging through the Bay against a developing north westerly, Luke wondered why the governor had not taken steps to maintain communications with his only supporter outside the St Mary's area. If Browne was his strongest ally why had the Governor not bothered to find out what was happening? Had Stone lost his faith in Browne? Perhaps Murchison might know something.

The Scottish sea captain was determined to keep his information general. He described the geography, avoiding any comment on the people. 'Browne's plantation covers three large islands that fill what, without them would have been a deeply indented half moon bay. In fact the islands fill the estuary of a sizeable river that enters the Bay through a North and South arm. His grant also includes hundreds of acres of undeveloped forest which he is hoping to allocate to new settlers. Some years ago he transferred the use of the immediate hinterland to his current tenants - Mr Richard Goodwin received land north of the North Arm, and Dr Matthew Sherman the land to the south of the South Arm.

Browne built his manor house on the most seaward island, West Island. For the first seven years his tobacco fields were on South Island. You will discover Colonel that the planters here use no fertilisers and simply clear further land to replace the depleted fields. His current fields are to be found on North Island while he allows his cattle and swine to run wild on South Island. West Island has a substantial wharf built out into the bay which can take the draft of the *Mary Jane*. We won't need to use our boats to unload.'

Luke persisted, 'So much for the plantation, what about Browne and his family?'

Murchison stared ahead. Finally, after a long delay he replied in little more than a whisper, 'Browne is a troubled soul. Very moody. One visit, he invites you to the house and entertains you as a gentleman. Next time he is rude and aggressive and treats you as a recalcitrant slave. I have carried many passengers from his plantation and several claimed that he was two different people – one, an affable charming patriarch, the other, a devious abusive monster who is violent towards his family and servants. He had a bad experience during the war which distorted his personality.'

Murchison suddenly shouted orders to his men, and they reduced sail. Luke felt the ship progressively lose speed as it headed for a cluster of islands that loomed into sight. Luke prepared his men for disembarkation, as Murchison was on a tight schedule. As the ship manoeuvred to come along side the wharf the *Mary Jane* was hit by intermittent musket fire.

Luke's men automatically grabbed their weapons, and primed their muskets awaiting their leader's orders. Murchison was initially flabbergasted, but quickly regained his composure. He shouted to those ashore. 'Jehu, Mr Browne. It's Captain Murchison. Why the unfriendly welcome?'

A man emerged from the undergrowth and made his way along the wharf. Luke did not recognize his former enemy. Browne replied, 'Sorry Murchison, can I trust you? Why are you here? This is not a scheduled visit. And why is your ship full of armed men? My old spy glass serves me well.'

'You old fool! Yes, I do bring soldiers, but they have authorization from Lord Baltimore to assist you.'

'No one told me,' replied an affronted Browne.

Murchison had a quick word with Luke, and replied to Browne, 'Send out your dugout canoe, and I will send their commanding officer ashore. You can inspect his papers. He knows you from the late war.'

Browne paled visibly, and appeared to tremble. His head was jerking involuntarily. He did not reply and wandered off into the undergrowth. Eventually a canoe emerged from further down the shoreline, and Luke carefully climbed down a rope ladder and waited for the canoe to come alongside. He managed to half climb and half fall into it. The canoeist, an ageing retainer, grunted an acknowledgment, and immediately headed for the shoreline adjacent to the wharf. Luke was still not sure of his reception from this disturbed planter.

4

LUKE CLAMBERED OUT, AND ALMOST FELL FACE DOWN IN the sand. As he scrambled to his feet he became aware of a middle aged man, whom he assumed to be Robert Browne, standing over him tapping a cane against the side of his boot. Luke strove to regain the initiative, 'Colonel Browne you won't recognize me. A decade ago I was Cornet Tremayne, attached to Cromwell's company of Parliamentary cavalry. You ambushed my troop, and then graciously allowed us to return to our quarters. I bring greetings, and this sealed letter from Lord Baltimore which explains my presence. May I disembark my men?'

Browne, who again began to shake, took the letter with some difficulty. He rested it on the stump of a tree and read it carefully. As he read he tapped a forceful rhythm with his cane against the tree. This accompanied the grunts and groans that his reading provoked. At last, staring intently at Luke, he commented, 'Welcome, Tremayne. Never forgot those bright blue eyes glowering at me, as you demanded your release, when you had absolutely nothing to negotiate with. Later in the war they would have shot you all. But in those early days both sides behaved as gentlemen. Sadly it changed so quickly. I heard you were one of Cromwell's favoured sons, and a brilliant cavalry commander. How does a Cromwellian officer find himself employed by a Catholic peer, and in this far flung Royalist colony? If I did not have this letter I would have suspected you were sent here by crafty old Noll Cromwell to assist my Puritan enemies along the Severn.'

After another interlude of silence Browne spoke, 'Forgive my rudeness, signal Murchison to unload your men and supplies.'

Robert Browne controlled his trembling and continued, 'There is no accommodation on this island, or on that containing our current crops. My shallop can take your men and supplies to South Island. We grew our first crops there, and a number of dilapidated huts are still standing. Your men will need to repair them. It will soon be thunderstorm season so make sure the roofs are waterproof. There are a number of canoes which you and your officers can use to return here for dinner. Build one for each of your men! They are the common form of transport between my islands, up river and inshore along the Bay.'

As Luke supervised the debarkation of his men and their transfer by shallop to their new home, he assessed his ageing former adversary. Browne was fifty but looked a decade older. His face was drawn, with prominent cheeks and a permanently flushed complexion. His former short crisp black beard was now grey, longish and unkempt. His hair was predominantly grey but with patches of white around the ears. He was plump, of average height and walked with a slight limp, the result of a wartime injury. Luke was not sure whether the cane, which seemed permanently attached to his arm, was a walking stick, a status symbol, or a weapon. Robert kept alive the Royalist predilection for bright colours. His breeches were an azure blue as were his stockings and the ribbons that tied the two below the knee. His white shirt, now somewhat grey, displayed considerable lace at the cuffs and collar. He wore a broad brimmed, low brow felt hat that was decorated with a faded blue ribbon and silver buckle which looked the worse for wear as the result of enduring numerous thunderstorms. On closer inspection Luke noticed that much of the clothing was stained, and there were numerous splits and inappropriate rips in Robert's doublet. And the man was ill. His hands shook and his head twitched - the physical manifestations of the troubled soul?

Later that day Luke and his sergeants, Andrew and John, joined the Browne family for dinner. Robert Browne introduced his wife Elizabeth, who despite the warm evening was dressed in heavy black apparel as was his daughter Priscilla. Luke was surprised that only one daughter appeared. Lord Baltimore had told him that Browne had four children. His sons James and Thomas, and daughter Lucy were absent.

Luke was disconcerted by Elizabeth's appearance. Her eyes were wide open and she stared vacantly into space like an inmate of Bedlam. Any attempt at conversation was cut short by a single nod of her head, and intermittently she sobbed almost silently. Her dress reflected a past opulence that would not have been out of place at the court of the late King. Over a black underskirt she wore a black gown, the bodice of which was studded with black pearls, all highlighted by a large lace collar and very large lace cuffs. Elizabeth was of minute stature with very thin limbs. She had a pale ashen face replete with purple and yellow bruises.

Luke's lack of female company over several months briefly gave him a favourable impression of Priscilla. She was a younger and larger version of her mother. She had a compact body and looked older than her twenty years. Her oval face had been browned by years in the Maryland sun which gave her an Italian or Spanish appearance. Her black-grey bodice suggested to Luke small taut breasts but his lust quickly dissipated. She kept her eyes downcast, and her complete lack of conversation convinced Luke that she was dull and boring. The only signs of animation from this troubled young lady were the continual glares directed towards her father, and an unpleasant habit of sucking her abnormally small lips. Luke was surprised to find a Royalist household, apart from the master, in such dismal array.

Robert eventually explained why, 'I have read the letters. You are indeed a military mission sent by Baltimore to check on my situation, and assess the loyalties of my fellow colonists. Your arrival is timely. Our family is in mourning. Two days ago our son Thomas died in strange circumstances.'

Luke extended formal condolences but knew it would break etiquette if he asked the obvious questions. One must never speak of the dead at table. There was a long awkward silence. Luke struggled to restart the conversation, 'Lord Baltimore suspected that you were having problems. What exactly has been happening here?'

'Ever since our arrival seven years ago the Virginian adventurers on Kent Island have fomented opposition to Lord Baltimore. In recent months the newly arrived Puritan settlers on the Severn added their weight to this opposition. Governor Stone and his Catholic supporters around St Mary's do not have the resources to contain these subversives. My settlement in this area, as a known supporter of Lord Baltimore, placed me close to the areas of potential insurrection. I regularly reported developments to his Lordship and to Governor Stone. About twelve months ago I was warned to stop, and encouraged to join the others in an attempt to overthrow his sovereignty. I refused. Things quietened down, and then in the temporary absence of the Governor, his deputy stupidly in the circumstances, formally declared for Charles II. Although Stone has now reversed the decision it gave the dissidents a cause. Rumours that the English republican government would withdraw Baltimore's jurisdiction added to the unease, and fuelled Puritan ambitions. My eldest son James was kidnapped a month ago and held for a week as a warning of what would happen if I continued to support Baltimore. A week ago at night a dozen canoes circled West Island and the intruders fired at random across the island – another warning.'

'Who is responsible?'

'Maybe the Puritans who want to create a colony free of Catholics, or the Kent Island men who want a greater Virginia. Both seek to overthrow Baltimore.'

Silence descended as the family and guests concentrated on the food. Luke enjoyed the freshly baked apple pie and craved for the taste of cheese. He remembered his mother's advice that an apple pie without cheese was like a kiss without a squeeze. At the moment he needed both.

The women withdrew, and Robert led the men to large chairs located in the entrance hall. Luke who had contained himself all evening now asked quietly, ' Sir, what happened to Thomas?'

'Two nights ago my family entertained at dinner my gentlemen tenants and neighbours, Goodwin and Sherman, and my estate manager, Tim Lipton. Towards the end of the meal Thomas suddenly slumped forward, and Dr Sherman, a Bristol physician in an earlier life, pronounced him dead.'

'From what cause?'

'No one knows, and I want you, as an outsider to find the answer. All judicial power on this plantation rests with me. Therefore as the local magistrate I formally empower you to investigate the death of my son.'

'Willingly,' replied Luke. 'Is there one of your servants that you could second to me?'

'Yes, I have just the man, Humphrey Norton - the man who paddled you ashore. He came out as a youth to the settlement at Jamestown, and has spent his life in the interior trading and living with the Indians. He lost some mobility in a series of accidents and misadventures. But his knowledge of the area - the plants, the wildlife, the tides and currents in the Bay, and the ways of the Indians is unsurpassed.'

'Then sir, my first request. Immediately make it known, as widely as you can, that we are soldiers sent by Baltimore to protect you, and his Lordship's interests, and any future action against you will bring reprisals. I believe that when there is trouble always look close to home. What can you tell me about your gentlemen neighbours?'

'Not much. Baltimore's agents selected them. They aim to make their fortune producing tobacco, and pay me as lord of the manor certain fees out of their profits. By the grant I am the magistrate for the whole area, and also commander of the local militia in which they are my fellow officers, and our combined workforce force of indentured and free servants provide the troops. Given this environment, all men are armed. Unlike England before the Wars you are entering a highly militarised community. Goodwin fought for the King, and still dresses as a courtier. He has appeared before me in my magisterial role on several occasions. He is a hard taskmaster, and his servants claim he abuses them but I could never satisfy myself that his discipline ever broke the law. I have had no complaints against him in the last three years. He was a womaniser and impregnated at least two of his female servants. There are now no women on his plantation, other than Indian girls who fraternize with his labourers. He flirted outrageously with Priscilla and Lucy, and my servants Abigail and Rachel. He now keeps to himself, and does not encourage visitors. In the last few years his men have stopped fraternising with those on the other two estates. He has become a recluse.'

'What about Sherman?'

'He was a physician from Bristol who had Puritan relatives in Virginia. These cousins then moved to the Severn. He had intended settling there, but Baltimore persuaded him to take up my vacant land.'

'So, even the inhabitants on your grant, masters and servants, are not necessarily supporters of Lord Baltimore?'

'That's right. I support Lord Baltimore. I assumed Richard Goodwin as a Royalist and possibly a Catholic, did the same, but if there is a breach between Baltimore and the new king he could have turned against his lordship. Sherman may be a Puritan, although I have not seen him exhibit the normal obsessive behaviour of men of that ilk. Gentlemen in this province, other than the Puritans, wear their old world religion lightly. They have one aim – to prosper. As for our workers they have no interest in politics or religion. They want to survive long enough to receive land of their own. Opposition to Baltimore is political, not religious. His opponents simply want independence to pursue their own interests.'

After many drinks, with all four men befuddled, Luke asked in a somewhat slurred manner, 'Can I see the body of your son tomorrow morning?'

Robert, who had been staring vacantly into space and talking quietly to himself, was suddenly energised back to reality by the question, 'No! Tom was buried the morning after his death.'

The soldiers excused themselves as Robert began shouting at the invisible demons which seemed to be tormenting him. Andrew was furious. He muttered to his companions that he had not volunteered for service in Bedlam. They were all glad to reach the sanity of South Island.

5

LUKE AND HIS MEN SPENT THE NIGHT IN THE dilapidated huts. The eventful day contributed to a restless night, and even a slight drizzle managed to seep through the roof, and dampen the spirit and the bodies of the unhappy soldiers. Next morning the tired and wet men were assembled, and Luke allotted the tasks for the day. Half the men were to repair the huts. The other half were to chip out several two man canoes. The officers would return to West Island, and investigate the death of Thomas Browne, and the general attempts to undermine Browne, and reject Baltimore's authority.

Andrew had noticed Luke's difficulty in handling the single man dugout on the previous evening. He volunteered to paddle alone, while Luke joined John Halliwell in the two man canoe. They had not pushed far offshore before the incoming tide swept them away from their destination towards the rocky southern shore of North Island. As John and Luke struggled to guide the canoe in the direction they wanted, the former suggested, 'Forget the high politics, and concentrate on Thomas's death!'

'I agree. One issue at a time. Let's recreate every detail of the fatal meal, and obtain Dr Sherman's professional opinion as to the cause of the death. If it is murder, then how and why was it committed?'

'There's a bigger problem,' replied John. 'If it is murder, how do we know that Thomas was the intended victim?'

'Yes. Why young Thomas? His father, elder brother or the guests would appear to be more appropriate targets, but we know nothing about personal relationships on this settlement except that with only one day's acquaintance it is obvious that the Brownes are a very troubled family. And we have only met three of them. We need to know much more.'

The two men ran their canoe ashore, soon followed by Andrew. They made their way to Humphrey Norton's small hut near the manor house. Robert Browne had already informed his servant that he was being seconded to Colonel Tremayne. Humphrey's face reflected his lifetime in the wilderness. It was wrinkled, rugged and olive in complexion. He had a small forehead, with a deep furrow and extremely bushy eyebrows. His dark brown eyes were bright and almost twinkled. His mousy brown hair was worn long, but most of it was contained under a light brown Monmouth cap. He wore a dark brown jerkin and grey breeches with brown stockings. His shirt was a light grey with a narrow plain collar and no cuffs. He was short but sturdy, and despite his age, a strong and healthy individual.

Luke explained that his men required huts and canoes, and he needed Humphrey to instruct them in these unfamiliar activities. Andrew returned to South Island with Humphrey where he stayed long enough to ensure that the men recognised that Humphrey acted on Luke's authority, and that his advice was to be followed. Luke and John turned towards the manor house just in time to confront a man whom they judged by the black bag he carried to be Dr Sherman.

Luke introduced himself, and made Sherman aware that Robert Browne as magistrate had appointed Luke to investigate Thomas's death. Sherman indicated a newly felled tree, and the three men sat along its recently debarked trunk. Sherman's appearance was unusual. The doctor was very tall, six feet six inches at least. He was incredibly thin with very long legs and unusually long arms. He had a long forehead, his eyes close together and ears set low in his head. He dressed as a gentleman with a wide brimmed and moderately highbrow black hat, decorated with a black ribbon and a rather small silver buckle. He had removed his doublet given the rising heat of the day, and his white shirt was complimented with large lace cuffs and an expensive lace collar. His breeches and stockings and the ribbons that joined them were also black.

'Doctor, did Thomas die of natural causes, or was he murdered?' asked Luke.

'Truthfully I don't know,' replied the gaunt beanstalk.

'No clues to an unnatural death?'

'None at all, except the death itself.'

'What do you mean?' probed Luke.

'Thomas died of a heart problem. He looked like many patients I dealt with in Bristol who had weak hearts. But Thomas was a young man who was exceptionally healthy. Tremayne, your precise problem is to establish what stopped Thomas's heart - medically I cannot help.'

'Are there poisons that would bring about this result?'

'There are, but they have to be administered over a long period, and there are usually residual signs. Thomas just went to sleep.'

'Do you have any such poisons?'

'Yes. Most poisons are also positive medicines if used in the correct dosage, or in combination with other ingredients.'

'Where do you keep your poisons?'

'I keep my medicines in a chest back on my plantation, but carry a few of them with me in this bag.'

'So someone might have taken one of your poisons and administered it to Thomas causing his death?'

'Theoretically yes, but I have no ingredients that would create such effects so quickly. Nor do I have the quantity that would be needed to have fatal results.'

'What about native Indian poisons?'

'I don't know much about them. Humphrey is the expert. He uses them to catch fish. He might be able to help.'

'Thank you doctor. Can you help us recreate the dinner at which Thomas died? What were the seating arrangements?'

'Robert was at the head of the table with Lucy on his right and Priscilla on his left. Elizabeth was at the end of the table with Richard on her left and myself on her right. Between Lucy and Richard was James, and between myself and Priscilla were Tim, next to me and then Thomas next to Priscilla.'

'Take me through the meal?' asked Luke.

'It was a simple two course meal. The first course was the inevitable corn fritter, on this occasion including pieces of previously roasted chicken, the second was roast pig with beans and corn.'

'Everybody ate the same meal?' asked John.

'Thomas didn't have any special food?' reiterated Luke.

'Not as far as I noticed.'

'Where were the fritters cooked, and who brought them to the table?'

'They were prepared by Abigail Hicks, Mr Browne's cook. She prepares meals in the cookhouse – a building separate from the main house to reduce the danger of fire. Both the fritters and the main course were transferred to the hall and kept warm in the hearth until we sat down to eat. Abigail brought two large platters to the table, one of fritters and the other of bread. The platters were passed around the table clockwise from Robert, which meant young Lucy had the last dip into the platters.'

'So there would be no way of knowing who would be eating a poisoned fritter if one existed?'

'Poisoning a fritter would predicate a completely random attack on the family and its visitors.'

'What about the roast pig and vegetables?'

'That was slightly different. There were three platters of roast pig which Robert had chopped into hunks with his machete, and three platters of vegetables. Lucy, Robert and Priscilla selected from one set of platters, James, Thomas and Tim from the next and the third set was provided for Elizabeth, Richard and myself.'

'Did you notice whether Thomas served himself or did James or Tim fill his plate?'

'I was too busy filling my own, and talking to Elizabeth to notice what the others were doing.'

'But Tim was sitting next to you.'

'I was talking with Elizabeth,' repeated Matthew.

'She can talk then?' muttered John sarcastically.

Luke asked, 'So any poison in the pork or the vegetables could not with any certainty be directed to Thomas?'

'Even with a random attack, if the poison was in the pork then James, Tim or Thomas were equally at risk of getting it.'

'You said that Robert had initially cut the pork into chunks. Who cut it into more delicate pieces for eating?'

'The men did not bother. We ate the chunks in our hands. There is no civilized eating in this settlement, Colonel Tremayne.'

'What about drink?'

'Before the meal we drank here sitting on this log. Everybody took a mug from a collection on a trestle table and filled it themselves from the barrel of Dutch beer that Richard had provided. No way could poison have been introduced either through the beer or the cups, and be sure of finding only Thomas.'

'Your evidence precludes a quick solution to our enquiry,' moaned Luke.

Matthew was silent for a while, 'Maybe not. While we were drinking Thomas dropped his drinking cup, and it broke into pieces. One of the other drinkers gave Thomas a replacement cup, already filled. If only I could remember who it was?'

'Don't worry doctor; some one will recall the incident. What's your view on Thomas's death?'

'Too many variables to be sure. If Thomas was murdered, apart from the replaced cup of beer, the attack must have been random, and not directed against him in particular. Seeking motives for such a general attack may get you closer to the truth, than trying to recreate the detail of the dinner. A random attack on the family in general could be part of the malevolence that has pervaded the Brownes over recent months. Probably it was another warning to back away from Lord Baltimore, and join the other malcontents. I'm convinced that the attack was random on the family and its guests. Thomas was just unlucky.'

'You imply Thomas was a most unlikely specific target. Why?'

'The powers within this estate are Robert, and to a much less extent his eldest son James and then the manager Tim. Thomas was a reluctant settler who avoided as much work as he could. He spent most of his time with Priscilla and his mother. He didn't fit into frontier life at all. Robert was about to send him back to England to be brought up by his uncle Charles on the Browne's English estates. His death will make no difference to the life on this plantation.'

'You alluded to the political context, and the possibility of a random attack on the family and yourself and Goodwin. What is behind these attacks?'

'Pretty simple, the inhabitants along the Severn River where I have relatives are seeking support from the republican Government in England. The Royalist settlers on Kent Island want to join a greater Virginia. Both groups in practice ignore Baltimore's authority. Governor Stone and the Catholic settlers along the Potomac are still loyal to Baltimore. Robert Browne is seen as a Baltimore stooge who keeps the Governor apprised of developments in the northern Chesapeake. His fellow planters see him as an unwelcome spy.'

'But are such political differences sufficient to provoke murder?'

'For the greedy any impediments to unfettered exploitation of men and resources is resented. Baltimore has placed restrictions on the exploitation of indentured labour, and the ill treatment of the local Indian. He also strictly regulates trade with the Indian, and with our Dutch and Swedish neighbours along the Delaware.'

Luke summed up, 'So doctor, it is your view that Thomas died from natural causes, or was the unlucky victim of a random attack on the family as part of the political struggle on the upper Chesapeake.'

6

Luke's questioning was cut short when Robert Browne emerged from the house. 'Thank God you're still here Matthew! Elizabeth is having one of her turns. Give her something to quieten her down!' The doctor re-entered the house.

Robert greeted Luke, 'Started your investigation? Matthew's a reliable witness, except where Priscilla is concerned.'

Luke noted the reference to Priscilla, but asked, 'Was Thomas murdered?'

The strain was telling on the ageing planter. He sighed and groaned as his face went through a series of contorted expressions. 'I would like to think it was natural causes but Tom was exceedingly healthy, probably because he exerted himself so little. He was a parasite, and sower of discord in the family. His effect on his siblings was such that I had decided to send him back to England, and subject him to the discipline of my authoritarian brother Charles.'

'Did his siblings hate him so much as to murder him?'

'No. Lucy and James's dislike of Thomas was no more than the usual sibling rivalry, except Thomas was never a serious rival to anybody. If anyone else in the family had been murdered, Thomas would have been my prime suspect. He had a chip on his shoulder.'

'And as the old maxim says, "By doing nothing one learns to do evil." Anything else about your family that would help my investigation?' probed Luke.

'It's no secret that my family is divided and disgruntled. James, Lucy and myself relate well together on the one hand, as did Elizabeth, Thomas and Priscilla on the other.'

'What caused the division?'

'Complex, but in essence Elizabeth, Thomas and Priscilla want to return to England. James, Lucy and myself want to stay and develop the plantation.'

'How did this basic disagreement work out in everyday activities?'

'No problem on the surface. The family does as I say. James is the heir not only to this plantation but also to our ancestral estates in England. His siblings must learn to obey him.'

'Have the family defied you or James?'

'Not actively. There is sullen resentment from Elizabeth and Thomas. Priscilla, since Matthew has shown an interest in her, appears to be finding some aspects of life in Maryland bearable, and her negative attitude is abating.'

Luke turned his attention to the dinner at which Thomas died. Robert's account confirmed the picture already given by Mathew. 'Robert, before dinner when you were drinking out here Thomas broke his mug. Who replaced it?'

'I selected the new cup, and Priscilla filled it.'

Luke's questioning was interrupted when Matthew re-emerged from the house and spoke to Robert. 'Elizabeth may be suffering from the death of Thomas, but at the moment she is experiencing a recurrence of malaria. I've told the servant to keep her warm when she shivers, and keep her cool when she runs a fever. It must run its course.'

Luke interrupted, 'This water land region must be rife with victims?'

'Yes,' responded Matthew. 'Half the workers have it. Dozens have died. It recurs once or twice a year which renders the victim useless in the field for weeks.'

While Luke chatted with Matthew and Robert, John Halliwell had moved to the back of the house to question the servants. Rachael O'Brien was too busy looking after her mistress. John eventually found Abigail Hicks alone in the cookhouse butchering a deer which Humphrey had obtained from the local Indians. John explained that his leader

Colonel Tremayne had authority from her master to investigate Thomas's murder.

Abigail Hicks was a sensuous young woman whose every movement and gesture raised the interest of most males – even the somewhat austere and moral John. Her long blond hair was only partially contained by her spotlessly white close fitting coif. She was not in a state of mourning that reflected either her rebelliousness, or the complete failure to enforce traditional English customs in this heathen wilderness. Her bodice was a deep red, set against a plain cream shirt with linen collar and cuffs. Her skirt was of dark grey largely hidden behind a lighter grey apron that was already spoilt by fingermarks from her kitchen chores. Her low cut tight bodice strained to contain large firm breasts which she almost forced against John. He was old enough to be her father but the large pouting sensuous lips temporarily affected his demeanour. He was glad that his Colonel was not conducting the interview. Luke's vow to avoid sexual encounters would be sorely tested by this saucy wench.

'Abigail, did you prepare the meal the night Thomas died?'

'Yes, but there was nothing wrong with it. Nobody else complained, and they all ate the same food - well almost.'

'Did Thomas eat something that the others didn't?'

'The boys - James, Thomas and Tim - do not like the sweet flavoured apple sauce that I provide with the roast. On their platter the pork was soaked instead with an herbal gravy that contained a lot of thyme and sage. It was a regular variation every time we had pork.'

'Was this variation known to the rest of the household?'

'Certainly. Given the general monotony of meals any variation is carefully noted by the others.'

'Was Thomas murdered?'

'How should I know? But he deserved to be,' Abigail replied.

'Why do you say that? His father admits he was a lazy parasite, but is that a motive to murder him?'

'Thomas was a viperous filthy beast. He kept appearing unexpectedly around the house and throughout the islands - as if he had been stalking you. We servants called him the Turd.'

'Did he molest you?'

'He tried, but I resisted him.'

'He molested other women?'

'Not really, he was easily stopped by his intended victims. He spent most of his time watching other men swive with their women. He was weird.'

'So he liked to watch others do what he couldn't? Could this have provoked his murder?' asked John.

'Most likely. While spying on the intimate relationships of the settlement he may have seen something that the participants did not want to be made known. If he was murdered it was to keep him quiet.'

'About what?'

'Forsooth, you are an innocent John. There are few women on this plantation. Men from the master down to the older boys need us. The Turd with his information and nasty personality could have caused a lot of trouble, especially for the married women on North Island, few of whom are faithful to their husbands.'

'Anything else about Thomas that might help our enquiry?' asked John

'Rachel, who does most of the housekeeping duties, constantly remarked on how often she found Thomas alone with his mother in a physical embrace. The Mistress did need a lot of comforting. She got none from the Master, or her eldest son,' said Abigail with a knowing look.

'Your not suggesting what I think?'

Abigail threw up her hands, 'Trust me, this is a strange and unhappy family. The world would be better off without them.'

'Let's go back to the dinner. If poison was given to Thomas through the sage and thyme gravy could someone had placed it there without you knowing?'

'Yes, Rachel and I carried the food from the cookhouse, and placed it around the hearth to keep it warm. Although most were outdoors drinking, the master came in to cut up the meat and I later saw Dr Sherman alone in front of the hearth. But even if poison was put in the gravy at that point the murderer could not guarantee that only Thomas would receive it. The herbal gravy was mixed with the pork before it was served so why did James and Tim survive?'

There was a long silence and then Abigail volunteered, 'Perchance the poison was on Thomas's hands.'

John was stunned – a simple explanation that he had missed. Abigail continued, 'Master cut the pork into large slabs. Thomas stuffed the pork into his mouth with his fingers.'

'So it could have been on his hands. Where would a murderer find poison in this settlement?' asked John.

'Dr Sherman has chests full of it, old Humphrey has a collection of English and native poisons that he uses largely to catch fish, and many of the men have obtained medicines from the local Indians that in the wrong quantity could be deadly. And Humphrey taught Miss Lucy all he knows. She probably has her own collection.'

'Poison on the hands is a possibility. What did Thomas touch that others did not?'

'He held a drinking cup in his hands for some time just before the meal.'

'Maybe the replacement cup had poison sprinkled over it? If Thomas was murdered who would you suspect within the household.'

'If Thomas had discovered some one's secret then everybody is a suspect. He may have seen a married woman with someone who was not her husband. Even the gentlefolk here are not innocents,' alleged Abigail, enjoying the opportunity to badmouth her betters.

'Are you suggesting that Mistress Elizabeth, Priscilla and even young Lucy have been nought with the servants?'

'Not necessarily with the servants. Look into Richard Goodwin's behaviour towards the women.'

'Why this plantation? Are there not enough women on his own estate?'

'No, he is a bachelor, and all his servants are men. My master on the other hand has encouraged married couples. There are twelve couples with six children, and twelve single men on North Island.'

'So the only women potentially available to the males on this settlement are three gentlewomen, two unmarried servants, and twelve married women on North Island

'Yes, unless they like the native girls.'

'Do any resort to the heathen?'

'Not on this plantation, Master forbids it.'

John sensed a tinge of bitterness in her comments about males. He also wondered which men she currently satisfied - a situation that might have coloured the views she had just expressed. He changed the topic.

'What if it didn't matter to the murderer which of the three took the poison. Was there anyone who had a grudge against James or Tim?'

'The labourers see James as a cruel and brutal taskmaster. Many were not prepared for the heavy manual labour that tobacco production requires and James forced the issue by punishing malingerers most severely. And there have been rumours about Tim and several married women. Everybody despised the Turd, but he could have been an innocent victim of an attempt on James by avenging workers or Tim by jealous husbands.'

'Tell me about other family members! Let's start with Lucy.'

'Miss Lucy is not the innocent young girl that her father dotes on. She knew about men as a young girl, and the gossip used to revolve around who stole her virginity. Since then she has been playing the field creating considerable tension - Mr Goodwin, Dr Sherman, Tim Lipton, and any number of servants and maybe her special Indian friend. Come to think of it she would have several reasons to murder Tom if he threatened to tell her father of her more lurid exploits. Since childhood she has been especially close to a Nanticoke boy whose father is the local war chief. Despite what I have just said, I like Lucy. She is a rebel, and an excellent woodsman. Old Humphrey and her Indian boy friend taught Lucy everything they knew. She is an uncanny shot. She can live unaided in the forest for weeks. When she doesn't get her way on the settlement she disappears for weeks into the wilds.'

'Is that where she is now? asked John.

'Probably. The spoilt brat is completely out of control. For a gentlewoman she behaves like a borrid bawd.'

7

ANDREW FOLLOWED HUMPHREY AS HE INSTRUCTED LUKE'S MEN ON the basics of hut building and canoe making. After the initial briefings Andrew sat with him on one of the large logs that eventually would be sawn into planks for the huts.

'Humphrey, you are privy to the secrets of the Browne household,' began Andrew.

'And they will stay with me,' interrupted the loyal retainer.

'Jehu! How can you remain loyal to a family of misfits? We have been sent to help them, but do they deserve our assistance?'

'Everybody has their demons,' Humphrey cryptically replied. 'Master's are a little more real than most.'

Andrew changed his focus. 'You have been in the Americas for over forty years?'

'I came to Jamestown as a lad but could never buckle under to the authority of the Governor, nor my masters. Living with the Indians suited me. I learnt very early how to grow the best tobacco. When I became too old to travel the interior I advised new settlers on how to grow it. There have been a constant stream of newcomers over the decades who did not have a clue how to get the best out of the land, and how to survive in the face of a difficult climate, mixed soils and often unfriendly Indians.'

'So Robert Browne is just the latest in a long history of employers who needed to learn the basics from you?'

'Yes, the Brownes were appalled to discover that there were no ploughs in Maryland, and the cultivation of tobacco required constant attention with the hoe, and manually removing grubs. Mr Robert misses his horses, but they are of no use here.'

'Who murdered young Tom?' asked Andrew.

'You think he was murdered? How come?' retorted the wily Humphrey.

'He was a healthy young man with no earlier signs of illness. The general consensus is that if death was not natural, he must have been poisoned. Who's the expert on poisons? Dr Sherman?'

'God's Blood! That stick is a charlatan. All book learning. Doesn't know the real power of the potions he has in his bag. I know more than most.'

'How are you an expert in poisons?' asked a cynical Andrew.

'Spoken like a green newcomer. Nature's cures need to be harvested from barks, roots, berries, the skins of toads, and certain fish in order to keep healthy, relieve pain, and catch fish or game. My grandmother was a cunning woman back in England with a vast knowledge of English herbs but I was too young to learn anything from her. My knowledge comes from the Indians of several nations. They have a massive range of potions to effect most desired outcomes. In the wrong quantities or mixtures they could be fatal.'

'Where are your poisons?'

Humphrey became defensive. 'Why do you ask?'

'If Tom was poisoned the potion must have come from Sherman or yourself.'

'Not necessarily, anybody can approach the Indians and obtain a range of potions.'

'Nevertheless let's concentrate on your supply. Where do you keep it?'

'On a bench in my hut, in pottery bowls. But these are the raw ingredients only. Unprocessed they have little potency.'

'Was there anything left lying about that could have killed Thomas?'

'A powder which I use to stun or kill fish –depending on how much you use. The Indians use a similar powder on their arrowheads to bring down deer. I do not know its effect on people. Perhaps the poisoner only wished to make Thomas sick but accidentally overdosed. This could be a practical joke that has gone sadly astray.'

'Who in the household has access to your poisons - and understands their effects?'

Humphrey was silent for some time. Andrew was about to repeat the question more firmly when the retainer quietly replied, 'There are no locks in this plantation. Everybody has access to my potions but only one person understands them. Both her Indian friends and I have given young Miss Lucy a detailed knowledge of herbal medicines. If this is an accidental poisoning you can rule out Miss Lucy. She would know exactly what she was doing.'

'Conversely if it was deliberate Lucy would be a prime suspect. Did she get on well with Thomas?' Andrew asked.

'No worse than the rest of the settlement. Thomas was not liked, except by his mother. He was a lazy, whining, trouble-making peeping Tom. If Miss Lucy had a reason to kill him so did dozens of others.'

Humphrey removed a flask from his jerkin took a couple of swigs, and offered it to Andrew. Andrew was taken aback by the potency of the liquor. Humphrey explained it was distilled by the Dutch in New Amsterdam to which he had added his own special ingredients. The men sat for some time regularly swapping the flask. Humphrey appeared deep in thought when he suddenly sprang to his feet. 'Jehu! The poor boy. It is probably too late. Take me back to West Island. I must speak urgently to the master.'

'What's the trouble?'

'Young Tom! He may have been buried alive.'

'Impossible, surely Sherman could tell whether Tom was dead or not?'

'No, not with the poison that Tom may have ingested. Indians bring down a deer and when you approach the animal, it appears dead. There is apparently no breathing. Yet within hours it wakes up and appears as healthy as before. Someone may have given this poison to Thomas as a joke. It backfired, and they thought they had killed him.'

Andrew returned to the manor house with Humphrey. Robert, Luke and John were gathered under the nearby tree drinking beer. As Humphrey explained his thoughts to Robert, Andrew simultaneously brought Luke and John up to date. A shaken Robert finally spoke, 'Humphrey, you must be wrong. I've seen dozens of men killed in battle, and had no difficulty separating those who still hung precariously to life with those who had passed over. Thomas was dead.'

Luke bravely intervened, 'Given the uncertain properties of the Indian poison that may have been used, can you be absolutely sure?'

'Even if Tom were buried alive he would now be dead. He could not survive all this time buried underground. Leave it be!'

Humphrey persisted, 'Master, I have seen bodies buried for days which when uncovered the victim recovered. All that is needed is air and water. There was air in the coffin which was built of green uneven planks which would have allowed water to percolate through the soil and into the coffin. Thomas's coma like state would have reduced his intake of air considerably. He could still be alive.'

'I will talk to Elizabeth and Priscilla,' replied Robert, as he sought to avoid a decision.

Robert entered the house. Luke, John and Humphrey heard a hideous cry which turned into a series of screams, interleaved with hysterical sobbing, and the clear repetition of the word, no. Suddenly Priscilla emerged from the house, and ran screaming towards Humphrey, 'You evil old man, filling father with such ideas. Listen to what you have done to mother!'

Priscilla wielded her father's cane in the direction of Humphrey. Luke grabbed her wrist. 'Unhand me sir! Or I will give you a thrashing also,' she shouted hysterically.

John tried to reason with her, 'Miss Priscilla, Colonel Tremayne must discover the circumstances of your brother's death. Don't you wish to know if he miraculously survives?'

Priscilla did not answer and strode back into the house ignoring her father as they passed at the door. Robert reached the men. 'You heard the response of my wife, and witnessed that of my daughter. Leave Tom where he is.'

Humphrey insisted, 'If he were buried alive every minute we waste could be his last. We must act now.'

Robert ignored the comment. Luke turned to him. 'Your final decision?'

'The body will not be disturbed,' was the emphatic reply.

Luke's response took everybody by surprise. 'I am sorry Robert. I have authority from Lord Baltimore to override all jurisdictions in his name – including your's. The coffin will be disinterred, and the body examined. You may be present or not.'

Robert's face went white, and then flushed as his whole body convulsed. He kicked everything in sight. and his language amazed the hardened soldiers. Robert could do nothing. His son was missing and his men except for Humphrey were on North Island. Luke, Andrew and John could call on twenty or more armed and trained men to implement Luke's decision. As quickly as his condition flared, it died away. He quietened down. He saw the value of finding the answer to Thomas's state when he was buried, without having to face the antagonism of his wife and daughter. The decision was out of his hands. Robert returned to the house, while Humphrey procured three shovels.

The soil was largely sand and the three men were so absorbed in their task that they did not see three figures armed with hoes creeping up on them. At the last moment a scream from near the cookhouse was heard. 'Watch out!' John recognised the voice as that of Abigail Hicks, and turned in time to deflect a blow from Priscilla. Andrew had not heard the warning, and took a full blow from the tiny but frenzied Elizabeth that knocked him out. Luke was able to fend off the attack from Rachel O' Brien. The women apart from Rachel were mouthing unintelligent obscenities at the diggers. Alerted by the noise Robert and Abigail ran to the burial site, and with John led the women back to the house. Humphrey offered his flask to the lips of the inert Andrew. He then disappeared for some time, and returned with a poultice made from the roots of numerous plants and applied it to the large gash on Andrew's head.

'Keep digging Colonel. Every second counts,' pleaded Humphrey.

Luke soon reached the coffin and with Humphrey's help lifted the lid. The body had not had time to deteriorate significantly. Both men examined Tom and nodded in agreement. He had long been dead. The two men then confronted the major question. Had he been buried alive?

'Humphrey are these marks on the coffin lid chisel marks, or the work of desperate finger nails?'

'I built this coffin. They are not my chisel marks.'

'Mercy, Thomas was buried alive,' concluded Luke.

'A horrible death. Perhaps sir, you could spare the family - and lie.'

'A good thought Humphrey, especially given the reaction of the women. Let's get this lid back on.'

'Wait, Colonel what is that pronounced mark on the side of the coffin near the head?'

'It's an initial which Tom has partially scratched out with his bleeding fingernails.'

'Tom is naming his murderer. This marking is the letter L,' declared Humphrey rather sadly.

'I'm not sure. It could be a badly formed T or even a J. In his state Thomas may not have known where on the coffin wall or lid he was writing. He could have been completely disoriented. The letter may not have been completed. I don't think it helps.'

Humphrey thought to himself. If it was an L it incriminates Lucy. This was one practical joke of Miss Lucy that had gone horribly wrong. He must find Lucy before Luke.

8

LUKE DREW THE INVESTIGATION TOGETHER, 'LUCY AS A MA-
LEVOLENT prank poisoned her brother, never intending to kill
him. When it miscarried, she ran off.'

'Too simple!' grumbled Andrew. 'The only facts against
Lucy are that she knows about poisons, and is missing. We
don't know how the poison was administered. And I'm still
not sure that Tom was the intended victim.'

John was also unimpressed, 'Your explanation suits Robert
Browne. His son was accidentally killed, and his daughter
would be free from any serious punishment. Nostalgia distorts
your judgment Luke. There are many avenues we have yet to
pursue. Tom was a weird voyeur. Many people could have had
a reason to remove him. Our priority is to unearth the secrets
of this settlement. We have scarcely begun.'

Next morning the three soldiers returned to West Island.
Luke lied to Robert about Tom's state when he was buried, and
the old planter revealed a moment of compassion, 'Glad the
boy did not suffer.'

Luke, despite his sergeant's misgivings then put his hypothesis to Robert, which was immediately rejected. 'Young
Lucy is a prankster, but I didn't see her in a position where she
could have given Tom the poison. It was Priscilla who helped
Tom with his drink, and sat next to him at dinner. Despite
what you suggest, I believe this was a random attack on all of
us, and Tom was the unlucky victim. You need to do better
Tremayne.'

Suddenly the frantic ringing of a bell interrupted the discussion. Robert turned to Luke, 'Trouble! Get your men over
here as fast as you can. Let's get down to the quay and see
what confronts us!' Luke sent John to rally his men. Robert

explained that there were watchtowers scattered through the plantations, each with its distinctive bell. Continuous tolling indicated danger, three short peals that vital information needed to be relayed to the community, and a long repetition of single chimes signified the all clear.

The bell that had rung was on the most westerly point of West Island which gave unlimited vision up and down the Bay. Within minutes armed workers from across the Browne and Sherman grants began to gather on the shoreline. Luke's men in full battle array soon joined them. A hundred or more canoes were heading down the Bay towards them. 'God's Blood,' muttered Robert. 'Susquehanna - the most warlike and powerful of the local tribes. Until recently they regularly sailed passed us to harass the Indians around St Mary's. Governor Stone signed a treaty recognizing their suzerainty over the Indians in our region, and they recognised Lord Baltimore's power over those in the south. Either they are about to break the treaty, or they are heading specifically for us.'

'Why would they be hostile towards you, Robert?' asked a suspicious Luke.

'They might be acting on behalf of the Severn River, or Kent Island settlers to remove me. Where is Humphrey when you need him? He speaks their language fluently, and is known to some of their chieftains.'

Humphrey had set out up river looking for Lucy but he heard the warning bell and hastened to return. He scrambled ashore and approached his master. He was silent as the canoes came closer. Eventually he spoke, 'This is bad. In the lead canoe is the war chief of the Wolf clan, the fiercest of the Susquehanna clans. They are raised only for the most serious military endeavours. Look at their weapons. The canoes bristle with muskets. They outnumber us by about three to one.'

Luke was impressed. The Indians were incredibly tall and almost completely naked with a skin of a cinnamon hue and painted in green, black and yellow stripes. As they drew closer their leader shouted in heavily accented English, 'I am Tamuagh, war chieftain of the Wolf clan, seeking permission of Mr Browne to pass through his plantation.'

Humphrey replied, 'Why does the war chief of the mighty Susquehanna wish to cross our lands?'

The war chief came ashore, and embraced Humphrey. They were an incongruous pair. The Indian was the perfect specimen of a man. Taller than Luke, and with his arm and leg muscles rippling, he gave the impression of amazing strength and agility. Humphrey by no means unfit for his age was at least a foot shorter. Humphrey introduced the war chief to Robert Browne who had the foresight to order his men to place their weapons on the ground. Luke was not happy at this gesture as Indian after Indian came ashore, and surrounded the settlers. Others landed along Goodwin's shoreline while the North Arm of the river was congested with Indian canoes. Humphrey explained, 'The Mohawks are raiding Susquehanna villages. While the other clans of the Susquehanna are defending the home villages, the Wolf clan has divided in half. This group have been ordered to cut across country, move up our river, conscript the local Nanticokes and come up behind the attacking Mohawks, cutting off their return to the Hudson River. A smaller group is to sail down the western shore of the Bay to ensure that the Piscataways do not use the opportunity to attack them from the south.'

Robert indicated to Tamuagh that he could pass through the plantation without harassment. The war chief signalled to his men, nodded to Robert Browne, saluted Humphrey and returned to his canoe. Very quickly all the Indians were heading upriver. Within ten minutes all trace of the Indian incursion had gone. Luke was amazed at the silence. This was then broken by a series of short peals of the warning bell, returning the settlement to normality.

Luke was astonished at the ease with which Humphrey had conversed with the Indian leader, and asked him how many local tongues he understood. The old retainer responded enthusiastically, 'Initially in Virginia I learnt the Algonkian language from the Powhatan – the same tongue as used by the Piscataway, the Nanticokes and the Lenape. Most of my life was spent in the wilderness with Iroquoian speaking tribes such as Susquehanna. When Tamuagh was a young man he and I travelled up the Susquehanna River, crossed the mountains and explored the headwaters of the great rivers flowing south. We went so far north that we met with the nations of the Great Lakes, and encountered many French traders and missionaries. Tamuagh was seeking supplies of beaver pelts. I acted as interpreter when he sold his purchases to English traders on the Chesapeake.'

Robert rudely interrupted, 'Enow old man! Where were you when the bell rang? You were not on the island.' Robert continued to rant and rave and appeared momentarily distressed as his ever present cane slashed the air perilously close to Humphrey. The retainer was obviously used to such tantrums and waited until Robert calmed down and replied, 'I was on the river heading inland to do a bit of hunting to give Abigail some game to cook.'

Suddenly John shouted, 'Listen! I hear gunfire in the distance. Quiet! There it is again.' The men looked at each other in alarm.

'God's death,' exclaimed Robert. 'The Susquehanna have gone berserk. Sounds like a massacre.'

'Let's get up river fast! Someone needs our help,' said Luke innocently.

'No way, you saw how many there were. We do not get involved. Come and eat! Humphrey, resume your hunting trip – and find out what that gunfire was about!'

Luke and Robert sat on a bench under the large tree and drank while they awaited the sergeants who had supervised the return of Luke's armed men to South Island. Luke was in no mood for diplomacy. 'Robert since I have been here I have not seen your eldest son or youngest daughter. Where are they?'

'After Thomas's funeral James went off to survey the further reaches of my grant for future cultivation, or allocation to new settlers. In the process he said he would keep a look out for his wandering sister who at a sniff of a crisis runs off into the forest. Thomas's death triggered her disappearance. I blame Humphrey. He taught her to survive out there better than any heathen.'

'Cuds-me Robert! Don't take me for a fool. Lucy kills Thomas accidentally, and big brother takes her away to prevent justice being done. You have kept them away so that my limited investigation cannot really get to the truth,' shouted a frustrated Luke.

'Rubbish Tremayne! Lucy will soon return. She always does, and this time the desire to see young Tim Lipton is an additional pressure. You'll have your opportunity to question her.'

Luke suspected Robert knew more about Lucy and James's whereabouts than he was admitting but his interrogation was halted by the return of his sergeants, and the appearance of Abigail Hicks. As she placed some corn fritters on a long platter in front of the men Luke immediately responded to the sensuousness of the wench. She faced him and curtseyed, 'Please to meet you Colonel Tremayne. I have been watching you. If you need anything don't hesitate to ask.' Her emphasis on anything could not have been misinterpreted. Luke had sworn to end his womanising days, but lust was already eroding that promise.

All through the meal Luke thought of Abigail. As the afternoon reached its warmest the group were about to disperse when John alerted the others to two canoes that had run ashore on the northern edge of West Island. Luke recognised Humphrey, and a tall well proportioned Susquehanna warrior who Luke noticed had a missing right thumb, and unlike those who had passed through earlier had red lines on his body in addition to the green, yellow and black. The condition of the third man shocked the group. It was Dr Sherman bleeding profusely from the mouth, and being dragged along by the Indian.

'Mercy me Humphrey, what's this?' asked a shocked Robert.

The Indian threw Sherman to the ground, and drew his bow and pointed the arrow at the bleeding doctor. Robert intervened, 'Humphrey, stop your friend, and get Miss Priscilla here to dress his wounds.'

Humphrey replied, 'You might wish to order Black Cougar to release the arrow.'

An appalled Robert muttered, 'What could justify the murder of an English gentleman by a savage?'

'Black Cougar is not the savage. Sherman is the barbarian. You gave Tamuagh safe passage. To the Indian your word is your life. The Indians travelled up river and were in sight of the Nanticoke village, which is within your plantation when several of them were killed by bursts of musket fire from the riverbank. At first a renegade band of Nanticokes was suspected. The Susquehanna returned fire, silenced the attackers and a small raiding party cut across country and caught up with the fleeing attackers. They were not Nanticokes. They were white men who, after their fingernails were removed, revealed all. They had been told to kill as many savages as they could.'

'Told by whom?' asked Luke.

'By their master, Dr Sherman,' replied Humphrey.

'How did you become involved Humphrey?' asked Robert.

'I was travelling up river and overtook Black Cougar paddling up stream with Dr Sherman. He told me what had happened. After their confession Sherman's men were freed and their master abducted. I was able to convince him to bring Sherman here rather than return him to the Susquehanna.

I claimed that you had given your word that Tamuagh could travel your land in peace, your word had been broken, and your honour impugned. It was up to you to inflict punishment.'

Robert turned to the prone Sherman, 'Matthew, why? You could have had us all massacred.'

Humphrey interrupted, 'I did not tell you the full story. Sherman broke your spoken word. Black Cougar removed his tongue. The doctor cannot answer.'

9

HUMPHREY WAS WRONG. BLACK COUGAR HAD MUTILATED MATTHEW'S TONGUE, not removed it - a symbolic act rather than an actual punishment. Nursed by Priscilla, and using Humphrey's and his own potions, Matthew was speaking, although indistinctly, within days. It was then that he summoned Luke to his bedside and whispered, 'I didn't do it, and my men are innocent. Humphrey's story is complete fiction. Not that I blame Humphrey. He accepted what the Indian told him.'

'Perchance you are innocent, but how do you know your men did not use the passing Indians for target practice?'

'In addition to tobacco growing, my men and I make considerable money from trading furs with the inland Indians, and we need the friendship of the local Nanticokes, and then further up the Indian trail, the good will of the Susquehanna. Why would my men jeopardize their major source of income?

They get no wages as indentured servants – just shelter and sustenance.'

'What exactly happened the day you were assaulted?'

'My men and I returned to our plantation after responding to Robert's warning bell. The men moved directly to a field some miles from the river. I was in my house working through some accounts when I heard distant gunfire. I went outside and moved across the plantation in the direction of the noise. Entering the woodlands along the river I suddenly felt an Indian knife across my throat, and found myself in the grip of that giant Susquehanna brave. Before I could speak he forced open my mouth and sliced into my tongue. The pain was such that I passed out. When I came to I was in a two man canoe, and my attacker was paddling us up river. I passed in and out of consciousness, and the next thing I remember was Humphrey overhauling us, and after a long conversation in the heathen language, which I did not understand, my captor and Humphrey turned around, and paddled back to Robert's house. You know the rest.'

'If you and your men didn't fire the shots, who did and why?'

'Black Cougar fired the shots - probably into the air - to create the basis of his fiction. It has more to do with his conflict with Tamuagh than a specific attack on me.'

Both men were silent for some time as Matthew gave himself another mouthwash. After spitting out the blood flecked wash into a basin Matthew quietly pleaded with Luke, 'Tremayne, prove my innocence!' Priscilla entered the room, and made clear that it was time to leave.

Luke returned to South Island and relayed to Andrew and John Matthew's version of events. Andrew asked, 'Do you believe him?'

'It is worth checking out. Andrew, talk to Sherman's men! John, revisit the scene of the alleged attack on the Indians,

52

and the subsequent assault on Sherman! I will go through his books.'

Later that day the three men reassembled. Andrew reported, 'Sherman's story is supported by his men. They claimed they were worming the tobacco crop on the other side of the plantation when they heard very distant gunfire. As it did not continue for long the men continued working the field. All of them had their fingernails intact, and they claimed nobody was missing.'

John related that although he walked up and down the riverbank he found no sign of musket fire along the riverbank, but did come across a trail of dried blood that validated Sherman's story. Luke verified from Sherman's accounts that he and his men derived considerable income from trading furs in which the Susquehanna were important partners.

Luke wondered whether the attack on Sherman was part of the same plot to undermine the Brownes, 'If it is, then the heathen, not the English must be behind it,' concluded Andrew.

'Andrew, it hasn't take you long to turn into an Indian hater. Why blame them?' asked Luke.

'It was an Indian brave who butchered Sherman's tongue, and Thomas probably died from an Indian poison.'

Next morning the three soldiers returned to West Island to discuss their conclusions with Robert. As they pulled their canoes ashore Luke called out to Humphrey who was shaping a new canoe. 'Morning Humphrey, can I ask you a few questions regarding the attack on Sherman?'

Humphrey grunted, and placed his adze on the ground. 'I know no more than I told you when I brought him back. I was still here when we heard the initial gunfire. Soon after I headed up river and after some time overhauled a two man canoe. I was shocked when I saw Dr Sherman half unconscious with blood streaming from his mouth. The Indian explained what had had happened which I have already recounted to you. I pleaded with him that my master should have the final say in punishing a man who had broken his word.'

'Was there anything in what the Indian said, or from your own observations that causes you to doubt his story?'

'No, I accepted his word.'

'Have you seen Black Cougar before?'

'Dozens of times. He is a real trouble maker. A medicine man as well as a warrior he carries out the dirty tasks that Tamuagh wants to avoid. He leads a small separate group of Susquehanna and is plotting to overthrow Tamuagh. Only last week I saw him leaving Mr Goodwin's landing beach just after dawn and paddle up river.'

'Why didn't you mention this before - an Indian snooping around the plantations. He could have murdered Thomas, kidnapped James and Lucy, and then assaulted Sherman. Andrew thinks the three events were Indian contrived, even before you mentioned this wandering heathen.'

'Many Indians cross the plantations. They trade with the labourers as well as the masters. What would the Indians gain from such attacks? Mr Browne is known as a supporter of treating the Indians as partners, and of signing a treaty with them as advocated by Lord Baltimore.'

'Browne has such views, but what about Sherman?'

'He has relatives among the Puritan settlers on the Severn. They treat all Indians as hostile. He may have negative views like many who live on the frontier, but I have not seen any sign of it since he took up his tenancy. Maybe this is a Susquehanna warning to all Puritans? The Susquehanna do not like the settlement on the Severn. It is too close to their home villages.'

Luke made his way to Matthew's room just as the recovering patient came through the door. 'Good to see you up and about,' Luke responded cheerfully.

'I was coming to see you,' uttered Matthew with a pronounced slur.

Luke spoke, 'Before you continue, we checked out your story and find it stands up. Something is happening on these plantations. The attack on you is part of a bigger story. For the present the source of this malevolence has me stumped. Andrew thinks it is an Indian plot, but I cannot see what they would gain.'

'Since I arrived here I have sensed a malevolent force. The Brownes are a very divided family. I would seek the source of the evil within that family, rather than with our Indian neighbours.'

'What did you want of me?' asked Luke.

'I am going to my cousins across the Bay to recuperate. They are among the new Puritan settlers on the Severn who have moved on from Virginia. If you really are here to inform Lord Baltimore of what is going on the views of the Puritans would give you a fuller picture.'

Luke agreed, but was immediately apprehensive. Lord Baltimore's man would not be welcomed on the Severn – a view which Robert Browne endorsed when Luke told him of the plan.

'Robert, is Matthew a Puritan spy?' asked a suspicious Luke.

'How can you tell what a man believes? As I have said before since he took up his land neither he nor his men have shown the usual obsessive behaviour, and high morals of that ilk. Maybe he was sent here to keep an eye on me, but his interest in Priscilla could have dampened his enthusiasm for politics. Why?'

'He has relatives on the Severn. He may be part of the Puritan conspiracy to overthrow Baltimore. To take up land beside Baltimore's strongest supporter would be a clever move.'

'I wouldn't jump to any conclusions based on attitudes of relatives. Guilt by association is far from valid in these complex colonial situations. Look at your own situation. As we both know the Civil War split families.'

Robert suddenly lost interest, and wandered off. Luke decided to question the women. He asked Rachel to inform her mistress. 'The mistress does not wish to see you, sir,' Rachel replied curtly.

Luke was in no mode to brook opposition. 'Tell your mistress that I will forcibly enter her room and interrogate her regarding her son's murder.'

Rachel slunk away and within minutes Elizabeth Browne entered the room. She looked even worse than she appeared at their first meeting. She looked decades older than her husband and could have passed for her children's grandmother. Her frown, and somewhat vacant look did not change. 'Mistress Elizabeth I regret the circumstances in which I must question you. Tell me what you remember of the dinner at which your son died?' asked Luke politely.

Tears welled up, and Luke began to despair that he would get any civil communication from this sad woman. 'Forsooth Tremayne, I have nothing to add. It was a meal like dozens that went before it. The servants prepared it in the cookhouse and brought it into the hall where it was kept warm in the hearth. My husband carved up the meat and placed it on three platters spread along the table.'

'Did you see your husband carve the meat and distribute it?'

'No, I was drinking outside with Dr Sherman and Mr Goodwin.'

'Did anyone enter the hall while your husband was carving?'

'Only the servants who brought in the vegetables.'

'Mistress Elizabeth, we suspect that Thomas died of poison introduced into his food. When could this have been done, and by whom?'

'Any of them could have done it.'

'Who do you mean?'

'Tremayne this is not a happy family. My husband and eldest son hated Tom. Both are unreasonable vindictive men.

56

James was sitting near Tom. He could have slipped the poison into the meal as he reached across the table for more food. Why has he disappeared? Lucy was always up to mischief and incessantly teased poor Tom. She could have helped her evil brother kill him.'

Luke was taken aback that Elizabeth suspected her eldest son of murdering her youngest and favourite boy, maybe with the help of her youngest daughter. He was fully aware of the tensions, and hatred that permeated her views. He probed further, 'But why? Why would James kill his own brother?

'Tom threatened to make public a family secret involving his father. James would do anything to protect his father.'

'What was that secret?'

'I learned a long time ago never to refer to it. I don't intend to tell anybody now. My husband would kill me if I did.' Elizabeth left the room as fast as her weary body could carry her - sobbing as she went.

Luke, somewhat disconcerted, went in search of Priscilla.

10

PRISCILLA WAS OBSESSIVE. SHE DEVOTED HERSELF INCREASINGLY TO HER deranged mother, and now applied the same uncompromising dedication to the recovering Matthew. Luke found her tidying the room in which Matthew had convalesced. 'Miss Priscilla, your brother was poisoned during his last meal. Did you see anything that might explain how it happened?'

'You are father's friend. Ask him!' came the venomous reply.

'Your father and Thomas did not get on, but would he kill his own son?' asked Luke surprised at the bitterness of the response.

'Father's treatment of Tom was worse than you know. I say no more. Father forbids family matters being discussed with strangers.'

'Miss Priscilla there is a possibility that the death of Thomas, the absence of your other siblings, and the assault on Dr Sherman are part of the same plot to discredit and destroy your family. Your father is unlikely to behind such a co-ordinated outrage.'

'You don't know father. He killed Tom, and because he believed Dr. Sherman and I were becoming close he had his Indian friend attack Matthew to warn him off. My siblings have run off because they are implicated in Tom's death. They will stay with their Indian friends until you leave. They can do what they like as far as father is concerned. If you are to be any use here Colonel, protect Matthew! His life is in danger.'

With that request Priscilla strode from the room, and nearly collided with Rachel O'Brien. Rachel was an austere young Irish Catholic who wore her religion openly in the form of a large crucifix, and the crossing of herself excessively in times of stress. She was small and plump with curly black hair, big brown eyes and a round face. Her bodice and skirt were black with a minimum of white linen collar and cuffs. Her apron was a drab olive brown and her coif a dull cream.

Luke sought her version of the fatal meal. She seemed relieved to talk about it. 'Abigail prepared the meat in the cookhouse and we took it into the hall, and left it in the hearth where the master carved it. Later we took in three platters of vegetables, and three empty platters on which we placed the carved meat. Abigail poured applesauce over two of the meat platters, and sage and thyme gravy over the third. After that we left, and had our own meal with Humphrey in the cookhouse. We did not re-enter the main house until Mr. Timothy came and told us of Thomas's death.'

'Anything unusual prior to Tom's death?'

'No, except that the master insisted on tasting the sauces that Abigail had prepared.'

'Could the master have placed something in the sauce?'

'Maybe.'

'But how could he be sure that Tom, and not James or Timothy received the poisoned gravy?'

'They may have been part of the plot, and the master told them not to eat the sauce. They were always fooling about with their food, switching trenchers and stealing each other's meal. It would have been easy.'

'Not so easy Rachel. Abigail said the sauce was mixed through the meat. The others would have had to refrain from the meat as well. All the men ate a hearty meal, including Thomas. Surely he was not so hated that his father and siblings would kill him?'

'Sir, I am the personal servant of the mistress, and she doted on her Tom. But I have to admit Mr Thomas was odd and nasty, and hated by everybody. He spied on couples. His only friend, apart from his mother and Miss Priscilla, was a renegade Indian who the Nanticokes had expelled from their community.'

'Did Tom molest you, Rachel?'

'All the males in this settlement try it on. Mr Thomas was no exception, but he did not persist. Abigail had more serious trouble with him. After her sweetheart who works for Mr Goodwin heard about it he assaulted Mr Thomas.'

'Surely an attack on the master's son by a worker on a neighbouring plantation would have been severely punished. Perchance this man resented his punishment and killed Thomas.'

'He had no cause. The master refused to punish him, and handed him over to Mr Goodwin who I hear reduced his rum ration by a pitiable amount for a week.'

'Nevertheless I will speak to Abigail's friend when I visit Mr Goodwin.'

Back on South Island Luke reported to his sergeants the evidence of the women. Elizabeth blamed her son James, Priscilla had put the finger on her father, and Rachel had incriminated both siblings and Tim Lipton. It was possible that James as he unobtrusively reached across the table, sprinkled Tom's meal. But Robert could not have doctored the sauce as both James and Tim had eaten it without any negative effects.

Andrew whose frustration and concern had been building for some days finally exploded. 'Luke, if the murder is part of a family feud, and not an Indian plot, the murderer is one of the Browne family - a family that it is our mission to assist. They are a collection of misfits or worse. We should cut our losses and return home. I don't want to help such a begrumpled family.'

'I have similar reservations,' admitted Luke. 'The family could be involved in Tom's murder, but the attack on Sherman, and the absence of James and Lucy need to be probed further before we leave.'

'What's our next move then?' asked John.

'I failed an earlier investigation because I ignored the ordinary people who probably know more than their superiors. I want you and some of the men to mingle with the workers on the Sherman and Browne plantations. Andrew and I will take Sherman to the Severn settlement. General Cromwell needs to know the precise nature of that enterprise. We will be gone seven to ten days.'

Luke borrowed Robert's shallop and headed out into the Bay and took advantage of an out of season strong south westerly which relieved the men from the arduous task of rowing. Luke, Andrew, two troopers, Matthew, Humphrey and two of Robert's labourers made up the party. The relatively heavy but light drafted boat almost skimmed across the surface as the wind intensified. Humphrey brought the vessel almost to Kent Island and turned due west until it reached the western shore of the Bay. The wind reversed and under Humphrey's direction the boat hugged the shoreline as it was rowed north towards the mouth of the Severn.

Andrew was the first to see them. What had in the haze first appeared to be some giant sea creature were dozens of Indian canoes heading south. Humphrey responded. 'I am sailing into the first inlet I can find. That looks like the other Susquehanna war party Tamuagh mentioned – a pre-emptive strike to prevent the Piscataways taking advantage of the Mohawk attack to weaken the Susquehanna.'

Humphrey ran the shallop ashore on a sandy beach in a narrow bay, not easily visible to traffic paddling south along the western shore. Luke asked, 'Why are we hiding? If they are after the Piscataways they will ignore us.'

'You can never be sure. The Susquehanna are no fools. They have defeated the tribes to the south, and Lord Baltimore is seeking a further treaty with them. The settlers on the Severn resent Indian power more than those on the Eastern shore, and the Susquehanna may at any time engage in a pre-emptive strike against them. These Indians may come ashore anywhere along the coast, travel overland, and attack our settlements at St Mary's or along the Severn. I lived with this tribe for decades. If their witch doctors tell the chiefs that the time is right to strike against an unsuspecting victim it will happen without any warning being given.'

Humphrey's word immediately proved prophetic. Instead of paddling past the entrance to the cove the whole war party entered it, and paddled towards the beached shallop. Humphrey whispered to Luke, 'We are seriously outnumbered and I don't recognise their leader.'

Humphrey greeted the war chief who approached the Englishmen accompanied by half a dozen braves. The two men conversed for some time and eventually Humphrey turned to his companions. 'The chief wants to know why we protect the beginning of the trail that leads directly to the camp of the hated Piscataway which they are about to destroy. They don't trust us – we go with them or they kill us. They fear we will warn the Piscataway, or if left here attack them from the rear on behalf of their enemy.'

'Tell them that we were heading north for the Severn, well away from the Piscataway.'

Humphrey after further discussion reported back to Luke, 'You and I will stay with the Susquehanna as hostages. All our muskets are to be confiscated. The rest of the men will leave immediately, and once into the Bay turn north. They will be escorted out of the cove and if they change direction a cascade of arrows will descend on them.'

Luke's men placed their muskets on the sand. The Indians pushed the shallop into the water. Andrew led the men back aboard and they rowed towards the head of the inlet accompanied by four canoes of Indians. Humphrey whispered to Luke, 'Lord Baltimore ordered that Indians were not to approach English settlements by land. Their approach had to be by the sea. You will soon understand why? They move through the countryside silently and swiftly. The Piscataways will not know what hit them.'

'Unless we warn them,' replied Luke.

'Why would we Colonel? Advice from an old hand. Never take sides in an Indian conflict if it can be avoided. Why would you want to help the Piscataways against the Susquehanna? You know nothing about either. Let the heathen fight each other. Do not get involved, especially on the side of the weak. Our sole aim is to escape. Trails intersect, and there is one that heads north towards the Severn not far along this east west path.

The Susquehanna moved along the trail in single file, but whenever trouble was anticipated the file spun out both left and right and formed an extended rank moving silently through the forest. While progressing in the latter formation the silence was broken by loud shouting, simultaneously accompanied by the swish of countless arrows directed against them. Luke and Humphrey hit the ground as the latter whispered, 'Play dead!'

The two men lay motionless as Piscataways wielding war clubs rushed at the surprised Susquehanna. They ignored the prone Englishmen, and raced toward their enemies. As the rivals engaged in man to man encounters now some distance from them, Luke and Humphrey rose and ran from the conflict. After several minutes a puffing Humphrey signalled for Luke to stop. The two men sat against a tree trunk on the edge of a small clearing. There was little undergrowth, and Humphrey indicated notches on a number of trees. This was the intersection of two Indian trails one of which ran north to the Severn.

Just as the men were about to rise and walk north, a herd of deer sauntered into the clearing where the grasses were palatable. Luke scrambled to his feet and moved around the trunk of the tree. He froze. A sleek grey wolf baring its glistening white teeth blocked his progress.

11

Intent on stalking the deer, the wolf after an initial snarl and prolonged stare at the human obstruction, moved on. Luke had never confronted a wolf before. He had no idea how to react. Humphrey had not seen the wolf that faced Luke. He was concentrating on four other wolves that were moving silently through the undergrowth on the other side of the clearing. Both men were transfixed. Then with military precision the pack struck, isolating a young deer and killing it within minutes.

As the wolves feasted, the men relaxed, and as quietly as Europeans could, headed up the trail towards the Puritan settlement. Humphrey claimed that no human had been attacked by a wolf along the Chesapeake. There was just so much food available. The dearth of sheep in the colony was due to the slaughter of them by wolves that appeared to relish an occasional change from venison. The colonists quickly discovered wolves had little taste for cattle or pigs.

After several hours of easy walking the two men came to a small stream, and refreshed themselves. Luke was hungry and tired. He reflected on the adage that an empty belly bears no body. During their march northwards Luke had seen several deer, but without muskets it was difficult for him to get close enough to the animals to bring them down. Luck was now with them. Near the stream at which they drank Humphrey was alerted to the buzz of flies. The source of their attention was a partly eaten carcase of a deer that Humphrey assured him had only recently been killed. Humphrey cut some of the unpolluted meat with his dagger and offered Luke a portion of the raw flesh. As Luke reached for his meat an arrow went through the edge of his shirt, and pinned him to the tree against which he sat. Simultaneously Humphrey fell across the body of the mutilated deer, an arrow protruding from his upper leg.

Luke removed the arrow that pinned his shirtsleeve to the tree, and moved to assist Humphrey. The wound did not look too bad, despite the blood, as most of the arrowhead still protruded from the leg. Luke extracted the arrow. Humphrey nodded his thanks and pointed with alarm over Luke's shoulder. Five Indians with bows drawn moved in for the kill. Humphrey protested. He was a blood brother of the Wolf clan, and friend of paramount chief Tamuagh.

Humphrey translated their reply, 'We betrayed them to the Piscataway. We warned their enemy, which led to the death of many of their braves, and now we must pay the price. I argued that as a blood brother I must be taken to the Susquehanna village and make my case to the elders. It was not the role of a war party to execute a brother. They are not in the mood to listen. They just cannot accept that without our help the chicken livered Piscataway knew they, the mighty Susquehanna, were coming. Their honour has suffered an immense blow, and we are to pay the price.'

'All is not lost. Listen!'

The babble of English voices could be heard, increasing in volume as the chatterers came closer to Luke and Humphrey. The Indians also heard it. They disappeared into the forest as quietly as they had come. Humphrey slipped into unconsciousness. Within minutes the noisy party reached them. Luke introduced himself as coming from Robert Browne's plantation on route to the settlement on the Severn. The leader of the new group formally presented himself, 'I am Edward Lloyd, a settler on the Severn and commandant of our Fort Providence. Your shallop reached our plantations earlier today. The situation was explained to me by your Sergeant Ford who is here with us.'

Andrew stepped forward, and embraced Luke who thanked the new arrivals. 'You saved us from certain death, but we must get Humphrey back to your settlement and have his wound properly dressed. He has lost a lot of blood.'

Luke was astonished that the Severn contingent consisted of over fifty men and he asked, 'Mr Lloyd, why so many men to find two missing Englishmen?'

'You were not our prime objective. We saw the war canoes pass Fort Providence, and feared that the heathen may land further down the Bay, and move up this trail to attack us. When your men reported that the Indians had gone ashore and taken you captive I raised the militia and marched south to confront them.'

'Happily your concern is misplaced Commandant. The Susquehanna were on a pre-emptive strike to prevent the Piscataway taking advantage of the current Mohawk attack on their home villages. Just now we were attacked by a remnant of the Susquehanna, who believed we had betrayed them. Five of them were about to finish us off when they heard you approaching.'

Lloyd spoke to some of his men, and then ordered the party to return to the Severn. He asked for Luke's dagger and sword, and also ensured that Andrew and Humphrey were completely disarmed. 'Sorry for this Tremayne but you come from Robert Browne who is no friend of God's people.'

Luke protested, but Lloyd simply replied, 'No discussion until we feed you, and dress the wounds of your man.'

Luke was fed within the palisade of Fort Providence. All those who had left the Browne plantation, except for Matthew Sherman, were confined to the fort. Commandant Lloyd was taking no chances. The Puritan leader led Luke to a large natural rock formation in one corner of the fort on which they sat. 'Sorry to be so cautious Tremayne, but you come from a plantation of the Antichrist. Browne is a stooge of the papist tyrant Baltimore, and in constant contact with the Papists at St Mary's. And Sherman informs me that you are soldiers sent specifically to assist Browne suppress subversives, of which we must number ourselves. So why are you really here? Sherman could have come here without your unnecessary involvement.'

Before Luke could answer a young man whom Luke vaguely recognised came across to them. 'Colonel Tremayne, I thought it was you. I recognized Sergeant Ford when he arrived earlier today.'

Lloyd was surprised, 'Harry, you know this man?'

Yes uncle, he was my commanding officer at Dublin Castle until I resigned to join you.'

Lloyd turned towards Luke, 'Even more interesting. Why is a senior military officer of the Parliament working for the papist peer Baltimore, and his Maryland lackey Browne?'

'Commandant, read this.'

Luke retrieved from deep within his clothing one of the authorizations he had received from Cromwell. Lloyd read it carefully, and turned to his nephew, 'Please keep to yourself the real identity of Colonel Tremayne and Sergeant Ford. Leave us!'

He then turned to Luke,' My question stands, 'What is one of Cromwell's senior serving officers doing in Maryland pretending to be working from a Catholic peer?'

'There is no pretence. I have authority from both Lord Baltimore, who now is not opposed to the new republican government, and from Cromwell to find out the true state of affairs in the colony.'

'Why associate yourself with the butcher of Beale Hall? You would have had more credibility amongst the independent settlers if you had based yourself at St Mary's, and assisted Baltimore's legitimate face in the colony.'

'What do you mean?'

'You don't come from Hampshire. For years before the war three local families divided political power between them – the Beales who are moderate Puritans; the Brownes, some of whom are Anglican although most are openly Catholic;

and the Lloyds, distant cousins of ours, who remain rigorous Puritans. Early in the war a royalist troop led by Browne attacked Beale Hall, and after the inhabitants had surrendered, they were all murdered in cold blood - men, women and children. The official blame was placed on Browne's deputy who was executed for the atrocities, but he maintained to the end that he was acting under the specific orders of his commanding officer. Browne protested his innocence but claimed that he was so shocked by the events that he resigned his commission, and left suddenly for Maryland. The gossip of the county is that Browne indeed was the author of the massacre.'

'Was he?'

'County gossip would give you an emphatic yes. There had been tension between the Brownes and the Beales for decades. It came to a head twenty odd years ago when Lady Elizabeth Trafford, daughter of an earl, who was betrothed to the heir of the Beale dynasty was suddenly married to Robert Browne.'

'So Mrs Elizabeth Browne comes from an aristocratic background, and was the subject of a love triangle involving Robert Browne, and a man who was later murdered by troops under his control. Why isn't Elizabeth Browne accorded her correct title as a daughter of a peer? No one refers to her as Lady Elizabeth.'

'It's a petty aspect of Browne's domestic tyranny. The Beale Hall affair prevented the King from knighting him for his service to the Royalist cause. As he has no title, within his family neither does his wife. He half killed his youngest son Thomas with brutal slashings of his cane when he provocatively addressed his mother as Lady Elizabeth. But to present matters. What happened to Sherman?'

'Sherman was the victim of an unprovoked attacked by a Susquehanna Indian, and had part of his tongue snipped off as a warning. As yet I don't know why.'

'I will be honest with you, Tremayne. Matthew was to be part of our settlement here. When Baltimore's agents were negotiating with us regarding a settlement on the Severn River they also mentioned that there were vacant tenancies on established plantations. Lord Baltimore was anxious to strengthen Robert Browne's plantation on the Eastern Shore. Our pastor in Virginia suggested that one of our potential settlers should take up the vacancy to keep an eye on the activities of a possible enemy. Matthew volunteered.'

'How do you communicate with your spy?'

'Routinely we send mail, as is the custom here, by Murchison's regular trips up and down the Bay. If there was an emergency we could use a shallop either way.'

'Thanks Commandant, you have put the Browne plantation in the broader context. Why did you accept Baltimore's offer of land and recognition, and then plot against him?'

'In Virginia Governor Berkeley rules with an iron fist, and has the majority of Royalist and Anglican settlers behind him. Puritans were persecuted, and put on notice. Maryland is chaotic. Baltimore's power is on paper only, and there is no unity amongst the settlers. We felt we could move here and build a new society, and eventually create a Puritan state on the model of Massachusetts.'

'So you are waiting your time to reject all traces of Baltimore's authority?'

'Yes, God's people can never accept the absolute rule of a Papist peer.'

Before Luke could comment a bell on the tower that looked out onto the Bay, was rung continuously. Luke and the Commandant climbed a mound from which they could see the cause of the alarm. A number of canoes were paddling north well out in the bay. It was a considerably smaller party than had headed south earlier. The Piscataways had taken their toll. This depleted Susquehanna war party had no designs against the settlers.

'Colonel, stay here overnight, and return to Browne's tomorrow.'

69

'Thank you Commandant. What happens to Sherman?'

'He is staying with a cousin for a while and will consider his return after he fully recovers. Try to unravel why he was attacked before he goes back. Without a clear answer he might be returning into a situation where he may suffer further harm.'

'His friend Miss Priscilla Browne certainly thinks he is still in danger.'

'Oh dear, I thought Sherman would be immune from the temptations of the Browne women. At least it wasn't that whore of a younger daughter.'

'What happens to his sub tenancy if he does not return?' asked Luke anxious to avoid a discussion of Matthew's personal life.

'He can maintain it if he places a manager in his place within two months. Otherwise it reverts to Browne who may then allocate it to anybody he wants.'

'We could leave the Brownes at any time, especially if we solve the murder of the youngest son, which I have undertaken on his behalf. My senior men are not happy to stay and assist a very troubled family. If you want to keep a presence there after we have gone why not send your nephew as manager of Sherman's plantation?'

'An interesting suggestion. I'll speak with former Cornet Harry Lloyd, and let you know our decision in the morning. He admired you as his commanding officer, and with him out of the road here, your Cromwellian connection can remain a secret.'

12

NEXT MORNING THE SHALLOP SKIRTED THE SOUTHERN COAST-
LINE OF Kent Island and then turned south along the eastern
shore of the Bay. Although assisted initially by the tide and
wind the latter dropped away and the men were forced to row.
Young Harry Lloyd, replacing the injured Humphrey, was a
valuable crewman. On arriving at Browne's plantation Luke
reported Humphrey's injury to Robert, and Harry Lloyd presented a letter from Matthew Sherman appointing him manager. Robert greeted them warmly and they drank Dutch beer
and nibbled on pieces of roasted chicken. Before they departed
Robert took Luke aside, 'I must see you in the morning. Lucy
has returned.'

Luke was enthusiastic. He believed Lucy's evidence would
fill many of the gaps in his enquiry. He met Robert for breakfast. Robert indicated that Lucy would be available for questioning when she rose for the day. Luke cooled his heels all
morning. Despite increasingly terse orders from her father
Lucy refused to leave her bedchamber and confront Luke.
Robert eventually strode into his daughter's room and Luke
could hear the almost hysterical rant of Robert, and the constant swishing of his diabolical cane. He moved away from the
door. Robert emerged and indicated that Lucy would be in
the great hall just prior to the serving of the midday meal to
answer any questions that Luke might wish to pose.

Robert had not cowered his daughter. She was still reluctant to talk to Luke. 'Father is the law here and he cannot
give away his authority to any passing stranger. You cannot
question me.'

Luke was surprised by the attitude of this young English girl
although she was hardly recognizable as such. Years spent in
the Maryland sun gave her a skin a colour that was scarcely

distinguishable from that of her Indian friends. In England she would have been a striking beauty with a peach like complexion. In this environment her skin colour was only one part of an appearance that was unkempt, and a personality that displayed few ladylike attributes.

Her beautiful golden red hair was cropped short, and her green eyes reflected a mischievous glint. She wore an olive bodice with thin linen cuffs and even thinner collar. Most gentlewomen in the colony with deference to the climate dispensed with the layers of petticoats that reflected status in England, and wore only one or two at the most. Lucy wore a light green long underskirt that was visible under her shorter darker green top skirt.

Luke stared at the girl, attempting to discomfort her. After a while he quietly commented, 'You are wrong young lady. I have direct authority from Lord Baltimore to override all jurisdictions. I am conducting a murder enquiry, and unfortunately your family, including yourself, are prime suspects.' Lucy sat on a bench in the hall exuding defiance, while Luke paced around the room, 'Where have you been since your brother's death?'

'In the forest. I have many hideaways - some I share with friends, and others are my secret. I have been moving between them, enjoying the sounds of the woodlands, and the companionship of the animals. I have deer that eat from my hand, squirrels that sit on my shoulder and a pet wolf that does not leave my side.'

'You love animals?' Luke asked, hoping to break through Lucy's resistance.

'They are more trustworthy than people,' she replied.

'Why did you run away immediately after your brother's death?'

'I did not run away. I simply avoided my mother and Priscilla.'

'Why?'

'Mother is not normal. If she were in England father would have had her committed to an institution. The death of her beloved son Tom unhinged her completely, and led to a vicious verbal attack on father, James and myself.'

'Why? Did she hate you all?

Lucy ignored the question, and continued the demolition of her family.

'Tom was even stranger than mother. He was a miscreant minnow who spent his life bearing tales, and stirring up discord - just for his own amusement. I hated him, and I am glad he is dead, but I did not kill him.'

'Did he do anything in particular to harm or harass you?'

'He spread it throughout the settlement that I was a whore, available to any man whatever race or religion.'

Luke changed the focus of his interview, 'Lucy, who do you think killed your brother and why?'

'Why is easy. Everybody, except mother and Priscilla, hated or despised him. He was hit by one of the labourers, and everybody cheered. Everybody had a motive.'

'You think Tom was murdered, and just didn't die from an unknown illness?' asked Luke.

'Father told me he was poisoned, but I did not have time to ask him when and how this occurred.'

'An unknown Indian poison was added to the trencher on which Tom placed his food.'

'By my troth, then only James, Tim or myself could have done it after Tom selected his trencher,' admitted a now interested and cooperative Lucy.

'That is why, James, Tim and yourself are my obvious suspects.'

Lucy was silent. Luke was astonished by her next comment. 'I killed him, sir,' whispered a suddenly contrite young woman.

'Tell me the full story,' said a patronising Luke, convinced the confession was a ploy in whatever game Lucy was playing.

'I am not the murderer, but I killed Tom.'

'God's truth girl! Don't speak in riddles! This is serious. You will hang.'

'Don't threaten me! I know what happened which completely destroys the witless case you have built up.'

'Then tell me wench!' Luke repeated with a degree of annoyance. He suspected the girl was playing with him, and making wild statements to get some sort of response.

'Tom was not the intended victim.'

'How do you reach such a silly conclusion?'

'Because as a prank I switched the trenchers around when they were not looking. The meal Tom ate was not intended for him.'

Luke was astounded. He had previously considered that Tom might not have been the specific target but a random victim if the whole family had been targeted. Perhaps that had been the right approach. Any member of the family would have satisfied the murderer, and all Lucy had done was to change the identity of the unlucky victim.

Lucy turned on Luke. 'Father should dismiss you. You missed the obvious.'

'Yes, Lucy I must rethink my investigation. Your exchange of the trenchers does suggest that the intended victim was a family member. When you exchanged the trenchers, was it limited to those that took food from the central platter?'

'No, I moved trenchers from my end of the table as well, Priscilla's and my own.'

'So, the intended victim could have been James, Tim, Priscilla or yourself?'

'Yes.'

'Lucy, if you were the intended victim, why?'

For the first time Lucy looked discomforted and blushed although it was hard to know with her tanned complexion. 'There are not many women here. Every man wants to bed or wed me. I have rejected many suitors but some continue to push their cause to the point of stalking me. One or two may be so distracted as to want to kill me. James warns me constantly not to underestimate the jealousy of men I have spurned.'

'Your brother is right. It is dangerous to play with men the way you have. Can you give me a list of the men who might have cause to kill you? Jealousy and humiliation are powerful motives. Now, on a related matter, did you see anything unusual while you were out in the forest that could relate to what has been happening here?'

'I was alone most of the time but I did meet Tom's strange Indian friend, One Ear. He was one of a kind with Tom. Weird. On seeing me he wailed loudly, wrung his hands and kept seeking my forgiveness. I ask him why he sought forgiveness, but he could only repeat incessantly 'sorry'. He was distraught at Tom's death.'

Luke noted that a discussion with One Ear might be useful, but Lucy had not finished. 'There was one other incident. After the Susquehanna had moved through the area taking with them a large body of Nanticokes I, following some deer, approached a clearing. The animals heard something and immediately changed direction. I soon saw the object of their concern. In the middle of the clearing was Mr Goodwin talking to a tall Susquehanna brave.'

'There is nothing unusual in that.'

'True, but what appeared strange was that after they parted the Indian did not head north to catch up with the rest of the war party. He headed south toward Sherman's plantation.'

'Now that is very interesting. Lucy, this chat has been very useful.'

Luke returned to South Island and spoke to John. 'What did you find out from the workers?'

'No surprises. Browne's men dislike him. He is too moody, swinging between affable master to vicious irrational bully. In his worse moods he is brutal and inhumane. Some showed me the welts they had received from Robert's cane. Life is made bearable by the overseer Tim Lipton who is seen as very fair, and relates well to all the men.'

Luke nodded, 'We have seen the dark side of Robert Browne ourselves, and it explains much of the tension and hatred that pervades his household.'

John continued, 'Sherman is admired by his men. They are all Protestants, probably Puritans, and have a work ethic that is not found amongst Browne's men. Most plan to move to the settlement on the Severn if Sherman does not return.'

'He probably will return, but in his place he has sent as an overseer a young soldier, Harry Lloyd who had served under me in the past. You might remember him from the Dublin garrison.'

John ploughed on, 'Richard Goodwin is seen as a man of mystery. His men do not fraternize with those on the other plantations, and he allows no casual access to his property. He approached Sherman offering to take over his land. The gossip is that Goodwin has regular contact with the Bay pirates, and with the riff raff on Kent Island. Some suggest he is an ultra-Royalist wanting to hand over the colony to the new King.'

'Clearly some one we must call on,' concluded Luke.

'There's more. One of Sherman's men claims some weeks ago towards dusk he was paddling up the river that separates Goodwin's land from Sherman's when he glimpsed two men run ashore on the Goodwin bank.'

'That's not so unusual is it?'

'No, but one of these men was a Catholic priest and the other was a strange Indian.'

'What do you mean by a strange Indian?'

'He was not a Piscataway, Nanticoke or Susquehanna. After I described the appearance to some of the other men one suggested by the cut of his hair he could have been a Huron from the Great Lakes of Canada.'

'A Huron this far south, and on this side of the mountain? Good work John! From what I heard on the Severn, from Lucy and now from you, we have hardly solved one problem and now we have several more.'

Next day, after the midday meal, Luke, Andrew, John, Humphrey and Harry met at Sherman's house now occupied by the young Lloyd. Luke opened the discussion. 'Gentlemen we still need to explain Tom's death, and to uncover what is afoot on these plantations. But one problem at a time. Tom's death could be a key to the more general problems. John take Humphrey with you and question this expelled Indian, One Ear! Try to find out why he apologised to Lucy for Thomas's death. Andrew, you will come with me. While I question Goodwin regarding the night of the murder, I want you to reconnoitre his plantation, and ascertain what if anything is happening there.'

'What about me?' asked Harry.

'For the moment you have you hands full taking over Sherman's plantation. I will keep you informed because we may need at some stage to call on you and your men to help us.'

Before Harry could respond they all heard the bell pealing out from Browne's watchtower. Luke was about to summon all the able bodied men in the vicinity when Humphrey interjected. 'No Luke, the bells are not warning us of imminent attack and summoning us to the muster point. This is announcing that the master has vital news to impart to his community.'

Before they took steps to find out what it was, one of Lloyd's men burst into the house, 'Miss Lucy is dead.'

13

Lucy had been found floating in the river, caught amongst the marsh grasses that edged the plantation of Richard Goodwin. Robert was inconsolable, Humphrey distraught. Later Luke accompanied by Humphrey examined the body. Both were taken aback. Humphrey exploded in a mixture of anger and surprise. 'Jehu have mercy! The lass was dead before she hit the water. She did not drown, she was strangled.'

Luke agreed. Neither man needed any expertise given the purple bruising around the girl's neck. Luke had seen several strangled bodies in his time. Lucy's neck did not reveal the usual two deeper pressure points of the thumb which normally dug deeper into the flesh. However given Lucy's thin neck the thumbs of her murderer may have overlapped. However there were four unusual indentations on the right side of her throat and neck.

Luke informed Robert, and then sent for his sergeants. Once settled around the table in Robert's hall he summed up the situation 'Another murder! Lucy was in the water for a very short time so let's establish her precise movements.' He turned to Humphrey, 'Given the direction of the tide where do you think she entered the water?'

'On Goodwin's side of the river a hundred yards upriver from where she was found.'

'We will proceed as planned before this latest murder. John and Humphrey, question One Ear! Andrew, you and I will visit Goodwin. While I interview the master wander along the river bank and see if you can find any trace of Lucy's presence.'

Luke and Andrew beached their canoe on a small stony beach, climbed the embankment, and set out in the direction of Goodwin's house. Four armed men blocked their path.

Their leader did not speak, but signalled to them to return to their canoe. Luke sensed that this was an occasion that demanded authority. 'Move aside churl, I have authority from Lord Baltimore to visit where I wish. Take me to your master at once or I will have you in the pillory in no time! My man will stay with the canoe. Move aside! If I do not return within the hour a party of armed men will search for me,' threatened Luke.

The chastened lackey did not reply, but motioned Luke to follow him, and waved Andrew back in the direction of the beach. As Luke walked through the tobacco plantation he noticed labourer after labourer hoeing vigorously with the most vacant of expressions on their face. Although within yards of each other there was no conversation. He saw why. At regular distances from each other were raised platforms from which armed guards supervised the workmen. On reaching a substantial building which was at least twice the size of Robert Browne's the group stopped, and its leader went inside. While he waited Luke noticed that all of the party that had apprehended them were still with him. Andrew had returned to the canoe without supervision. Luke smiled.

His escort emerged from the building accompanied by a house servant who indicated that Mr Goodwin was ready to receive him. Luke followed the servant to a small room off the hall in which a man of military bearing was arising from behind a large desk. So this was the mysterious Richard Goodwin. He was an impressive figure. A well built man of about average height he was dressed to perfection as a courtly cavalier. His doublet was of dark blue with slashed sleeves revealing a light blue underlining. His wide collar was of the most intricate lace as were his equally large cuffs. His breeches were the same colour as his doublet and were tied at the knees by light blue ribbons. His stockings were a sky blue and large silver buckles set off his black shoes. His black hat with a very broad brim, lowbrow, and blue band with a large silver buckle, lay on the desk.

But this man was no fop. His long black curly hair fell loosely over his shoulders partially covering a rugged face that was badly scarred on its left side – a scar that Luke had seen sustained by many artillerymen, and his left hand showed similar disfigurement. This man had seen much military action. His brown eyes were large and accentuated by the lack of eyebrows obviously a result of the same trauma that had caused his considerable facial injuries. A short black beard was immaculately trimmed. Some people, unlike the Brownes, did not let their standards fall, even when placed in a rough and rude environment.

'Welcome Colonel. I expected you would have paid me the courtesy of a visit before this.'

'I am sorry for the delay sir, but Mr Browne asked me to investigate the murder of his son, and then Dr Sherman had to be taken across the Bay. You saw service in the late wars?'

'And before that. I served as an artillery officer in an English regiment in the French army during the European war which I spent besieging Spanish towns in the Netherlands. I had many a cannon blow up in my face. Unfortunately our late King did not understand the value of artillery, unlike that devil Cromwell, and I spent our civil war as a reluctant cavalryman. Now how can I help you?'

'Thomas's murder. Can you tell me anything about that fatal night which could help me uncover the killer?'

'Was he was murdered?'

'Yes, what other explanation would you have?'

'Poisoned himself accidentally,' replied Goodwin as if it was the only sensible conclusion.

'Evidence?'

'Tom was a strange lad. The whole family is strange, as you probably realize, but Thomas outstrips them in weirdness and nastiness. Everyone despised him, and his only friend apart from his mother was an equally strange Indian misfit, whom the Nanticokes had expelled from their community. The two freaks chewed, smoked and imbibed all sorts of strange mixtures. Tom had a heavy cold in the days before he died and when he arrived for dinner on that fatal day his father grunted that the lad had spent it all with the creature they call One Ear. Tom told me that his Indian friend had given him a potion to cure his cold. That's what killed him.'

'An explanation that certainly warrants further investigation. At this very moment my men are questioning One Ear.'

'And yourself Tremayne? Why are you really here?'

'I've come to talk to you about Tom's death.'

'No, I don't mean this social visit. Why are you in Maryland, and equipped with absolute authority from Lord Baltimore, and a considerable number of armed men. I've noticed your company move around the area. You are professional soldiers.'

'We are soldiers on a fact finding mission for Lord Baltimore. He realises that his power is being flouted, and he wanted an on the spot assessment of the real situation. We came to Browne's plantation first because he was seen in England as the one firm supporter of Lord Baltimore in the north of the province, after the raids, rebellions and invasions of the last few years. Where do you stand on these issues?'

'Tremayne, am I likely to tell you that I am opponent of Baltimore, and will lead the next rebellion? I fought for the King in the recent wars, and Parliament's execution of him has confirmed my prejudices however they may play out in Maryland.'

'I take that to mean you are keeping your options open. If you are not an enthusiastic supporter of Baltimore why take up a sub tenancy on this plantation?'

'Simple, after the first war ended I heard that Browne who had fought with a close relative of mine had established himself in Maryland, and was looking for tenants of gentry status. After Parliament's victory, and their confiscation of our family's property I decided to migrate here. I knew nothing of the local politics or where Browne's loyalties might lead us.'

There was a moment of silence before Richard Goodwin deliberately changed the focus of the discussion, 'I heard Robert's bell earlier today. What's the latest crisis besetting my unfortunate neighbour?'

'Miss Lucy has drowned,' lied Luke.

'God's Blood, that man must have offended a witch,' exclaimed an obviously surprised Goodwin.

'I am also trying to establish the events leading up to her drowning. Did you see Lucy today?'

'No, I don't encourage visitors, even friends. Miss Lucy makes the men restless. She would only come here if I invited her. I probably would have, but the last I heard about her was that she had run off into the forest following her brother's death. Could her body have floated down from up river?'

'No, it had been in the water less than hour, and given the tides Humphrey Norton suggests she entered the water from your land not far from where I came ashore. From what you have said Miss Lucy could turn heads. Were any of your men in a permanent relationship with her?'

'No. I retain a team of effective supervisors who watch the workers day and night. Unless it happened off the plantation, I would know about it – and I don't let my men leave the plantation.'

'Your men don't always obey your orders. Didn't one of them leave here and attack Tom Browne on West Island for molesting the sensual Abigail Hicks?'

Richard smiled. 'That was a set up. I wanted to teach Tom the Turd, as the workers call him, a lesson. His father's discipline was brutal but ineffective, and his gentry status prevented any of the lads from physically assaulting him without my protection. I asked one of my men to give him a beating, and I would prevent his prosecution.'

Luke was surprised, and thoughtful. A man confesses to having his neighbour's son assaulted, could he have ordered the murder of the daughter? Luke changed the topic back to Lucy, 'How would you explain the girl's entry to the water on your side of the river?'

'Many possibilities. Given her interest in plants, butterflies and birds she may have seen something fascinating on my side of the river, paddled across and in reaching out for whatever it was, overturned her canoe and drowned.'

'That could be true up to the point of overturning the canoe. Humphrey told me that young Lucy could swim like a fish. Unless she was knocked unconscious an overturned canoe would not have worried her.'

Richard rose from behind his desk. The interview was being terminated. 'Is there any other way I can help you Colonel Tremayne. I must complete my correspondence to catch Captain Murchison's ship, and get my letters to Jamestown as soon as possible.'

'I am sorry to have interrupted your writing. I got a whiff of melted sealing wax as I came in. One last question - why do you encourage Indians to move in and out of your plantation at will?'

'Nothing unusual about it. Browne has liberal views regarding the Indians and allows the Nanticokes free run of our lands, especially to fish and hunt. I don't like it, but it is part of my tenancy agreement.'

Luke exaggerated, 'Be that as it may, but it has been reported that a tall fine looking Susquehanna brave, and an Indian of a tribe not known in this area has been seen here, and with you in the forest on several occasions. It is a curious if not dangerous relationship given the ambivalent attitude of the Susquehanna, who tried to kill me on the Western shore earlier this week.'

'Not at all, tobacco pays slowly. I make more money trading furs with Indians far inland. To avoid other European and

Indian go betweens my Susquehanna warrior has direct access to furs that would otherwise go to New Amsterdam or Quebec. He liases with me on behalf of his people. The strange Indian was one of his suppliers from beyond the mountains.'

'He was accompanied by a Catholic priest.'

'Yes, I am trying to tie up a deal for furs directly with the Indian nations over the mountains. The priest is a missionary among these people and acts as an interpreter for them with the Europeans.

'Thank you Mr Goodwin.'

'See you again at Miss Lucy's funeral. Fare thee well.'

Luke was escorted back to the riverbank without a word being spoken. Andrew was waiting quietly chewing tobacco. The two men were closely watched until they were mid river. They allowed the tide to take them to West Island. 'Well Andrew did you find anything?' asked Luke as they dragged the canoe up the beach.

'Not much. A cow grazing along the embankment has crushed many of the grasses and reeds and destroyed any footprints that may have existed in the soft soil. Just up from the spot where Humphrey estimated Lucy might have been pushed into the water I smelled burning leather. I headed in the direction of the smell and saw a group of Goodwin's armed men just ahead of me. I returned to the canoe and waited for you.'

'Humphrey told me that Lucy had a canoe unique in this region. Instead of being carved out of a log Lucy had a canoe like those of many of the inland Indians – skins stretched over a frame. It was much lighter and less likely to sink. The burning leather may have been someone trying to remove evidence that Lucy had been on Goodwin's land. They were burning Lucy's canoe.'

14

JOHN AND HUMPHREY RETURNED TO SOUTH ISLAND A FEW minutes after Luke and Andrew. Luke reported Goodwin's comments and Andrew's discoveries. Humphrey spent so much time nodding vigorously that Luke thought it might be some trauma associated with Lucy's death. The retainer could hardly contain himself and exclaimed, 'Mr Goodwin is right regarding Thomas's death, and the smell of burnt leather may well be Lucy's canoe. We must recover the evidence.'

'Why do you agree with Goodwin?' asked Luke.

Humphrey looked at John, seeking approval to relay the information they had gleaned from One Ear. John nodded benignly. Humphrey continued, 'I asked One Ear why he felt responsible for the death of his friend. Thomas and he dabbled with potions and poisons, and One Ear was expelled from the tribe because he misused his knowledge of poisons to bring about the accidental death of a tribal elder. He kept Thomas supplied with powders and potions to cover every conceivable complaint. Thomas always thought he was ill.'

'So Goodwin was spot on?'

'Not quite. A few weeks back Thomas asked One Ear for the poison that his people used to stun deer because he wanted to frighten one of his siblings. One Ear refused to give him the powder, unless he also took with him an antidote in case the victim received an overdose. It is difficult to adjust the dosage for humans.'

John picked up a cornet that lay on the table and blew a fanfare, proclaiming theatrically, 'We have solved the so-called murder of Thomas Browne. Tom poisoned the meal of one of the other dinner guests probably with no intention of killing them. Lucy swapped the trenchers around, and Thomas unintentionally poisoned himself. He declined so rapidly that he had no time to use his antidote.' The group agreed. Thomas had died due to accidental poisoning administered by himself, and Luke would formally record it as death by misadventure.

'Richard Goodwin appears a breath of common sense in this mad house of a settlement. Could he help with Lucy's death? asked Andrew.

'Maybe, but he denied seeing Lucy in recent days. Andrew take Humphrey back to Goodwin's tonight and recover any fragments of the burning leather! First thing in the morning let's question the whole household as when and where they last saw Lucy.'

This questioning elicited routine answers. Lucy had arisen late, and around noon had headed up river in her canoe. Rachel O'Brien alone could fill in the detail. 'I gave Lucy her breakfast very late in the morning. She complained that Colonel Tremayne's questioning had tired her out. I left the kitchen for a few minutes to get some hot water, and I returned just as one of the labourers left the kitchen. He might have been one of our own. He was vaguely familiar.'

'Why did you prepare breakfast for Lucy? Where was Abigail?'

'She was delivering the midday meals for the workers on North Island.'

'How was Lucy after the labourer's visit?'

'Highly elated. She said she had just received good news, and was going up river to take advantage of it. She paddled across the river and moved upstream along Mr Goodwin's bank. I went back to my chores.'

The soldiers considered Rachel's evidence. Luke concluded, 'Lucy was enticed by good news to paddle upstream keeping close to the Goodwin bank. Perhaps she had a meeting arranged with someone?'

'News about her brother James?' Andrew asked.

'Why would Lucy be concerned about her brother? She knew where he was,' John commented.

'Maybe she was told he was coming home, and went to meet him?' replied Andrew.

'Robert must tell us where James is,' said Luke.

Robert was sitting on a bench in the hall of his house. Luke was struck with how untidy and unkempt Robert's house and people were, when compared with those on the Goodwin estate. Robert motioned Luke to take a seat beside him. His eyes were red, and he appeared very distant. Luke tentatively broke the ice. 'Robert, I know how and why Thomas died.' Luke explained his conclusions, and Robert seemed comforted to know that Tom had not been murdered, and that he had not intended to kill anybody. Luke continued, 'Lucy may have been enticed to her death by news about James. Where is he? You must inform him of Lucy's death.'

'James is in the hinterland surveying virgin land for its future division into new plantations.'

'Cuds-me Robert! If that were the case his sister would have gone with him, or at least come across news of him during her sojourn in the woodlands. She had no contact or knowledge of him while she was away.'

'Lucy would not have gone to meet James. She knew exactly where he was, and that he is not due to return for months.'

'Stop dithering Robert. Where is James?'

'All right, but keep this to yourself. Tobacco does not grow as well here as in Virginia so most planters on the upper reaches of the Bay deal also in furs. Goodwin has a special deal with the Susquehanna to extract furs from up the Susquehanna River. I obtain my furs further to the north and with the help of the Lenapes. We have a trading post within Swedish territory. It is a breach of my agreement with Lord Baltimore under which I hold these lands. During the season James operates the post - buying pelts from the Indians and ensuing they are shipped to Europe on Swedish or Dutch vessels - a breach of English government policy, whether Royalist or republican.'

'I can see why you and Goodwin keep your trading a secret. Neither Baltimore nor the English Government would approve. A total ban on the use of anything but English ships for colonial trade is about to be passed by the Parliament. Confiscation of all goods found on non-English ships will be the penalty and it will be enforced by English warships.' Luke returned to the personal. 'James should be told about his sister's death. I'll tell him. Tim Lipton could come with me and operate the trading post if James wants to return.'

'It will take days, and Lucy will be buried tomorrow. We cannot in the name of decency delay the burial any longer. James may wish to return, and Tim knows the way. He has assisted James in the past, and is a partner in the trading venture. Take all of your men as you will be outside the lands of the Nanticokes and Susquehanna, and you can never be sure of the reaction of our Swedish and Dutch neighbours!'

'I can't take Humphrey. His wounded leg would not take him such a distance. Is there any native speaker that could come with us?'

'No, only Humphrey and Lucy were fluent in the local languages,' replied Robert as tears welled up in his eyes. 'Besides if Tim goes with you, I need Humphrey to overseer the tobacco fields.' As Luke left he heard the overthrowing of benches and tables as Robert went into another of his uncontrolled fits. Luke kept walking.

Next morning Luke's men assembled on the northern edge of Sherman's plantation intending to follow the river upstream. Luke put aside all pretence. They were soldiers on a mission. His men were dressed as such, and the officers would be addressed by their rank. Only one thing was missing from a normal patrol led by Lieutenant Colonel Luke Tremayne. There were no horses. An infantry patrol was the first for most of his men. Tim was waiting for them at the start of the riverside trail.

To this point Tim had avoided Luke, and the Colonel wondered why. Perhaps given James's absence, Humphrey's secondment to Luke's unit, and the daily care required of each tobacco plant Tim was plainly overworked. No wonder he was keen to join Luke's expedition when Robert put the suggestion to him. The young man wore a red jerkin and grey breeches and his off white shirt had neither cuffs nor collar. His cut down cavalry boots revealed dark grey stockings. His straight black hair was cropped in the manner of the Parliamentary cavalry. He had a round chubby face, blue eyes and a mouth that remained partially open revealing white gleaming teeth.

Just after the men moved off a labourer came running after them. He whispered to Luke that Harry Lloyd wanted to see him urgently, but did not want to be seen by Luke's expedition. Luke was impressed by young Lloyd and reasoned he would not make unnecessary requests. Luke asked Andrew to lead the group to the clearing near One Ear's roundhouse, and wait for him there. Luke turned back and approached Sherman's house and was met by a very agitated Harry who asked, 'Colonel, who is that young man in the red jerkin?'

'Robert Browne's overseer, Tim Lipton.'

'No he is not. I went to school with him on his father's estate, and we served together for a couple of years in Ireland under Colonel Monk. He is Sir Timothy Beale.'

'Any relation to the Beales of Beale Hall?'

'Yes, he is the current head of the family, and should control extensive lands in England but the courts have yet to accept his identity.'

'I thought all the family had been killed.'

'Yes, so did everybody else, especially the Royalist butchers who committed the crime. Tim was left for dead but managed to crawl away, and at the same time drag a body of one of his servants and place it beside his parents and siblings. When the butchers counted the number of bodies in the family group it appeared correct. Tim was declared dead at the time, and the family lands and title passed to a distant relative.'

'Harry, this is critical information. You have given us a new prime suspect. Why would the survivor of a massacre be found on a plantation owned by the man who allegedly committed the atrocity, other than gain revenge?'

Harry continued, 'I don't think you or your men are under any danger, but if Tim is behind the deaths of Thomas and Lucy, James could be the next victim. Was Tim eager to go with you?'

'Yes, he was. I must catch up with my men. For the moment keep this to yourself! We will confront Beale when I return. According to the current plan he is to remain at a trading post on the Delaware for some time, but now I will make sure he returns with us.'

Luke caught up with his men who with Humphrey and One Ear were resting in a clearing. Humphrey had paddled upstream earlier to talk to One Ear. At their last meeting the previous day when Luke had lamented Humphrey's absence from his mission and the lack of an interpreter, the old woodsman said that he would talk to One Ear who spoke all the local languages, and knew the terrain as far as the Ocean. Luke protested that One Ear might understand the Indians but as he couldn't speak English how could he help?

'It's all an act. One Ear speaks perfect English. It was probably the only occasion where Thomas helped another individual. One Ear's fluency is Thomas's sole positive achievement,' Humphrey commented.

He also reported on his and Andrew's nocturnal visit the previous evening to the site of the burning leather on Goodwin's plantation. 'It was no help. The charred leather was from water bottles that had presumably sprung a leak. It was not part of Miss Lucy's canoe.'

'Will One Ear come with us?' asked Luke bringing the discussion back to the present.

'Yes, I told him it was something he could do for Thomas. I will inform the Nanticokes of Lucy's death, and get them to approve your mission through their land. They don't take lightly anyone who is friendly with an expelled member of their village. You become guilty by association. Do not leave until I gain permission from the Nanticoke chief. Two thirds of your journey is through their lands, and you pass close to several of their large villages. It is not until you reach Delaware Bay, and progress north that you reach the lands of the Lenape, who are nevertheless kinsfolk and allies of the Nanticoke.'

'I will come with you, and present myself to the chief.'

Humphrey whispered, 'A good move, but you don't have a choice. Don't react! We are surrounded by Nanticoke warriors.'

15

A tall Nanticoke warrior emerged from the trees with twenty or more of his comrades, encircling Luke's company. The Indian leader greeted Humphrey cordially, but was obviously furious that the Englishmen were associating with One Ear. The two men engaged in a vigorous discussion for several minutes. Humphrey motioned Luke to join them, and introduced him as Colonel Tremayne representative of the great white sachem, the Lord Baltimore, who sought permission to cross Nanticoke lands to find James Browne, and inform him of his sister's death.

Before Humphrey could finish the shocked Indian interrupted, 'Not Miss Lucy?'

Humphrey nodded affirmatively, and continued. 'Colonel Tremayne, this is Straight Arrow, war chief of the Nanticokes. His son and young Lucy grew up together.'

Straight Arrow, visibly shaken by the news, turned to Luke, 'You cannot cross our lands with the detestable one,' as he pointed at a quivering One Ear. 'My son, White Deer, will go with you. He will do it for Lucy.' After a few words with Humphrey, Straight Arrow and his men disappeared, as quietly as they appeared.

Humphrey explained to Luke. 'White Deer had a good reputation throughout the Nanticoke lands but more recently is under a cloud. He and Lucy were very close. She taught him and his father English. With him you should cross the peninsula without problems. Difficulty will be communicating with the Dutch, German and Swedish settlers you will meet before you reach James. Be careful! The western bank of the Delaware River is the colony of New Sweden but the eastern bank contains isolated Dutch settlements. Don't get caught in the crossfire as both Swedish and Dutch Governors are determined to control the Delaware.'

'Don't worry Humphrey. I served for three years in the Dutch army, and Andrew fought with the Swedes for almost a decade. We will get by.'

After some delay White Deer arrived at One Ear's clearing where Luke's company had waited. He was naked apart from a breechcloth and headband holding a white and a grey feather. His hair was in long braids. He carried a spear, across his back were a bow and a full quiver of arrows, and a war club dangled from his waist. He approached Humphrey, 'Lucy was my friend. Her brother should know she is dead.' Before Humphrey could respond White Deer turned to Luke, 'Father says you are an important person. I take you to James, then I slay the person who killed Lucy.'

'Jehu boy! First we must bring James back, and then we can find Lucy's murderer,' replied Luke. White Deer nodded, and moved out in front of the group with Luke following close behind. One Ear, mouthing obscenities, scampered off in the opposite direction. The trail was clear and there was little dense undergrowth, although as they headed east this became increasingly thicker. As one moved inland the constant burning by the Indians nearer the Bay was less evident.

Luke took the opportunity to question Tim, whom he motioned to walk with him. 'Tell me about yourself. Why are you in Maryland?'

'I fought for Parliament as soon as I were old enough. Because of what happened during the war I have not been able to inherit my property. Lawyers have spent years on my behalf with growing success. Without the income from the family properties I had to earn something. I come from the same area as Mr Browne, and discovering from his brother that he was in Maryland I sailed here on the off chance that he could employ me.'

Luke smiled inwardly. Tim told the truth, neglecting only one key factor - his real identity. Luke tried to provoke him into a few indiscretions. 'I find it strange that a dedicated soldier of the New Model army, works for a retired Royalist who left England under a cloud. You could have stayed enlisted, and found a career in the army until the courts returned your estates.'

'As you have?'

'Yes.'

'I had no desire to become governor of some embattled English outpost in western Ireland or the isolated Highlands of Scotland. Here, the climate and the native inhabitants are at least pleasant. In addition to my salary as overseer, I have my own small plot of tobacco, and have become a partner with the Brownes in the fur trade. I am getting back on my feet, irrespective of what the courts decide. Are you not doing a similar thing? A senior officer of the New Model Army working for the Catholic Royalist, Lord Baltimore?'

Luke was open with Tim, 'Not quite. I have a double remit. Lord Baltimore wishes to discover what is happening here, but so does General Cromwell. The group around you is an active unit of the English army under the direct control of the Lord General.'

'And what will you report to your dual masters?'

'One word, chaos. I cannot see how Lord Baltimore can enforce his authority on these divided and isolated communities, and from Cromwell's point of view, while there is some sympathy for his cause along the Severn, most of the settlers are concerned with survival and then profit. Royalist Virginia should absorb the whole Province. Independent of the politics there is a strange malevolence here that emanates from Browne's plantation. How can you work with such a troubled family?'

Luke received an intriguing response. 'If only you knew the full story. However as far as I am concerned my courtship of Miss Lucy cancelled out the problems I had with the rest of the family.' Tim turned away but not before Luke noticed tears rolling down his cheeks. Why had no one mentioned Tim's interest in Lucy?

White Deer ploughed onwards, but the over dressed and less able Englishmen tired quickly. Luke was forced to stop in a small clearing, and his men relaxed, sitting on fallen logs. They took swigs of water from their leather bottles, and nibbled at crisp cold corn fritters taken from their knapsacks. Andrew nonchalantly kicked up the fallen leaf residue that had built up against the logs where he sat. The whole group heard a buzz coming from the leaves beneath Andrew's kicking feet. White Deer dived at Andrew, and pushed him over the log to its farther side. He was too late. The sergeant writhed in pain.

White Deer shouted, 'Rattlesnake! I find herbs.' With that he disappeared into the forest, while a trooper dispatched the snake with a lucky swipe of his sword.

Luke had no experience of snakes. He had no idea what to do. He turned to Tim. 'You must have dealt with snake bites?'

'Not really, the dangerous snakes around the plantation disappeared once we cleared the land. Only a few harmless corn snakes remain in the fields. Occasionally copperheads or rattlesnakes bite people in the forest. The victims rarely survived The exceptions were those who were found by the Indians immediately after such a bite. They administered life saving potions. Young White Deer is your sergeant's only hope.'

Andrew was helped to remove his leggings. The area around the wound was swollen, and oozed liquid. He complained of the pain, unusual for Andrew, and moved in and out of consciousness. When conscious he called for a drink and emptied Luke's bottle in one session. Luke knew that time was of the essence. If White Deer did not return soon, it would be too late. One of his men suggested Luke cut out the infected part. He seriously considered it. The area around the bite looked disgusting. He had seen many a battle wound caused from musket shot, sword jabs and slices, and artillery fragments, but they never deteriorated while you watched. This did.

White Deer returned, and after placing his hand on Andrew's forehead and pricking his hand with a thorn, smiled. 'He still has feeling, and breathes freely.'

'Then there is hope?' asked Luke.

White Deer nodded, as he sliced and crushed a handful of herbs on a log. He placed a macerated mass of plants on the wound, and put the remainder in Andrew's mouth to chew and swallow. The Indian relaxed. 'I have done all I can. For the next two days the potion will work, but the sergeant will get worse before he gets better. My medicine and the snake venom fight inside his body. The spirits will decide the victor.'

'What can we do?' asked a worried Luke.

'Keep him quiet, cool his fevers, warm his chills, and above all do not move him.'

'Stay with him,' pleaded Luke.

'No, without me you will go much further than you need. There is a village of my people just ahead. Leave the sergeant here! Women from the village will nurse him where he lies. They can repeat my potions at regular intervals. Wait here. I will arrange it.'

Luke explained to Andrew the plan for his care during his decreasing moments of consciousness. Andrew did not want to be left alone and asked that one of the troop stay with him. Luke agreed. White Deer returned with two women, one old and the other seductively young and beautiful. He explained that the older woman was the keeper of the village's herbal secrets, and a great healer. The other woman was her daughter, who was learning her mother's art. Luke was loath to leave Andrew as the sergeant shook violently, and threw himself about as if fighting some invisible enemy. White Deer assured Luke that this was a good sign. His medicine was defeating the venom. Luke was unconvinced. White Deer must stay with Andrew. Tim had made the journey to the trading post on several occasions. He could lead them to James.

White Deer was firm in his refusal, 'Follow the white man and you waste a day. The white men follow up the rivers that flow west and then down those that flow east. They then follow the coast north until they reach the bay and river you called Delaware – the land of my cousins, the Lenapes. Moving north crossing the mouths of many streams slows you down. My trail runs along the slight ridge that separates the east from the west flowing rivers. When you are far enough north you move down the nearest river to the mouth of the Delaware. It is easier, and quicker by almost a full day.'

Luke eventually reluctantly acquiesced, and with one last look to fuel his fantasies he watched the young Indian woman placing more herbs on Andrew's oozing wound. A sudden look of concern passed over White Deer's face. He was glad that Nanticoke braves from the village would keep an eye on their women as they nursed the white man.

Luke's apparent lust towards the young Indian woman lost him some respect in the eyes of White Deer. Nevertheless White Deer remained determined to help Luke on behalf of Lucy, who he had adored as a sister. If he were not the chieftain's son, and Lucy not an Englishwoman their relationship would have been very different. As the group moved forward both White Deer and Luke were thinking of women - both inappropriately.

Further along the trail Luke could smell smoke. White Deer looked at him, his face sketched with alarm. 'What's wrong White Deer? Your people regularly burn the undergrowth?' asked Luke in response to the obvious distress of the Indian.

'This is not the season for burning. And that is birch bark burning. There are no birches standing in this part of the forest, but our villages use birch bark. A village is burning.' Soon smoke swirled through the trees. White Deer ran ahead. They reached a large cultivated clearing, in the middle of which was a circular mound. Until very recently this extensive raised area had contained rows of well developed corn in its centre, surrounded by beans, and these in turn by numerous squash plants. The vegetables had recently been roughly harvested, and only crushed remnants of the plants remained. Beyond the mound were the round houses of the village, some still burning fiercely, while the rest smoked intermittently.

White Deer strode bravely into the centre of the village. Luke's men primed their muskets and cautiously followed the young brave. The white men were troubled by the eerie silence, broken solely by the sound of exploding wood and collapsing houses. Not only was the village burning, it was deserted.

16

WHITE DEER ADDED FURTHER TO THE DISQUIET OF THE soldiers by putting his hands to his mouth and uttering a long, loud disconcerting call. He repeated this eerie exercise several times. Eventually there was a rustle in the undergrowth, and Luke motioned his men to point their muskets in the direction of the noise. White Deer held up his hand for them to hold their fire. An elderly Indian emerged from the undergrowth, and warmly embraced White Deer. The two men talked for some time, and the old man turned towards the undergrowth and repeated White Deer's peculiar call. Gradually other Indians emerged - twenty elderly men and women, and a dozen or so children. There were no young men, young women, or babies.

White Deer gathered the group around him. He spoke quietly to them for some time after which the refugees moved off down the trail the white men had just come up. White Deer explained, 'The Susquehanna demanded our warriors join their attack on the invading Mohawks. They moved out with the Susquehanna war chief. Later a few Susquehanna returned led by Black Cougar. He rounded up the women and their babies, stole the crops, and set fire to the village.'

'What do you know about Black Cougar?' asked Luke

'Black Cougar haunts the settlements of the white men. Lucy and I saw him with men from Goodwin's plantation. He is an evil one. His people fear him as he has the protection of the evil spirit, Okee. He wishes to replace Tamuagh as paramount war chief of the Susquehanna.'

'I have met him. He mutilated Dr. Sherman. Where are the old people and children going?'

'Back to the same village that is nursing your sergeant. They will stay there until their warriors return. I am sure that

Tamuagh is ignorant of Black Cougar's actions. It's getting late. We can stay here for the night. Black Cougar harvested the crops so roughly that your men may find enough corn and beans to gather for a meal.'

At the end of the second day Luke could smell the ocean, and within minutes the trail led them onto a sandy beach just where a large river entered a bay. Tim was amazed. It had taken a full day less than he expected. A few miles up the Delaware, and along the Christina River they would find the Swedish settlement where James Browne had his trading post. Several ocean going ships were anchored in the bay and along the river. Many were Dutch and a few Swedish. Others bore flags of various German states. None were English, French or Spanish.

It was dark by the time they reached Fort Christina. A sentry shouted from a tower within a palisaded area demanding identification and purpose. Luke answered in English, and was making no impression until he mentioned James Browne. The soldier signalled him to proceed beyond the fort in the direction of a substantial log cabin that overlooked a natural rock quay. White Deer left the group to visit the Lenape, promising to return in the morning.

Tim and Luke found James drinking alone in an extensive cabin that was both warehouse and living quarters. The room was stacked high with pelts, which James had been sorting by the light of a gigantic candle. James had long locks of dark reddish hair that fell untidily around his shoulders and concealed much of his moonlike face, with an unkempt red beard and hazel eyes. His snub nose and wide mouth gave an overall impression of a somewhat stupid character. He was grossly overweight for a young man and his green jerkin and matching breeches were straining at the seams. His lace collar and large cuffs once white were badly soiled and somewhat yellow - in all, a typical slovenly Browne.

James was surprised to see Tim who introduced Luke as a Colonel Tremayne sent by Lord Baltimore and General Cromwell to ascertain the situation in Maryland, and who had been commissioned by his father to investigate the death of his brother. James replied, 'God's mercy! You have not come all this way to question me about my turdish churl of a brother? That dissembling miscreant deserved his fate.'

'No James,' replied Tim with a tear in his eye. 'We bring very sad news. Lucy is dead.'

James placed his head in his hands. Distress turned to anger when he learnt that his sister had been strangled, and her body thrown in the river. He was further shocked to hear of the mutilation attack on Dr Sherman. The cabin was big enough for Luke and all his men to camp down for the evening but the offer was never made. James could not conceal his contempt for inferior types, especially soldiers of the republic including their Colonel. Luke, sensing the strained atmosphere excused himself and settled his men along the base of the palisade that surrounded Fort Christina, and then quite deliberately returned to the cabin. James had after much thought decided to return home. Tim, to Luke's surprise, immediately poured cold water on James's resolve. 'Don't be rash James. You can do little to help the investigation, and Lucy is already buried. You would be better off staying here, and accumulating those precious pelts. Sleep on it before you finally decide.'

Luke wondered why Tim wanted to keep James away from the plantation, or was it to keep him at Fort Christina. He didn't appear the mercenary type anxious to obtain the maximum pelts possible. A more sinister thought crossed Luke's mind. Maybe Tim was planning to engage a local Swede to ensure that James had a fatal accident.

James's reply put an end to Luke's speculation. 'It's a bad season. My Lenape suppliers are not able to obtain any more pelts from further inland for months because the Susquehanna are deliberating usurping the supplies. I received a consignment yesterday. I have made arrangements to ship it aboard the Swedish merchantman anchored alongside the Rocks. The ship is almost full, and ready to leave on the mid morning tide. I will be ready to return home as soon as my pelts are aboard the ship. The captain is anxious to leave as soon as possible with a full load so I should negotiate a good price.'

Luke rejoined his men under the stars, and despite the coolness of the evening was soon asleep. Next morning James half heartedly welcomed White Deer. The two men were awkward with each other, despite their reiteration of happy boyhood memories involving Lucy. James changed the subject too quickly commenting with a hint of jealousy, 'Two days to get here following your heathen trails, rather than the three it always takes me.' White Deer affirmed, from conversations with his Lenape cousins, that the supply of pelts had been blocked further inland by the Susquehanna and their Iroquois enemies, both of whom wanted to redirect the trade to the established French and English colonies.

Luke's men assisted Tim to load the furs aboard the ship that displayed a colourful spotted cat as its figurehead and its name, *Leoparden*, painted in bright yellow and black along its side. James finalized his negotiations with the Captain. Suddenly a large group of local Indians emerged onto the Rocks. They wanted White Deer who after a lively discussion with them approached Luke. 'Colonel, we cannot return the way we came. My brothers have just learnt that the Susquehanna changed direction and are now south west of here and the Mohawks are moving against them. There could be a major battle between us and home.'

Luke understood the situation. He ran towards the ship and shouted to James. 'I'm coming aboard I must talk to the Captain.' Luke skipped up a bending plank. James was put out. 'I don't need help from a rebel soldier to negotiate a profit.' Luke ignored, but would not forget, this unnecessary rudeness. He turned towards the master of the ship. 'Captain, I am

Colonel Tremayne on a mission for Lord Baltimore. Where do you sail from here?'

'That sir is a secret. Loose talk alerts pirates who move up from the Caribbean searching for a full load of expensive cargo such as we carry.'

Luke was surprised at the captain's excellent English until he realised that the man was indeed English, 'Captain, my unit and Mr James Browne cannot return to his plantation overland due to Indian war parties. If you are heading south can you take us, at a fee, and land us well down the coast?'

'I am heading south to meet with a fleet of merchantmen which gather at the Hampton Roads to convoy back to Europe. The coast from here to there consists of miles of sandy beaches where my boats can get you ashore. Can you pay in English silver?'

The soldiers and White Deer came aboard, and soon the *Leoparden* left the quay and swung out into the Christina River. As soon as it was out of sight of the Fort, and approaching the confluence with the Delaware River the merchantman found its way impeded by a frigate flying the French flag. Its boats, loaded with musket firing troops were already in the water, approaching the merchantman from both sides. Simultaneously the frigate began to pound the merchantman's sails with its cannons.

The captain of the Swedish merchantman had no time to slow, and faced imminent collision. If he tried to pass the French vessel – *La Glorieuse*, he risked running his ship aground on the riverbank. He shouted to his men, 'Prepare to repel boarders.' Luke organized his troops who picked off several of the attackers with accurate musket fire. The French had not expected this show of military firepower. The poorly armed merchantman was better defended than they had expected. As the wind took up the sails and increased his speed the captain had little option but to ram the obstructing ship. Sensing danger the French frigate began to turn which enabled the Swedish merchantman to bring its small cannons into play. Simultaneously the more heavily armed adversary directed a cannonade into the canvas of the Swedish ship.

The boats of *La Glorieuse* had by now attached themselves to the side of the *Leoparden* and the invaders tried to climb aboard. The French were astonished to be welcomed by twenty experienced soldiers. These English veterans were ably assisted by many of the *Leoparden*'s crew who had seen service with the Swedish army. The French who managed to reach the deck were dispatched by sword and dagger. Luke engaged in a one to one sword fight with a blue uniformed officer who led the invading party. He was no amateur, and sensing the strength and experience of the opposition soon ordered his men to return to their boats. He was a typical professional soldier. He would not die needlessly, but rather live to fight when the odds were in his favour.

The ships passed each other - the *Leoparden* at top speed while the almost stationary French frigate was slowly turning to follow the Swedish ship down the river. Luke and his men with considerable help from the crew repelled the last invader. As Luke and the captain looked aft they could see the frigate gaining on them. This time it would draw alongside the merchantman and a full scale attempt to board would take place. The Swedish ship had only two small cannons on each side of the vessel. *La Glorieuse* had at least two rows of six on both port and starboard.

Luke wanted to move the cannons from the port side and lash them on the deck on the starboard above the existing gunwales but there was no time. The constant cannonade into the sails of the *Leoparden* slowed its pace, and the French were almost alongside. Luke grabbed the wheel. Those on the upper deck were alarmed as Luke turned the ship into the path of the oncoming frigate. Each time the frigate moved to the other side of the river to draw level, Luke turned the merchantman into its path. This process forced *La Glorieuse* to reduce sail to avoid ramming its prey. It dropped back. The *Leoparden's* captain having taken back the wheel concluded that the Frenchman had decided to wait for open water, where its speed would place the merchantman at its mercy. They were not safe but they had bought time.

Luke was seriously alarmed. These were not pirates or privateers. They were highly skilled French troops - on a French man of war.

17

'WHAT WILL THEY DO NEXT?' ASKED LUKE.

'They want ship and cargo. They will not ram us. That's why your tactic worked. They fired their cannon into our sails and rigging. The damage there can be quickly repaired. They carefully avoided the hull and the masts. This is a very professional attack.'

'Very,' agreed Luke as he explained his concern regarding the presence of French troops aboard the *La Glorieuse*. 'What are you going to do? The French will have plenty of opportunity as you sail south to achieve their end,' asked an increasingly alarmed Luke.

Before the captain could reply, the ship's lookout uttered a series of loud imprecations, and the captain smiled. As the *Leoparden* left the river and entered the Bay they sailed between two large Dutch merchantmen whose open gun holes indicated that they were heavily armed ships of the type normally seen in the East Indies. The captain visibly relaxed.

'Thank you Colonel Tremayne, for your help. Our brother merchants will deal with our pursuer. Those two merchant-men have more armaments than many a warship. They will blast our French friend out of the water. They will then escort us to the Roads.'

'Where did they come from?' asked Luke somewhat surprised at such naval firepower.

'They left Fort Christina yesterday afternoon. They must have seen the Frenchman heading this way and decided to investigate. On hearing gunfire they took up stations at the mouth of the Delaware.'

The conversation was completely blocked out by cannon-ade after cannonade from the Dutch, and a pathetic reply of the now heavily outgunned French frigate. Completely de-masted the stationary *La Glorieuse* began to sink as the Dutch cannon fire was directed below the deck line. The *Leoparden* was now out of sight, and Luke did not see the French ship disappear into the waters of Delaware Bay. Some hours later hugging the shore of the Atlantic Ocean the Swedish ship was eventually overtaken by the two Dutch merchantmen, and af-ter some friendly gunfire and exchange of signals the captain informed Luke that the Dutch would stand by out to sea while he came as close as he could to the shore to put Luke's party onto the sandy beach.

As the Swedes rowed them ashore in two of the ship's boats Luke relived the battle. He was proud of his men, and the Swedish crew who showed a remarkable degree of military professionalism. He had always admired the military train-ing of the Swedes which most of their adult males had to en-dure. White Deer who used his war club with deadly effect also pleasantly surprised him. As the French boarders reached the level of the deck they did not know what struck them as White Deer swung his weapon with precision and power.

On the other hand Luke was furious with James and Tim. Where were they during the action? Luke disliked James with a growing intensity. He lined up his party on the beach and with muskets pointing to the sky they gave a formal farewell to the three merchant ships which soon disappeared beyond the horizon. Luke moved his men off the beach onto the grassy bank of a small stream that trickled across the sand. He sent White Deer inland to establish their precise location. James and Tim were slow to move off the hot sand and appeared to be engaged in a heated discussion. James pushed Tim who retaliated with an even more deliberate shove. The pushing quickly escalated. Punches were thrown. Luke moved to push them apart.

'No, Colonel leave us be,' shouted Tim.

James snarled, 'Keep out of this Colonel. It is a matter of honour, something you knavish Roundheads never understood.'

Luke was incensed. 'We must be in the colonies. At home honourable men would not resort to fisticuffs like a common brawler. What are you swords for? And a master would never fight with his overseer.'

The soldiers gathered around the combatants, who having removed their jerkins resumed the fight that consisted of wild punches and attempts to throw the opponent to the ground. Luke's men shouted encouragement to one or other of the fighters, and began to take bets on the outcome of the conflict. The confrontation escalated. Knowing what he did about Tim, one part of Luke was concerned for James's safety; the other half hoped he would get the beating of his life. This could be a carefully staged fight to enable Tim to 'accidentally' kill the son of the man who had murdered his family. Luke's fears increased when Tim seized a lethal sized rock from the edge of the stream, and raised it above his head to crush James.

Luke moved to intervene, but James having picked up a large branch knocked the rock from Timothy's hand. Following through he flung himself at his opponent. The two men fell into the sand, pummelling at each other as they wrestled their way into the stream itself, which now revealed streaks of red as both men bled from the nose and Timothy also from his mouth where James had landed a number of effective punches. Luke's men who had clearly laid heavy wagers on the outcome became almost obsessed, and encouraged the combatants to continue the fight. The noise level on this deserted American beach rivalled that of a drunken brawl in a Dublin tavern.

Luke was now increasingly disinclined to get involved. He would find it difficult to stop the fight against the wager driven enthusiasm of his own men. Perhaps these planters were not the cowards that their absence from the shipboard fight suggested. The two men now stood face to face, their feet firmly embedded in the wet sand and continued to slug it out. Tim's superior fitness was beginning to tell. Both men delivered blow after blow, and both staggered a couple of times, then out of the blue Tim delivered a short sharp jab that connected with James's jaw. He doubled up, fell to the ground and remained motionless.

As his men worked out their wins or losses on the result, Luke moved in to assist James. Before Luke had time to question either man over their vicious conflict, White Deer came running along the shallow creek towards them. 'Be quiet! The Susquehanna are nearby.' When he realized what had been going on he glared angrily at both the combatants. Their behaviour dishonoured Lucy.

'Susquehanna this far south?' queried Luke.

'Yes, a small party that may have detached from a larger group, hunting and recruiting more braves. Fortunately they are now heading north.'

'Where are we?' John asked.

'Perfectly placed. We could not have landed in a more appropriate spot. If we follow this stream to the ridge, the nearest west flowing river is that which flows through your settlement,' replied White Deer.

Luke could not claim credit. He admitted to John that the landing place had not been his choice but based on the convenience of the Swedish merchantman and its Dutch allies. White Deer had a different explanation, 'The spirits have smiled on you Colonel. I will scout ahead and wait for you at the source of this stream. It will be nightfall by then. Beware of the approaching thunderstorm! This stream will become a dangerous torrent within minutes.'

As the group progressed up stream Luke was determined to question each of the brawlers before they had time to come up with a mutually agreed story. While John made sure that James did not catch up with Luke and Tim, the former began the inquisition. 'Well what was all that about?'

'Nothing that concerns you Colonel,' replied Tim.

'Pittikins. We have had two murders and one vicious assault, therefore any sign of disagreement may have a major bearing on my enquiries.'

'No, my fight with James was a result of our mutual interest in a woman whom honour prevents me naming.'

'That won't wash Tim. The only gentlewomen on all three plantations are James's sister and mother. So your mutual interest must be a servant, or the wife of one of the workers. If it's one of Browne's servants, I guess it is Abigail Hicks. And servants are not protected by any code of honour, or so many English gentlemen tell me. If it is Abigail how can you reconcile that with your professed love of Lucy?'

'I am not an English gentleman,' Tim lied rather solemnly.

Luke was tempted to reveal that he knew of Tim's real identity which placed him firmly within the gentry class, but he held his tongue and changed the topic. 'If you are not a gentleman then why did you assault James, who clearly is. Such activity could have fatal consequences for you. In law it can be construed as petty treason.'

'In England yes, but in Maryland status has to be earned. Wealth and physical strength are basic here. James has to prove he is a better man than I – and he can't,' Tim proudly announced.

'I sense an element of bitterness in your attitude to your betters. If you hate such gentlemen why are you working for the Brownes?'

'I have no bitterness towards the Brownes. I am just comparing this colony with the situation in England.'

'So you insist that James and you were fighting over Abigail Hicks?'

Tim did not reply, and made it clear that he would not discuss the matter further. The group did not reach the source of the stream. As White Deer had predicted they were hit by a ferocious thunderstorm with lightning strikes very close to the group. As the stream increased in volume and speed, Luke led his men well away from the bank and decided to shelter under a canopy of well leaved trees, risking the branches that broke and fell within feet of them. Although unhappy with the situation Luke made camp for the night.

Most of the men were asleep before darkness fell. Luke was not one of them. He lay awake reflecting on Lucy's murder, and whether the conflict between Tim and James had any relationship to it. Hours into darkness he was surprised to find White Deer beside him. The Indian realising that the group had been stopped by the thunderstorm had retraced his steps. His question to Luke was direct. 'Were the white men fighting over Lucy?'

Luke replied, 'Why would they be fighting over Lucy?'

'You know little Colonel.'

'Well tell me White Deer! We both want to find Lucy's killer. You don't think that James or Tim were responsible. James was miles a way, but Tim had opportunity.'

'They did not kill her with their own hands, but they made her death happen.'

'How so?'

'I will not say bad things about my friend Lucy but she was a troubled spirit. She left her home many times, and came to the forest or my village to find peace. I only reveal some of her secrets now to help find her killer.'

Luke was ready to receive what might be most vital evidence in his investigation so far when White Deer disappeared as quickly as he came. Looking over his shoulder Luke saw why. In the darkness a figure towered over him. It was that obnoxious jackanapes, James Browne.

18

'WHAT DID THAT REDSKIN WANT?' JAMES ASKED WITH A touch of distaste.

'Just reporting back,' lied Luke.

'Question him regarding Lucy's murder!'

'Why? I thought Lucy, you and he were the closest of friends.'

'When we were children, yes, but in the last year the relationship has cooled.'

'Why?'

'With her attitude to men, Lucy was fast becoming an outcast from decent society. Any man regardless of class or colour provoked her interest.'

'What are you suggesting? Your sister slept with the heathen?'

'I don't know. But until last year both Lucy and White Deer were planning a future together. Then the elders of the Nanticokes told him to cease his association with Lucy. They were now of the age when both should be available to marry - but not to each other. My father who let Lucy do what she wished, was surprised to find that her obsession with White Deer was so intense.'

'Did he agree with the Indians that the relationship should stop?'

'Yes, it never entered his head that an English gentlewoman would entertain such thoughts. To him Lucy's association with White Deer was a childhood friendship, in which Lucy learnt many of the native skills.'

'Interesting, but how does it make White Deer Lucy's murderer?'

'White Deer was so infuriated by his tribe's decision, and so infatuated with Lucy that if he could not have Lucy no one else would.'

'But why would he wait so long. I understand that Lucy and Tim have been in a relationship for several months. Did anything happen in the last few weeks that would have set White Deer on such a course?'

'Yes, Lucy, to spite Tim, started once again to find casual lovers. This could have pushed the redskin over the edge.'

'Any evidence?'

'No, but he had opportunity. Indians move in and out of our settlement without being seen.'

Luke suddenly changed focus, 'What's the problem between Tim and yourself? You were friends, despite the difference in status.'

'There is no difference in status. Tim comes from a gentry family deprived of their lands and titles during the war. He came to the colony to recreate his fortune, while his lawyers try to regain his rights. As usual in Maryland with its lack of women we were fighting over a sensuous female. She had been my regular partner for years and then I discovered that Tim was also enjoying her favours. I told him to cease his interest in the wench.'

'We both should get some sleep,' said an overtired Luke, who rudely pulled his blanket over his head.

Next morning the group moved out, returning to the bank of the stream which had ceased to be dangerous. White Deer and Luke led the way. The Colonel was anxious to continue his discussion of the previous evening. 'How were James and Tim responsible for Lucy's death?'

'Lucy was in love with Mr Timothy. She believed he was about to talk to her father about marriage. Then she discovered him with a servant. She was distraught.'

'Tim's betrayal might be relevant, but where does James fit in?'

'Lucy told her brother about what had happened, and James laughed at her. He said gentlemen slept with servants as a right, and it would continue to happen throughout her marriage. He told her to grow up, and accept Tim's behaviour as normal. Lucy was very upset. She left home and came to my village. She was determined to teach Mr Timothy a lesson. She was obsessed with the need to punish him.'

'What form was this lesson to take?'

'She said what's good for the gander is good for the goose —she explained these words to me.'

'So Lucy threw herself at other men, who may have overreacted to her provocation?'

'Yes, Lucy liked men, but she did not give herself totally to anyone. I know. She was not a bad woman. Saying no to a new lover caused her death.'

White Deer decided he had said enough, and moved ahead of the party. Luke signalled for Tim to walk beside him. 'I heard your explanation yesterday of what went on between James and yourself. Who do you think killed Lucy and why?'

'Why is easer, who is difficult. Lucy was very popular with numerous men, and she had in her youth and inexperience teased a lot of would be seducers. A frustrated and disappointed lover probably killed her.'

'And that was not you?' Luke asked without warning.

Tim was visibly shaken. His whole body tensed and his face became flushed, and he replied defensively, 'What an outrageous suggestion. What has James been saying?'

Luke noted the reference to James and replied, 'James said nothing, but others say you and Lucy were to become betrothed, but she caught you with a female servant and ended the relationship there and then. She then found a new lover to punish you. You, Tim are a major suspect.' Tim, clearly upset, dropped back to the main body of soldiers.

In the late afternoon White Deer reached an intersection of the trails. He, accompanied by Luke and a trooper, took the trail north to the village whose members were nursing Andrew. John took control of the main party and continued west towards the settlement. Luke spent the night on the edge of the village with Andrew and the two troopers. White Deer returned to his own village and the two Indian women who had nursed Andrew returned home, as did their menfolk who had remained hidden in case of trouble from these untrustworthy white men. Andrew had fully recovered and was anxious to hear what had happened. Luke described the shipboard battle. Andrew was crestfallen. It had been almost a year since he had seen action in Ireland, and that was an unimpressive siege in which the cavalry played little part.

Andrew changed the subject, 'Was White Deer reliable?'

'Yes, an excellent guide, and played his part in fending off the French attack. Why do you ask?'

'He is not popular with his own people, according to my old nurse'.

'How do you know? The woman spoke no English, and you know less Nanticoke.'

'I didn't need to. The younger woman was infatuated with White Deer and made her feelings very evident. Her mother berated her, and indicated that he was not a good choice. I used hand signals and finally the old woman understood my question of why White Deer was not a good match for her daughter. She pointed to Trooper Ackroyd and myself and with her hand movements outlined the shape of a European woman. White Deer has lost face and reputation because of his association with a white girl, whom I assume was Lucy Browne.'

'That fits what I have been told. He was very close to Lucy, but just how close? So it affected his relationship with his own people. One Ear might know more.'

Next morning the four soldiers made their way to One Ear's small hut. He was not pleased to see them, and was somewhat alarmed. Luke quietened his fears, and played on his need to feel important. 'We need your help to solve the murder of Miss Lucy. How friendly was she with White Deer?'

'Until a year ago White Deer treated her as his wife. When she came to the village she stayed in White Deer's round house - just the two of them.'

'Did Straight Arrow and the elders of the tribe approve of this?'

One Ear warmed to his account and Luke could detect his hatred of White Deer colouring the telling. 'No, it was totally unacceptable. Several leaders within our community expected him to wed their daughters, and Straight Arrow planned that his eldest son would marry a Susquehanna to improve relations between the two nations. With us final say in family matters rests not with your father, but your mother's brother. White Deer's uncle absolutely forbade him to continue his relationship with the girl. He ordered White Deer not to see her again.'

'How did White Deer react?'

'I don't know. No one tells an outcast anything.'

'Don't play games with me! You move about the woods unseen. You see and hear things all the time.'

'He did not stop seeing the girl,' One Ear admitted. 'The elders were furious, and Straight Arrow embarrassed. If he were not the war chief's son White Deer would have joined me in exile.'

Luke changed tack, 'Is there anything you have seen that might have a bearing on the murder?'

One Ear remained silent for some time as if desperately searching his memory for some incriminating evidence against his enemies. He finally spoke, 'I did see Straight Arrow, well away from his village, talking with a tall Susquehanna warrior. Perhaps he was arranging a wife for his wayward son.'

'Was there anything about this Susquehanna that could identify him?' asked Luke.

'He was very tall and he did not have a thumb on his right hand.'

'Black Cougar,' uttered Luke.

As the four men trekked homeward Andrew mused, 'Perhaps that unfortunate redskin has solved the murder for us. White Deer continues to bring disgrace on his people by his obsession with Lucy. Straight Arrow has to save the family honour. He asks Black Cougar to kill Lucy.'

'Black Cougar enters our investigation at several critical points. The marks on Lucy's throat could have been made by a man missing a thumb,' admitted Luke.

'I knew it. The heathen are responsible,' exclaimed Andrew.

'No, I don't agree. If all the participants were English your explanation might be feasible, but the redskin doesn't think the way we do. Straight Arrow has known the Brownes for almost a decade. Lucy and White Deer grew up together. If their friendship was as damaging as One Ear suggests Straight Arrow and Robert would have put an end to it long since. Robert would not have wanted his daughter to be anything more than a friend to White Deer. I am sure that is all she was. In recent times Lucy has been besotted with Tim, not White Deer.'

Andrew stopped in the track, 'Luke, that's the answer. White Deer loses Lucy to Tim and kills her.'

'I've already heard that explanation from that dissembling knave, James Browne – a Royalist turd of the worst kind.'

The soldiers reached their South Island base around noon where the whole group ate the usual corn fritters which included pieces of freshly cooked fish that one of the men had caught in the deep South Arm of the river. They were relaxing with mugs of West Indian rum when a single shot rang out in the distance. 'I think that came from Goodwin's plantation,' John remarked.

No one was concerned with this not uncommon sound, until the bells began to peal some half an hour latter. Luke paddled to West Island. Humphrey met him at the landing and announced, 'Jehu Colonel! There is a curse on this household. Mr James is dead. He has been shot.'

'What happened?' asked a stunned Luke, who could not completely obliterate the thought that the gentleman churl had received his just desserts.

'After his long absence Mr James was to meet Mr Tim on North Island to assess progress of the crops. I walked with Mr James to the riverbank, filling in some the events that had occurred since he left for the Delaware. He found a canoe, paddled towards North Island. I turned away to come back to the house when a single shot rang out. I turned and saw Mr James slumped in his canoe. The tide was pushing it back towards this island. I waded out into the water and recovered the canoe and body.'

Luke offered his condolences to Robert, after which he inspected the body. There was one musket shot to the heart, either an incredibly lucky shot, or the work of an extremely capable marksman. The murderer was beginning to show his hand. Luke asked Humphrey to return to the scene of the crime with him and asked, 'Did James row with his back towards his destination?'

'No, he paddled facing the direction in which he was headed.'

'The wound indicates the shot entered the body at a reasonable angle. Point out the exact course James was on!'

'He was headed for the small sandy beach where you can see a number of canoes. It is the accepted point of entry from West to North Island.'

'So the shot came from North Island, well to the left of the landing beach – maybe from those trees on that small headland jutting out into the river. Let's see what we can find.'

19

TIM APPEARED AS THE TWO MEN APPROACHED THE LANDING beach on North Island. 'Coming to help crush some worms?' he asked jokingly. 'What was Robert's bell about? I was at the other end of the island, and have come straight here.'

'James has been fatally shot.'

'God's mercy, he was to meet me here an hour ago. He did not appear so I returned to the fields. I had just rejoined my men when the bell tolled.'

Luke asked, 'How many men are working on this island?'

'There should be twelve, but today there are only eight and myself.'

'Are they armed?'

'No, they all have weapons, but while they work these are left in the tobacco hut which you can see here on your left. All eight were at the far end of the island with me. The worms are out of control so we are all busy removing them. Smell my shoes! I have crushed hundreds this morning.'

Luke volunteered assistance, 'Tomorrow I'll send four men across to help you. But for the moment Humphrey and I are moving towards that small headland. You are welcome to accompany us. The fatal shot came from there.'

The three men entered a patch of uncleared forest that constituted the small headland. Their search was fruitless. There was little undergrowth so that nothing appeared to have been crushed by the feet of an intruder, and there was no gun powder or shot to indicate the position of the shooter. Humphrey crossed the headland, and moved down to the river facing Goodwin's land and shouted to Luke, 'A canoe was aground here some time ago but the incoming tide is obliterating all trace of the visit.'

There was no certainty that the canoe that had run aground on the headland during the ebbing tide had anything to do with the murder. Someone may have beached his canoe there, and attempted to spear the fish that congregated around that part of the river. Humphrey found no footprints to show that any one had disembarked. The three men returned to the landing beach. Tim went with Humphrey to West Island to offer his condolences to the Brownes, and Luke paddled directly back to South Island.

Luke called his troop together, and they immediately reminded him of the brutal brawl between Tim and James. They raucously speculated that perhaps Tim had finished the altercation earlier that day. Luke called for silence and explained, 'Tim is not who he claims to be. He is Sir Timothy Beale, the sole survivor of a Roundhead family that a Royalist troop under Robert Browne wiped out. Because it was believed that all members of the family had been killed, the title and lands went to a distant cousin. Now that Tim has reappeared, his relatives are resisting a request to hand over the title and property, claiming Tim is an impostor. Tim has the strongest of motives to return an eye for an eye. Browne wiped out his family. Is he progressively wiping out the Brownes?'

The response from his men was unexpected. There was a cacophony of disapproval and one trooper spoke for the rest. 'If that be true Colonel, why are we persecuting one of our own, and supporting that blackguard Browne? Let Sir Timothy kill them all. Better still, execute Browne for the massacre and we can all go home!' Andrew and John's sympathy for such views calmed a potentially dangerous situation, as did Luke's acknowledgment that he was also sympathetic to their position.

The following day just after dawn Luke briefed four of his men on what he wanted them to extract from the workers in the field as they went about removing worms from the tobacco plants. 'It is terrible work especially as the heat increases. Find out Tim's movements yesterday morning especially where he was at the time James was shot. Humphrey will show you how to remove the worms from the tobacco plants.'

'A waste of time,' muttered Andrew. 'They all hated James. They, like us, are so sympathetic towards Tim that they will not provide any incriminating evidence.'

Mid morning Luke and the sergeants returned to West Island. As they approached the big house Harry Lloyd joined them just as Tim emerged from within. He was speechless when he saw Harry, who after a moment's delay embraced his former comrade. The two men engaged in an agitated yet whispering discussion. Luke put an end to the charade. 'Tim we know your real identity. Let us now tell Robert!'

Luke found Robert, and they all gathered in a disused tobacco shed, which was cooler than the house. Luke began, 'Gentlemen, three related facts interest me. Robert you left England because of what is known locally in Hampshire as the massacre of Beale Hall, most of your problems have only occurred since Tim arrived, and Tim is in fact Sir Timothy Beale, rightful possessor of Beale Hall, and sole survivor of the family your men massacred. '

'That cannot be. The whole family was killed. My captain told me that he counted the bodies personally, and no one had escaped,' replied an incredulous Robert, who once again began to tremble.

'Tim, explain!' commanded Luke.

'Yes, I was shot and stabbed. I can show you the scars. As the hooded butchers moved through the Hall I managed to drag the body of a servant whose face had been so mutilated that he was unrecognisable, and place it beside my parents and siblings. I put my cape around him, and quickly disappeared through one of the secret panels.'

'Was it Colonel Browne who carried out the massacre?'

'The men were masked. For years I assumed it was Browne and I came here to obtain justice – but not to kill anyone. The first time I heard Robert speak, I knew it was not the voice of the man who gave the orders to kill my family.'

'Robert, what did happen at Beale Hall?'

Robert was in a state. He was possessed by a cold fury which made it difficult for him to speak coherently. Slowly he pulled himself together, 'After our artillery had reduced the Hall's defences my cavalry troop was ordered to occupy the smouldering Hall, and take the family prisoners. I had partly completed the task when I received orders to immediately report back to my commanding officer. I told my deputy to finish the business at hand.'

'What happened next?'

'Well I didn't see it, but at the court martial it was elaborated in great detail by members of my troop. My Captain misheard my order. He thought I said finish them off, when I said finish the job, by which I meant escort the family to a place of detention.'

'Even if you said what you think you did, there is considerable justification for the interpretation your captain took. After all there was a history of bad blood between you and the

Beales. Why were your men wearing hoods if they were going about legitimate wartime activities?' goaded Luke.

'We were operating in our home localities. The men wore hoods so that none of their activities could be held against them when peace returned. But the officers were strictly forbidden to conceal their faces.'

Tim interrupted, 'The man who gave the orders to wipe us out wore a hood.'

'Yes, I learnt at the court martial that Captain Goodes, my deputy had put on a hood.'

'What did the court martial determine?' asked Luke.

'Goodes was found guilty of giving the orders, and was shot the next morning. I was advised to resign my commission and remove myself from the country. That is why I came here. The officers of the court martial like you Luke, were not totally convinced that my orders were as innocent as I claim.'

'And were they? Did you order the execution of the Beale family?'

Robert's trembling and jerking began again and his face became contorted, reflecting a demonic horror that only he could see, and his reply was almost inaudible, 'I don't remember, but the demons say I did.'

The reply confused Luke, who had neither understanding nor appreciation of the other world. He decided to change the subject hoping that Robert would regain his composure - or was it his sanity?

'What sort of person was Captain Goodes?'

'Maurice Goodes was a professional soldier. He and his brother fought in an English regiment within the French army, but returned to England at the outbreak of our Civil War. He was an infantryman, a crack marksman who quickly adapted to the cavalry,' replied Robert.

'Was he from Hampshire? Could he have had a personal grudge against the Beales?'

'No, he had a northern accent, and had been with the French army on the Rhine for almost a decade.'

'Was he a Catholic fanatic? Did he have an obsession about the Protestant Beales?'

'No, he was a professional soldier fighting for the King against those that supported Parliament. He was not a man of ideas or prejudices.'

'Robert, you realize that your answers suggest that while you had a motive for the massacre, Goodes had none.'

Robert looked a complete wreck. He was strained and emotional. Luke noticed his hands were still shaking. 'Robert did you ever meet Goodes's brother?'

'No.'

'Could your neighbour, Richard Goodwin be Goodes's brother?'

'Why would you think that?'

'Goodwin fought for the French, and his name is similar. People using a false name often keep it close to their real one.'

'Both parties could be lying, but Goodwin was an artilleryman stationed in the Netherlands, whereas the Goodes brothers were in the infantry on the German frontier. In addition Goodwin is a gentleman of considerable status, the Goodes were professional soldiers but of obscure background,' answered Robert.

'It's still a possibility. I have to assume everybody lies. What a mess! Two of your children have been murdered, and maybe we got Tom's death wrong. Perhaps he was the first victim. Someone is wiping out your family.' Luke turned towards Tim, 'You can see Sir Timothy why you are my prime suspect. Your family is wiped out; therefore you do the same to that of your family's murderer. My only problem with such a hypothesis is that there is not one piece of evidence as yet to convict you.'

Robert who had regained his equanimity spoke, 'Luke, continue to investigate the murders. I could understand Tim's hatred of me, but here he has never shown himself anything but an excellent overseer, a great friend of James, and more recently a serious admirer of Lucy. I spoke to her on the day she died about her relationship with Tim, and she confessed that she would be very happy to marry him, despite their recent tiff. Let's all continue as we are, until you can find an answer to what is happening. But I am sure the attack on my family stems from the present, not from my Hampshire past.'

'Robert, did you intervene at any stage to stop Lucy seeing White Deer?'

'No, but I did make clear that her relationship was not to get too close. White Deer's uncle came to see me. Young White Deer seems to have thought at one stage that Lucy was to become his wife. His family put an end to it, and I co-operated with them. Enough questions Luke. I must rest. Lipton's real identity has confused me. It brings back bad memories. If only I could recall the details.'

'Could White Deer have killed Lucy and James?' asked Luke, anxious to assail Robert in his vulnerable state.

'Lucy maybe. He had a motive, but what did James do to upset him?' replied Robert.

The group dispersed, but before Luke had gone far Tim caught up with him. 'Colonel I must tell you the truth regarding my recent altercation with James. It began aboard the Swedish merchantman. I criticised him for going below deck when the attack began.'

'Yes, I was disappointed at your inaction,' commented Luke.

Tim ignored the reference and continued. 'James had changed his mind, and did not want to return home. The news about the Indian conflict led him to believe that the Susquehanna would be so weakened that they would not be able to hinder trade with the inland. He had been paid for his furs with a bill of exchange, but also a large amount of Swedish silver. With his Swedish silver, and the reopened trade routes he had dreams of an immense and immediate fortune. Secondly, he took an immense dislike to you, and hated strangers investigating his family. He irrationally blamed the Parliamentary victims of the massacre at Beale Hall for his father's predicament, and the presence of New Model soldiers on his father's plantation seemed to unhinge him. Rather than have to put up with you, he decided to jump ship and return to Fort Christina.

'How did he intend to leave the moving ship?'

'He wanted to jump overboard, and allow the tides to push him ashore somewhere along the riverbank. I told him this would be fatal, as the weight of his silver would have carried him down. He cannot swim. He just laughed'

'So why didn't he escape?'

'When he was poised to jump not only were musket shots whistling past his ear, but the French were scrambling up the sides He scurried below deck looking for a convenient porthole to escape through unobserved. He couldn't find a porthole that didn't lead him into the arms of the boarding French. He then decided he would sit out the fight, and bribe the French victors to let him disembark.'

'This incensed me. I hit him from behind, and knocked him out. I then headed for the upper deck to join the fight, just in time to see you at the wheel, and the assailants dispersed.'

'So the fight that developed on the beach was James retaliating for you knocking him out?'

'In part only. He was furious, not that I hit him, but that the hit prevented his escape to unimagined wealth. James like his father had a nasty streak. He then accused me of killing Lucy.'

20

'WHY WOULD HE DO THAT?' ASKED LUKE.

'My indiscretion with Abigail hurt Lucy deeply, and forced her to punish me by making herself available to all and sundry. I am sure one of these fleeting lovers killed her. James blamed me for creating the tragedy, and I blamed him for not taking his sister in hand, and controlling her activities, which in the end proved fatal.'

'Because of her treatment by James and yourself, Lucy sought comfort from White Deer. Did White Deer have a grudge against James, other than James's insensitivity towards his sister?'

'Not that I know of.'

'Humphrey and I found the marks of a canoe that came ashore on the headland from which James was shot. An Indian could have silently floated down the river, killed James and returned up stream. Can you suggest other possibilities?'

Tim responded, 'While James was away the workers were involved in some activity which they were determined to hide from James. When I said this morning that James would be coming across to North Island one of them became deeply distressed.'

'But you told me Tim that all eight of your men were at the far end of the island when the shot was heard.'

'Yes, but he may have paid a friend to fire the shot.'

"Did any of your workers have time from when you told them about James's visit to contact anybody else?'

'No.'

'Methinks young Tim that you are trying too hard to place the blame anywhere but on yourself. I am placing your under arrest by confining you during the day to North Island where your current fields are, and here during the hours of darkness. One of my men will be with you day and night.'

ଦ୍ଧ

It was dark before Luke's four troopers returned from the fields. Their report was simple. Tim was not with his men for much of the morning. He went to meet James but did not return until well after the shot was heard. He left them again almost immediately, when he heard the bell tolling. Luke asked, 'Did his men indicate whether he could have shot James, and returned to the fields when he did?'

'It would have been possible if he had run some of the way, but they thought it unlikely.'

Luke dismissed the exhausted soldiers, and turned to Andrew and John, 'Regarding James's murder, we have two suspects –Beale who has strong motive and possible opportunity, and White Deer who probably resented James's participation in the campaign to prevent him developing a more permanent relationship with Lucy.'

'There is a third suspect,' Andrew announced.

'Who?' said Luke somewhat taken aback.

'You assumed that James had his upper body directly facing his landing site. If his body was turned significantly at the time, the source of the musket ball may not have been the headland you designated. It could have come from across the water, from the mainland – from an unknown assailant within Goodwin's land.'

John asked, 'That is much further away. Luke, did you find an exit wound for the shot or is it still within the body?'

Luke blushed slightly, 'I did not look. The body is prepared by Priscilla for tomorrow's burial. I will ask her if there was an exit wound.'

The following afternoon Luke and his men attended the funeral – a simple ceremony in which Robert read from the

126

Book of Common Prayer. The workers from the Browne and Sherman estates attended, but only Mr Richard Goodwin came from his plantation. Significantly missing was Elizabeth Browne, the deceased's mother. After the interment Luke took Priscilla aside, and asked her about the wounds. She was adamant there was no exit wound.

Luke thought about this for some time. His war experience was such that he knew that if a shot encountered bone if may be deflected and slowed within the body. It was too late to try and find where in the body the shot was lodged. While the absence of an exit wound suggested the shot could have come a fair distance, it did not necessarily rule out the closer source of the headland.

The soldiers were about to return to South Island when the heavens opened - not with the threatening thunderstorm, but with a cannonade of fairly heavy calibre artillery. It took Luke some time to comprehend that close inshore an armed merchantman, flying no identifying flag, was blasting away at West Island as it sailed by. The firing stopped as quickly as it began which left Luke confused. If it were a serious attack the ship would have anchored off shore and bombarded the plantation relentlessly, and probably put men ashore to continue the assault. This must be a warning of worse to follow, or simply passing harassment of an unpopular plantation owner. Was it part of the giant enterprise against Browne? – the precise nature of which still eluded Luke.

Apart from the demolition of a disused tobacco hut there was no damage. No one was wounded or killed, although following the death of her children the attack sent Elizabeth into another of her frenzied fits of spleen and irrationality. It was left to Priscilla to calm her disturbed mother. Why had Elizabeth not attended her son's funeral?

Andrew was relaxed concerning the attack. 'It has nothing to do with the malevolence that breeds on this plantation. They were having a bit of fun, and testing their cannon.

The attack was not serious, and they did not waste much ammunition.'

Next morning Luke was surprised to see Humphrey, who with the death of James had returned to Robert Browne's direct service. 'I thought we had seen the last of you for a while,' teased Luke.

'Yes, the master has made me overseer of this year's tobacco crop on North Island, and Sir Timothy has replaced Mr. James as manager of the whole plantation.'

'So why has such an important man deserted his fields to visit we lazy soldiers who are still abed so early in the morning,' joked John.

'I have news,' replied Humphrey

'Which is?'

'Two of the labourers, recovering from a bout of malaria, were well enough to paddle north along the shore of the Bay to a small inlet within which are shoals alive with fish. The inlet represents the northern edge of Mr Goodwin's plantation.'

'And what did these fishermen hear or see?' queried Luke.

'Anchored just off shore was a large armed merchantman.'

'The ship that attacked us yesterday?'

'Yes.'

'So what's the great news?' asked the ever cynical Andrew.

'When the ship anchored in the inlet it was flying the French flag, and they were close enough to read its name, *Notre Dame des Carmes.*'

'Now that is interesting!' uttered Luke.

'The presence of a French frigate in the Delaware, and another armed French vessel in the Chesapeake must be connected,' mused Andrew.

'How long was the *Notre Dame des Carmes* anchored in that inlet? Maybe some French sharpshooters came ashore, and moved through Goodwin's plantation, and took a shot at James,' John said, thinking aloud.

'Far fetched,' said Luke dampening the speculation.

'Not necessarily,' interrupted Andrew. 'Whoever shot James was an excellent marksman. I've seen no evidence that Beale or White Deer have such skills. James may have had some secret deal with the French, and your help in stopping the French board the *Leoparden* could have led them to believe James had double crossed them. They took their revenge. After all, James did nothing to help you repel the French boarders. Perhaps he gave the French information about the Swedish ship's cargo and itinerary?'

'A fanciful tale! The timing is all wrong. We have just returned from the Delaware. There is no time for news of what happened there to reach a French ship isolated in the Chesapeake,' countered Luke.

Humphrey left, and Luke visited the Browne household to probe the absence of Elizabeth from the funeral. He knew that he would not be able to see Elizabeth, and hoped that Priscilla or Rachel O'Brien would be more helpful. It was a vain hope. Both women simply stated that Elizabeth was unwell, and attending the funeral would have made matters worse. He considered confronting Robert on the matter. Lost in thought, he collided with Harry Lloyd.

'We are both on the wrong island,' joked Luke.

'I'm on my way to see Tim. I need his help with a few technical problems that these bloody tobacco plants create. Why are you here?'

'I came to find out why Elizabeth missed the funeral. Perhaps I have become too suspicious. Her grief must have been overwhelming. I shouldn't be looking for hidden secrets as an explanation,' admitted Luke.

'Yes, you should. And I can answer your question. Elizabeth hated James, and it goes back to the circumstances of his birth, and the long term mutual hatred of the Beales and the Brownes.'

'How do you know these things?'

'You forget Colonel that the Beales, the Brownes and the Lloyds, my distant cousins, were all leading gentry in a very small portion of Hampshire. It was common gossip two decades ago, which my cousins accepted as truth, and which was endorsed by Tim Beale during our service together.'

'What's the explanation?' asked Luke.

'Twenty five years ago Elizabeth Trafford, now Browne, was betrothed to Ralph Beale, Tim's uncle. Just before the wedding it became obvious that Elizabeth was pregnant, and not to Ralph. The father was Robert Browne. Both families forced Robert and Elizabeth to marry, and the early offspring of the forced marriage was James.'

'But why did Elizabeth hate James?'

'Elizabeth was not a willing partner in his conception. Robert raped Elizabeth and ruined her life. Every minute of James's existence reminded her of that traumatic event. She was deeply in love with Ralph Beale who died defending Beale Hall during the later Browne attack.'

'Tim is aware of this history?'

'Yes.'

'It strengthens Tim's motivation to wreak revenge on the Brownes,' Luke concluded sadly.

'But it also creates another suspect,' commented Harry.

'Who?'

'Elizabeth Browne.'

'What! Organize the killing of her own son?' queried a cynical Luke.

'The woman is mad. She has money in her own right. Out here a few shillings would buy a killer.'

Harry had raised a possibility Luke had not considered. He asked aloud, 'Is Lady Elizabeth really mad, or does she feign her illnesses to cover a murderous conspiracy?'

Harry had no doubts. 'Don't you think it is strange that Lucy and James were murdered so soon after the accidental death of her favourite, Tom. What greater revenge could she have against her vicious husband than by killing his favourite children, after losing her beloved son? This interpretation explains why these murders have occurred when they have.'

'No, Harry, mothers don't kill her own children. Besides she is so small and weak and watched like a hawk by Priscilla and Rachel. They would have to be part of it.'

'Maybe they were. All three attacked you and others when you wished to exhume Tom's body.'

Luke changed the topic, 'I know you were only a few months on the Severn, but did your uncle hear anything suggesting the imminent creation of a French trading post or colony in this region?'

'There were rumours among the Susquehanna that the Iroquois victory, and their attempt to monopolise the furs of the Great Lakes had forced the French with their Huron allies to look elsewhere to break the monopoly. They could send their goods across the mountains to the Atlantic coast. Uncle suspected they would use the Swedish and Dutch settlements along the Delaware as neither country exerted much control there. The French frigate that tried to capture the *Leoparden* may have been an escort for a number of French merchantmen. It is too early in the season to gauge what is really going on.'

'If the Delaware is the probable site of French intervention why was an armed French merchantman in the upper reaches of Chesapeake Bay? Could one of the maverick settlers on Kent Island be a front for a French trading post?'

21

'NOT LIKELY, UNCLE TOLD ME THAT WHILE THOSE SETTLERS are
not Puritans, and hate Lord Baltimore, they are down to earth
English Protestants who would not have a bar of anything
French or Catholic. Most of them want a greater Virginia.
They are indifferent to whether the Governor is Royalist or
republican. They want an independent collection of wealthy
planters doing their own thing, and in no way controlled by
community norms or rules. There they differ from my uncle's
settlement. He wants to create a Puritan Commonwealth on
the model of Massachusetts in which God and the community
rule.'

'Andrew thinks James did a deal with the French, double-
crossed them and they killed him.'

'Possibly, and it is much more likely that the Catholics at St
Mary's, and on the plantations here would do a deal with the
French, rather than the settlers along the Severn or on Kent
Island.'

'One word is starting to dominate my thoughts regarding
the situation here, both personal and political. That word is
chaos,' concluded a tired and frustrated Luke.

Luke felt, given his general commission from Cromwell,
that it was now far more important to investigate the French
connection than concentrate on the two murders. Andrew
who had fought for the Swedes in the Thirty Years War disagreed. 'What's the concern? France was our ally against Spain
in the European War. Spain, not France is the enemy.'

John supported him, 'France is weak. It's in the middle of a
Civil War. Their princes, and the magistrates and populace of
Paris have risen against the government of Cardinal Mazarin,
who rules in the name of a boy king, Louis XIV. France poses
no threat.'

Luke responded, 'Maybe but French activities in the Americas have a very religious intent. The most powerful man in Canada is the Catholic Bishop of Quebec, and the most effective agents of French power are the Black Robes, les robes noir.'

'What are they?' asked Andrew, genuinely ignorant of the term.

'Papist priests, mainly Jesuits - a name bestowed on them by the Indians of the Great Lakes.'

'Jehu!' gasped Andrew, 'They are already here.'

'What do you mean?'

'While I was recovering from my snakebite I heard my two Indian nurses mention les robes noirs. I had no idea what it meant except it sounded French, and I wondered why Indians so far from a French colony knew such words.'

'Significant!' exclaimed Luke. 'Let's question the women with White Deer as our interpreter. On the way I want another chat with One Ear. This time let's paddle up the river instead of using the trail. It is prudent to know as much about that river as we can. It's the main concourse for the area, including possible murderers. Humphrey can teach us some of its secrets.'

Within the hour the four men in two canoes proceeded up river. Humphrey had been reluctant to leave the tobacco fields, until Luke provided several of his men to help out. Progress was reasonably slow as Humphrey pointed out the vagaries of the river - parts where it flowed faster than expected, the sluggish deep pools in which one could easily drown, and the shoals and rocks that were hidden except in the lowest of tides. Luke was surprised to find there were sections of white water where canoes had to be carried around the obstacle. He had assumed this was a quiet tidal river, which was navigable at least by canoe, almost to its source.

The need to leave the water coincided with the path to One Ear. The paddlers left the canoes below the rapids. The smell

133

of burning birch was overwhelming as they approached the renegade's roundhouse. It was well alight. Luke burst through the flames, and emerged immediately carrying the limp body of One Ear. Luke placed him on the ground. He was dead.

'Murdered,' stated Andrew, without looking at the body.

'Why do you say that?' asked Luke.

'He didn't burn to death. He didn't die of smoke inhalation. He could have easily escaped the fire, - if he were alive when it started.'

'And look at his contorted face,' exclaimed Humphrey. 'He's been poisoned.'

'He could have taken poison, and then set his hut on fire,' said Luke defensively. 'He had lost his only friend. His community continued to hate and punish him. He had nothing to live for.'

Andrew was strident, 'Pretty convenient for Straight Arrow and White Deer, and maybe some of their white friends. A man who knew the Indian gossip, and through Tom, the secrets of the white planters, is dead. No, this is another murder.'

The soldiers moved on to the Nanticoke village. Word had preceded them and White Deer was waiting to receive them. Luke immediately reported One Ear's death. White Deer was openly delighted with the news, 'Good! The elders were not happy that in addition to his misuse of poison, he had begun to spread false rumours about Lucy and myself, causing much disquiet. He was told to use his knowledge of poisons to expedite his journey to the spirit world where his unhappy soul might find some solace. He lived badly, but he has apparently died with some honour. Was there another reason for your visit?'

Andrew was not convinced that One Ear had committed suicide, but chose not to comment. Luke answered White Deer, 'When Andrew was recovering from his snakebite he heard his two nurses mention, "les robes noirs". I must talk to these women about the black robes? Are there French Catholic priests in the neighbourhood?'

'Until about six years ago there were Jesuit missions near St Mary's. They refused to accept Lord Baltimore's authority and rejected his policies. When your Civil War began at home the Protestants here forced the Jesuits out. There are rumours that they have returned, and set up a mission to the south of us - well away from other settlers. But they are English. I do not know of any French connection.'

The men reached the nurses' village. White Deer sought out the old woman and her daughter, and explained to them what Luke wanted. They gabbled continuously, interrupting each other until White Deer raised his hand to stop them. 'They know nothing first hand. The refugees from the village that had been burnt by the Susquehanna told them that when the Susquehanna arrived they asked for the Black Robes, but their community knew nothing of any planned meeting between the Susquehanna and French priests.'

Luke had already decided that this was so serious he must get an urgent message back to Cromwell. Luke drew John and Andrew aside and asked in a whisper, 'Who is behind this? The French Government is divided. It could be one of several groups. Maybe there is a Jesuit plot hatched without reference to the French government?'

'In that case why are there French ships on each side of this peninsula. The priests could have come from the ship on the Delaware, the ship on the Chesapeake, or moved up from a suspected English Jesuit mission to the south of us,' commented John.

'Maybe they were disembarked by the frigate on the Delaware, and the merchantman on the Chesapeake was waiting to pick them up after their meeting with the Susquehanna,' speculated Andrew.

'If this is an evangelising mission by the Jesuits with a small number of Indians, they would cause no difficulties for Lord Baltimore, or the government of the English Republic. The local Protestants can deal with the problem in due course as they did in the past,' concluded John.

As the soldiers made their way back to their canoes Humphrey shocked Luke with his quiet comment, 'White Deer lied.' Luke waited in a state of surprise for Humphrey to continue. He took his time. Eventually he explained, 'White Deer ordered the women not to reveal what they knew about the Black Robes. The argument between the women was that the young girl wanted to follow White Deer's directive, while the older woman, whom we know is not very sympathetic to White Deer, threatened to tell us the truth even if she had to find someone else to translate for her. White Deer quietened her by lying to her as to what he told you. He must have thought I was out of earshot. He knows I speak Nanticoke perfectly.'

'Well, Humphrey in what particulars did he lie?'

'Apparently a Susquehanna warrior with a missing thumb, our friend Black Cougar, and our favourite Nanticoke war chief, Straight Arrow, had visited the village that was later burnt, on two successive full moons to await les robes noirs. They never arrived.'

'Why would White Deer lie?' asked Andrew.

'The simple explanation is that he is protecting his father, but I suspect something momentous is going on which might involve the French, the Jesuits, the Susquehanna and the Nanticokes. Therefore I want a volunteer - Andrew or John - to return to England immediately, and report to Cromwell. You will not return as we will all be out of here within the month.'

The journey down stream was in complete silence. Neither sergeant wanted to leave. On returning to their island Luke drew straws. John lost and would leave for England next day, boarding Captain Murchison's sloop around noon. When the ship arrived Luke was at the quayside to farewell his sergeant and was surprised to find a familiar passenger disembarking.

136

'Welcome back Matthew, I did not expect you so soon. You have been missed. There have been more murders since you departed. Your help would have been invaluable. Harry Lloyd will fill you in.'

Some days later, before Luke had left South Island, Harry Lloyd arrived. 'What brings you here so early in the morning?' asked the Colonel.

'Matthew has returned, and wishes to be his own overseer and manager. You have lost your sergeant. I have no income, and wish to resume my military service. I would like to join your unit.'

'What rank did you hold in Ireland?' asked Luke quietly

'Cornet, junior Lieutenant of Horse.'

'Harry, we are a cavalry unit, but have no horses in Maryland. We are temporarily an infantry section of musketeers. I appoint you to the rank Lieutenant. You will assist me and Sergeant Ford to lead the group.'

'What's my first mission?' asked the eager recruit.

'I have three problems - the murders of Lucy, and James, the general malevolence surrounding Browne's plantation, and now the French connection. Lucy could have been murdered by Tim Beale, White Deer or an unknown disappointed lover.'

'Or a random victim of the wider conspiracy to destroy the Brownes,' added Andrew who had joined them, munching some crisp corn bread.

'Agreed! With James, the murderer could have been White Deer, Tim Beale, a disappointed French partner, his mother, or anybody involved in a bigger conspiracy. What is behind such a wider conspiracy may have many aspects to it. It may be related to Browne's past, to his support for Baltimore in this largely hostile area, or there may be no such conspiracy all. As for a French connection we have the solid evidence of French ships on either side of the peninsula, and talk of an expected rendezvous between local Indians and settlers and the French

137

priests. As the men finished breakfast Browne's bell rang out. Luke now recognised this as information and not a warning summons. Luke, Andrew and Harry crossed over to West Island, and immediately went to the beach beside the quay where Luke had first come aground, and where a crowd had gathered. Humphrey left the group and walked towards them. He simply stated, 'God's Blood! You will not believe this.'

Luke pushed through the crowd and lying on the beach, with Dr Sherman examining him, was the prone body of a man dressed in a black cassock and wearing a large crucifix – a Black Robe.

22

MATTHEW ROSE FROM THE INERT BODY, AND INDICATED THAT the priest was alive. Luke helped carry the unconscious man to Robert's house, where he was laid on James's bed. Priscilla and Rachel removed his wet clothes and dried his body. Matthew, who could do nothing more until the priest recovered consciousness, gave Luke a preliminary report, 'The bruise on his forehead, that now looks like a plum, both in size and colour, suggests he hit his head rather sharply. His general condition is excellent. This is not an austere missionary priest, who has walked hundreds of miles from the inland to get here. This cleric enjoys a privileged life. And he was in the water for only a few minutes.'

'He came ashore from the French ship that sheltered in the inlet north of here, and in moving south to the Jesuit mission he slipped on the rocks, hit his head, and the tide brought him ashore?' speculated Luke.

Andrew, as ever, had a different interpretation. 'He came across from the Delaware to meet with the Susquehanna. While paddling down the river the treacherous current caused him to lose control of his canoe. He hit his head on a protruding branch, tumbled into the water and was carried by the fast current to where he was found.'

'Great imagination gentlemen, but this man was not washed ashore,' stated Matthew firmly. 'Did you not see his footprints in the sand? He tried to cross the North Arm of the river. In the process he slipped, hit his head on a rock which rendered him unconscious. The cold water revived him long enough for him to reach the shore, and then he collapsed again.'

The discussion was interrupted by a clamour from the room where the priest lay. Priscilla was screaming at someone to leave. Matthew, alarmed for the sake of his patient, entered the room as Abigail Hicks beat a hasty retreat. He turned to Priscilla who was red faced and upset. 'What's going on here? The man deserves some respect.'

'That hussy Abigail! Rachel and I had stripped and dried the comatose body, and dressed the priest in one of James's shirts. I turned around and found Abigail, who arrived uninvited, rifling through the wet clothes. I reprimanded her. She ignored me, and approached the body of the priest, and lifted his shirt.'

'Why did she do that?'

'I don't know. It was then that I ordered her from the room,' Priscilla explained.

Matthew returned to the hall where Robert and the three soldiers were waiting. They all adjourned to the shade of a large tree, and Robert ordered Abigail to bring some cold chicken and corn fritters. The warm late morning and a liberal supply of beer induced drowsiness. Andrew was dreamily looking north towards the river, and across it to Goodwin's estate when his face expressed alarm. 'Trouble?' he whispered.

Richard Goodwin and ten of his men were paddling towards them. Robert, obviously ill at ease at this unexpected visit in strength sent Rachel to North Island to summon his men. Andrew, even more quickly, headed for South Island to raise the troopers. Robert, Luke and Harry hastened to intercept Richard at the landing beach. Despite the weather he wore a burgundy doublet with slashed sleeves, revealing a bright blue underlining. His breeches and stockings were of the same burgundy hue, as was his hatband. Robert humorously commented, 'Well Richard, do I hand over the island to your invasion force now? I have not seen your men outside your plantation for years.' Luke and Harry did not smile, as their hands moved to the hilt of their swords.

Richard eased the tension that later Luke found difficult to explain. Richard was light hearted and friendly, but could not resist a gentle taunt. 'With a large body of professional soldiers on your plantation I would be a fool invading with ten men. Recent events have spooked all of you. Why would I want to invade my friend and neighbour? My visit is to offer my help. A priest was found on your beach. As a Catholic I have come to give him refuge, if that is agreeable to you. I have plenty of room. I have entertained priests before, and most of my men are Catholics, and could well benefit from his presence. I brought these men to carry him home. If there are any goods washed up with him, or found on his person I'll take them as well.'

'Nothing was found near him on the beach, but to be truthful we did not search it thoroughly,' replied Robert.

'He had a golden crucifix around his neck and an expensive ring on his finger. I will ask the women who undressed him if there was anything else. He is still unconscious, and cannot be moved until I ascertain the extent of his injuries,' pronounced Matthew.

'He hasn't spoken yet?' asked a surprisingly quizzical Richard.

'Not a word,' said Luke picking up on Richard's apparent relief. Luke decided to push the issue, 'And he won't be leaving this house until he does. There is so much going on here as you imply that every new development needs probing. Why are you so interested in his possessions, Richard? Do you know this man?'

Before he could answer Rachel announced that the priest was stirring. Luke immediately asked her, 'Did the priest have any possessions on his person?'

'Yes, a leather purse strapped around his waist.'

'Did you open it?'

'No, Miss Priscilla took it, and returned it to him just a moment ago, when he awoke.'

All the men tried to enter the priest's room at once. Luke barred the way, 'The doctor should see the patient alone, and then I will question him. After that if Robert and the priest are agreeable, then Richard you may have him.'

'You are taking your role a little too seriously, Tremayne. What possible role could this priest play in your murder enquiries? Maryland is full of Catholics and several priests – all protected by law. This is not Puritan England,' commented Richard with a hint of exasperation at Luke's overt prejudice and sense of importance.

Richard and Robert were unhappy, but Luke's large frame continued to block the doorway. The arrival of Andrew and the soldiers intimidated Richard's men, who now took themselves off to loll under a distant tree. The priest confirmed Matthew's interpretation of events. He tried to get across the North Arm at low tide, hit his head, passed out, came to in time to wade ashore and then collapsed. Matthew introduced Luke as special envoy of Lord Baltimore, which seemed to be good news for the priest, who responded in perfect English, 'I am Father Renaud of the Society of Jesus. I am also a special envoy, in my case on behalf of the French leaders of my Order.'

Before Father Renaud could continue Richard pushed into the room, and inundated the priest with a torrent of French. Both men became highly agitated. Luke who only had a smattering of French could make out very little of the conversation. He could contain himself no longer. 'Enow Richard, what are you arguing over?'

'No argument. I know of Father Renaud. He was to meet with various people over the last few weeks, including myself, but was attacked before the encounter took place. He is now hoping to make his way south to his English brothers further down the Eastern shore.'

Luke noticed the priest's face as Richard spoke. It expressed mild concern, and as Luke caught his eye he smiled nervously. Luke asked, 'Father are there other French Jesuits in the area?' The priest nodded affirmatively, and a tear trickled down his face. Luke continued, 'Where are they?'

'We were three, and were to meet the leaders of the local Indians and others. We were delayed and missed the first scheduled meeting because of inter-tribal warfare. On the second occasion we had almost reached the designated meeting place at the agreed time, when we were attacked. We made camp beside the river that flows past here. During the night I sensed that there were others in the area. I crawled away from the dying fire, and then I heard a struggle, and muffled voices. I dared not move. At dawn I returned to our camp, and found my companions gone. I knew of Mr Goodwin and moved down river to find his place. However the number of Indians and Englishmen using the river, or its banks concerned me. I moved inland and reached the coast at a small inlet just north of here. I walked around the headland looking for Mr Goodwin's house. I missed it, and was eventually confronted by a wide but what appeared to me, mistakenly, a shallow river.

I saw this residence from across the water and tried to reach it. You know the rest.'

Matthew interposed, 'That is enough; this man has experienced a nasty blow to the head. We must find some clothes for him, and then Richard you can take him home as that is where he was heading before he became lost.'

Robert spoke, 'Father, help yourself to James's clothes, and meet us in the hall. I will return your clothes when they are dry.' The locals withdrew to the hall and after some time Father Renaud emerged looking a little strange, as James's clothes were too large for him. He contented himself with a drab coloured jerkin over the white shirt and baggy olive breeches and black stockings tied up with olive ribbons. He remained hatless. Richard left the group, and re-emerged several minutes later.

'I was just checking that the Father had not left anything behind.'

Luke was not fooled. Richard had gone to Father Renaud's temporary bedroom and searched it. But for what? Richard was clearly in a hurry, and called his men to the house to carry the priest. The men brought with them a stretcher. Renaud waved the men away and walked hesitatingly towards the canoes. Suddenly he faltered and looked like falling to the ground. Luke grabbed him and as the inert body pressed against him, Luke felt a hand push into his doublet. Richard ordered his men to place Father Renaud on the stretcher, and headed for the river. He announced to the others, 'It will be easier to get him home while he is unconscious, than to revive him here. Good day gentlemen.'

After Goodwin and his men left Luke announced, 'There is more to that priest than meets the eye. He is a great actor.'

'What do you mean?' asked Andrew.

'That final collapse was an act.'

'To what end?' queried Harry.

'Let us see,' replied Luke, as he placed his hand into his doublet and revealed a sealed letter.

'I don't understand,' said Andrew who was sometimes slow to pick up on developments.

'When Father Renaud fell forward in his fake faint he thrust this into my doublet. He clearly did not want it to fall into Richard's hands.'

'Well open it!' said Andrew.

'Not so fast. Let's examine it first without breaking the seal. It may be more politic to deliver it to the intended recipient unopened, and gain his trust, than present a broken seal which would immediately create suspicion,' argued Harry.

All examined the unopened letter. It was addressed to Father Austin and bore a seal which Robert identified as that of the Jesuit order. Luke asked, 'Does anybody know of a Father Austin?'

Robert answered, 'Before they were driven out a few years ago by Protestant insurgents Father Peter Austin was one of the Jesuit priests located at St Mary's. If the rumours are correct and the priests have returned to an unknown location on the eastern shore to the south of us, then Austin might be their leader.'

'So you think Father Renaud, in addition to what he told us, was on a mission to get a message or orders through to Father Austin?' asked Luke.

'Priests don't go wandering around the wilderness carrying official seals of the order. This letter has come from Quebec or from Europe. And given Renaud's excellent physical condition he is a high powered envoy from the Jesuits in Canada or from France itself, who travelled here in the relative ease of a French ship. Renaud is not here to broker some deal about fur trading. It is much bigger,' commented Harry Lloyd.

'Then open the letter!' demanded an excited Andrew.

23

'No,' cautioned Luke, 'Father Renaud trusts me to deliver the message.'

Harry, who had first encouraged caution changed his position, 'Opening the letter is not a breach of trust. You must know its contents in case it is taken from you. Renaud does not know your basic role as a Cromwellian soldier, but trusts you as an envoy of Lord Baltimore. You owe it to Baltimore to discover what the Jesuits in his province are up to.'

Andrew exploded, 'You've lost your perspective Luke. This letter is central to our mission for both Baltimore and the General. I agree with Harry. Open the damn thing!'

Luke did, and declaimed deflatingly, 'God's Blood, It's in Latin.'

'What did you expect, French Catholic priests writing in English?' teased young Harry.

'Well, it's addressed to an English priest. Any of you able to translate?'

Harry took the letter which read,

Fidus Austin,
Ali volat propriis. Deus vult. Divide et impere.
Fronti nulla fides. Perfide X. Quantum mutatus ab illo. Experte
credite

Le Jeune

'It is brief and cryptic. Are his sermons as short?' joked Andrew.

'Papist priests don't preach many sermons. Preaching God's word is anathema to them,' sermonized the Puritan Harry Lloyd.

Luke lost his patience, 'Enough argument! What does the letter say?'

Harry translated aloud.

Faithful Austin.

She flies with her own wings. God willing. Divide and rule. No reliance can be placed on appearance. Perfidious X How changed from what he once was. Believe one who has had experience.

Le Jeune

'Well what does it mean?' asked Luke.

'Straight forward,' Harry stated brashly. 'Whatever they are planning has to be achieved on their own. They cannot trust X, who has changed his position.'

'This is a letter warning Austin not to trust X, and to proceed on the enterprise alone,' summarised Andrew.

Luke commented gloomily, 'More problems. What are the Jesuits planning? Who is X? And who is Le Jeune?'

'Humphrey can help. I'll get him.' offered Matthew. Within a minute or two Humphrey joined them.

Luke asked him, 'You have been in the Americas for over four decades. Have you come across the name Le Jeune?'

'Paul Le Jeune, yes, not only do I know the name, I have met him.'

'That's a start. Continue!' requested a delighted Luke.

'Le Jeune is the most famous of the Black Robes. Years ago when I went inland across the mountains with the Susquehanna, we met a party of Huron who had with them a French priest. He was a brave man who had suffered greatly, but who eventually became a hero amongst them. Only recently I heard that he had returned to France, and was now responsible for all the Jesuits in Canada.'

'That solves one problem quicker than expected. Experte credite, believe one who has experience. From what you say this Le Jeune is unsurpassed for experience, and is now in a position to control the French Jesuits in the Americas. This letter comes from France. Renaud is carrying Le Jeune's warning to Austin not to trust X.'

'We can speculate all day as to the identity of X. Find Austin, deliver your message, and see what the Catholic proprietor's envoy can discover,' commented a slightly sarcastic Andrew.

Luke ended the discussion. Humphrey returned to his hut, Andrew and Harry to South Island, and Matthew to his plantation. Luke remained and sought Robert's permission to interview the women. He asked Priscilla and Rachel if there was anything unusual about the body of Father Renaud, and of any possessions other than the leather pouch that he had on his person. Priscilla replied, 'This is no frontier priest. His body is perfect in that it revealed no scars or blemishes. His hands are soft. He is a man used to the good life. His under garments were of the highest quality. I don't know what was in his leather pouch, but apart from a large ring and gold crucifix which he wore, he had no other possessions.'

'Priscilla, what was the argument with Abigail about?'

'Rachel and I had finished drying and dressing the priest when Abigail strode in, examined his body which was lying on its back and turned it partly over to examine the man's back. I told her to show some respect.'

'Did she explain her actions?'

'No, she then went to the pile of wet clothes on the floor and rummaged through them. That is when I lost my temper and shouted at her to leave.' Rachel agreed with her mistress's account. Their memories of events worried Luke. They differed in some ways from what they had told Matthew at the time. Did such minor differences indicate the women had concocted a new story? Was it significant?

Luke found Abigail with a large pot of simmering water into which she was throwing numerous cut vegetables, and a freshly plucked chicken whose feathers were scattered around the cookhouse floor. She was an untidy cook, but personally very presentable. Given the heat, Abigail, in the privacy of the cookhouse had removed her coif. Her blonde hair cascaded down over her shoulders. Her white shirt and green bodice struggled to contain her unusually large breasts. Luke was temporarily transfixed above all by her large green eyes, and large sensuous red lips, which she licked seductively with her tongue, as she chopped the carrots and turnips.

'So Colonel, at last you have me all to yourself. What would you have of me?' she asked with her eyes twinkling at the obvious nuances of her question.

Luke was tempted. His promise to stay celibate as a gesture to a lost love, was fading with time. Abigail came close to him and rubbed her long blonde locks into his face, and whispered in his ear. 'My hut is just a few yards away, and this soup can look after itself for some time. And it is so hot in these clothes.'

Luke's lust overcame his heart - and mind. He was reacting physically in anticipation. She led him by the hand from the cookhouse to her hut, where gently yet purposely he undid her bodice and removed her shirt. This left her dressed in her low cut see through chemise, against which her already erect nipples were protruding invitingly. Luke's mouth could not resist them, and through the now sodden chemise he nibbled and sucked until Abigail responded with deep breathing, and eventually cries of ecstasy as she shook with delight. Luke undressed, except for his shirt, and the two lay together on the low large bed as Abigail gently, and then with increasing vigour, caressed the powerfully aroused soldier. At last she led him home, and Luke retained enough control to at first gently, and them with increasing aggression, thrust away until in a series of screams of delight Abigail came again and again.

The two lay quietly for some time. Abigail broke the silence. 'Where have you been, my big soldier? Compared with

148

you, the so-called men on this settlement are but inexperienced boys. Before we start all over again, why did you want to see me, other than to swive me stupid?'

Luke did not feel like questioning Abigail in these circumstances, but duty was slowly replacing lust in the control of his activities. 'Why were you examining the unconscious body of the priest?'

Abigail giggled, 'I have weird habits. I have never slept with a priest. Catholics treat them as gods. I wanted to establish in my own mind that they were mere mortals. I was satisfied.' The amused look on Abigail's face indicated to Luke that she was teasing him. He moved on.

'Why then did you rummage through the priest's clothing?'

'Colonel you're a man of the world. Servants struggle to survive. I saw the gold crucifix and a large ring. I thought there might be other pieces of jewellery about his possessions, but Miss Priscilla had removed a large leather pouch which probably contained any other valuables.'

Before she could say any more Luke's tongue and lips found her mouth, and their mutual level of arousal increased rapidly, when this almost heavenly state was interrupted by Rachel calling from the cookhouse. 'Abigail, are you there? Your soup is bubbling over, and Miss Priscilla wants something to eat.' Abigail dressed quickly, and returned to the cookhouse.

Luke waited sometime, made his way back into the house, and asked Robert. 'Did you find Goodwin's behaviour regarding the priest somewhat strange?'

'In what regard?' Robert replied.

'He is not a very generous person, and usually keeps to himself, yet he was here in minutes with a large body of men to relieve you of Father Renaud. Then he became engaged in a heated discussion with the priest who showed signs of distress. The fact that Renaud thrust into my doublet a highly secret and important document is proof that he did not want it to fall into Richard's hands. Is Goodwin the mysterious X referred to in Renaud's letter?'

'Maybe, Richard is an entrepreneur. He is an opportunist. He takes advantage of any incident. He is desperate to increase the fur trade with the interior, and French priests have great influence over the Indian suppliers. He probably wants to use Renaud's good offices to improve his business opportunities. After all he was scheduled to meet Renaud in the forest along with the Susquehanna,' Robert concluded.

'If Richard is an innocent entrepreneurial neighbour, then why did we panic when he arrived with ten men?'

'With everything that has happened to us this last year I have become uneasy about Richard. This is largely because of the secrecy that has enveloped his plantation in recent years. He has greatly increased his work force, and kept them confined to his plantation. He has become the great unknown right on my doorstep. Secondly over the last few months he has ceased to openly support Lord Baltimore, but has expressed enthusiastic support for the new King.'

'Then given your problems it could be the Catholic Royalist Goodwin, and not the Puritans on the Severn that is your real enemy.'

'Perhaps so, but I do not think he is a murderer. He is a gentleman.'

Luke took his leave, but as he departed Robert implored him to continue the investigation of Lucy and James's death.

Luke now felt no sympathy for Robert, and his priority was clear. Both Lord Baltimore and General Cromwell needed to know what the French and the Jesuits were up to. The murders must take second place to the questions raised by the two French ships, and the presence of Father Renaud. He would talk it over with Harry and Andrew. Later he would return to Abigail. Lust was out of the bottle. It would be impossible to put it back.

After dark when Abigail's duties at the manor house had long finished, Luke paddled silently across the river, and made his way furtively to Abigail's hut. She was not there. He had just missed her. As he looked north he saw, in a moment of moonlight that penetrated the overcast sky, a female form paddling across the river towards Goodwin's. He could not be sure, but his jealousy convinced him it was Abigail.

Disconcerted, Luke stumbled back towards his canoe, when a figure suddenly loomed up in front of him. He went for his sword but the limping figure spoke, 'I don't need to ask why you are wandering across the island in the middle of the night. I wondered how long it would take for her to claim your scalp. Be careful Luke! She is a pleasant wench, but not all that she appears.' It was Humphrey. He assumed that Luke was returning from Abigail. A frustrated Luke found his canoe, and paddled furiously as he contemplated the fickleness of women.

Humphrey arrived at Luke's hut before breakfast the next morning. 'I should have mentioned this to you last night, but you had other things on your mind. Yesterday there was an argument on North Island between Sir Timothy and one of the workers. The man resented being accused of malingering when he claimed his absence from the field was a persistent call of nature. The end result of this resentment was that the complainant approached me with an interesting story.'

'Concerning what?'

'Mr James's murder.'

'Tell me more!'

'The man claimed that in talking to your soldiers, whose intentions he immediately saw through, he was deliberately vague about Sir Timothy's whereabouts at the time the shot was heard. He now claims that Sir Timothy was definitely in the critical area at the time of the shooting.'

'A suspicious change of story to get back at his overseer,' Luke observed coldly.

'There is more. At the end of the day the men return their hoes and barrows to the storage hut near the landing site, where their muskets are also stored. Our complainant noticed that his musket was not exactly where he had left it. On inspecting it he instantly realised it had been recently fired. On closer examination of the hut he saw that powder and shot had been spilt.'

'How do you link this with Tim?'

'On the ground near the spilt powder he picked up a small red button – Sir Timothy's favourite red doublets and jerkins have such buttons,' Humphrey quietly observed.

24

'Tim had the opportunity, and the means to shoot James?' recapitulated Luke. 'I still can't believe that Tim would kill James in such a cold blooded manner, except as the final manifestation of deep seated vengeance that we know could have existed. Nevertheless he does not appear to me as a ruthless killer, but it doesn't look good for him.'

Luke reported to Andrew what the old retainer had revealed. Andrew promptly excused himself to return to his hut as he had something to show Luke. In a few minutes Andrew returned and placed on Luke's small table a button identical with the one produced by Humphrey. Luke looked at Andrew, 'Where did this come from?'

'Goodwin's plantation. When you asked me to see if I could find any evidence of Lucy's presence I found it on the beach along from Lovers Cove. With everything that's happened I completely forgot about it until now.'

'God's mercy! This places Tim exactly where we think Lucy met her death,' Luke said sadly.

Harry sauntered in, and being apprised of the new evidence was immediately critical, 'Tim is being framed. It is just too neat. He loses two buttons, each of which is found just where a killing took place. To me it proves the opposite. Tim is not a murderer, but someone, the real killer, is trying to incriminate him.'

'I would love to agree,' responded Andrew. 'Just because evidence is unearthed which clearly points the finger in one direction, we cannot dismiss it by suggesting it's been planted. We are all are too sympathetic to Tim, but we cannot ignore the growing evidence against him. We cannot cast aside the basic fact that Sir Timothy has the most powerful of reasons for annihilating the Browne family. Puritans like Beale believe in an eye for eye. Good God Luke! we have fought beside many of that ilk. He probably believes he is Jehovah's avenging angel – and I for one hope he finishes his mission.'

Luke, Harry and Andrew caught up with Tim just as he was about to leave for the tobacco fields. Luke was direct, 'Tim do you recognise these buttons?'

'Yes they are mine. I wear red all the time. I have several red jerkins and doublets. I am glad you have found them. They are hard to replace in Maryland. Where were they found?'

'One was found in your storage hut on North Island, and the other on Goodwin's plantation just along the beach from Lovers Cove.'

'The first I understand. I am always in and out of that hut, but the second baffles me. I have not been on Goodwin's land for months.' Tim blushed and said in a much quieter voice, 'Except for Lovers Cove.'

'What's this Lovers Cove?' asked a too eager Harry.

'It is not really a cove. It is a sandy beach off the North Arm of the river which leads to soft grassed sand dunes interspersed by numerous low shrubs that can conceal one couple from another. Behind it is a steep precipice. It can only be approached by water, and Goodwin does not bother to police it as he does the other boundaries of his property. Maybe I lost my button there, and it was washed downstream.'

'Did you take Lucy to Lovers Cove?' asked Andrew.

'Yes, several times. '

'When was the last time you went there with Lucy? asked Luke.

Tim was silent for some time prompting Andrew to repeat Luke's question. Eventually Tim whispered, 'On the day she died.'

'God's Blood! exclaimed Luke, 'Why didn't you tell us this earlier?'

'You would have over reacted - as you are now.'

'So be it. Exactly when and where did you last see her?'

'Lucy and I were anxious to make up after our tiff following my activities with Abigail. We met at Lovers Cove late morning after I sent one of the labourers to advise her of when and where. I left her around noon, and returned to North Island. She was still at Lover's Cove when I paddled out of sight along the northern shore of North Island.'

'So you enticed Lucy away from West Island, strangled her, dragged her body into the water, and the current did the rest. She tore off one of your buttons in her desperate attempt to save herself, and it too was taken by the current. Lovers Cove is where Humphrey, with his knowledge of the tides and currents, suggests the body entered the water,' concluded Harry, determined to be the Devil's Advocate to help his friend Tim.

Luke was less strident, 'The evidence is circumstantial, but it places you, Tim, in areas where you could have killed both Lucy and James. I won't proceed with this now, but be aware that you remain a prime suspect for the murder of James, and now also a suspect for the murder of Lucy.'

Andrew turned the enquiry to James's murder. 'Tim, I can't get my head around your movements on the morning that James was killed. You left your workers and walked to the landing beach in time to meet Mr James. You waited for some time and when James did not appear you headed back to the fields. Where were you when the shot was heard? Were you still near the landing beach, or were you almost back to where your labourers were working? If you were still near the landing beach why did you not investigate the sound of the shot? If you were well on your way back to your men, why did you take so long to reach them? If I try to recreate what happened on the island on that fateful morning there are about ten to fifteen minutes missing from your account.'

'Sergeant, I can answer your questions, but as it involves another person. I would like to speak to that party before I answer,' replied Tim.

'So you can cook up an alibi,' interrupted Luke.

Tim relented, 'When I went to meet James I checked some of the goods in the storage hut. A woman joined me there, and after making love for some time we left the hut separately, and disappeared in different directions. Not much later I heard the shot, but decided not to return in case my partner and I ran into each other, or third parties. I waited for over ten minutes just off the path in case people came to investigate the shot. I wanted my liaison to remain a secret. I eventually returned to the men in the fields and stayed there only a few minutes when I heard Robert's bell. I came back to the landing beach and met you.'

'And the name of this woman? Andrew demanded.

'Abigail Hicks.'

Luke was taken aback. 'As soon as Lucy dies, you return to the arms of your real lover. Another motive to kill young Lucy.'

On reflection no one was really surprised that Abigail had quickly replaced Lucy in Tim's affections. Luke was irrationally very annoyed. Tim went to the fields, Andrew and Harry returned to South Island, while Luke sought out Abigail. She was even more sensuous than Luke remembered from the previous day, as she deliberately ran her tongue over her large red sensuous lips. 'Colonel you must have more to do than tempt a poor servant woman?'

'Abigail, this is serious. We have evidence that points to one person as the murderer of both Lucy and James.'

'How can I help? I have told you all that I know.'

Yes, you have, but I now have questions that on the surface may not appear relevant to my initial inquiries. Did you and Tim meet in the storage hut on North Island on the day of James's murder?'

'Colonel that question sounds like one from a jealous lover rather than a military investigator. In my circumstances I cannot afford to detail my sexual activities. I only survive by letting my current lover believe he is the only person in my world.'

'Do you visit Lover's Cove often,' continued Luke. The girl's sensuality was getting through to him but her answers were vital to his investigation. 'Abigail I must insist on answers, or I will have to take action against you for obstructing my enquiries.'

'Forsooth Colonel, what would you do to make me talk? But I will not risk your ire. I have been at Lovers Cove with several men, and with Tim on at least three occasions. On the morning of James's death I took corn fritters from the cookhouse across to North Island for the workers' midday meal, which I do every day. As I took the food to the storage shed, which was the regular arrangement, Tim arrived saying he was to meet James who had not turned up. We filled in time together.'

'Where were both of you when you heard the shot?'

'Tim left the hut well before me. You men dress much more quickly after such activities. I was already back on West Island when I heard the shot. I had seen Humphrey talking to James as I paddled home. He had not yet started his trip to North Island.'

'Did Humphrey see you paddling across?'

'No, he had his back to the water, but James saw me.'

'Things don't look good for Tim. Could he could have killed the Browne siblings?'

'Not Lucy. He loved her. Women in my position spend a lot of time listening to their current partner talking about the love of his life. The last few times I have been with Tim he has sobbed about Lucy. He could never kill her'

'Maybe this sobbing was remorse for killing her, when he was unstable?'

'Tim is one of the most stable people I know. I must get back to work, but I will be free two hours after dark if you want to question me further,' said Abigail as her tongue once again flickered seductively around her lips.

'A final question. What colour doublet was Tim wearing in the storage hut on the day James died?'

'Tim always wears red. I have not seen him in any other colour.'

Abigail left the cookhouse, and moved into the main house. Luke returned to South Island. There was something not quite right with the accounts of Tim and Abigail. But what was it? Were they in a conspiracy together? The soldiers reviewed the situation. Luke finally admitted sadly, 'All the evidence points to Tim as the murderer of Lucy and James, despite my reluctance to accept it. It must be a campaign of revenge against the man who is thought to have ordered the massacre of his family.'

'At last you are seeing sense,' said Andrew, 'so what are you doing about it? If Tim is the murderer and he is progressively wiping out the whole family you cannot allow him free run of the settlement unless you tacitly agree with his mission.

'What should I do?' asked Luke.

Andrew was blunt. 'You have three choices. The legal option is to arrest, formally charge, and transport him to the Governor at St Mary's. If you consider your prime responsibility is to stop the killings then quietly kill him as we did in Ireland with troublesome recalcitrants. Thirdly you can ignore the evidence, forget about the murders and concentrate all our energies on getting to the bottom of this French involvement.'

'The evidence against Tim is still circumstantial. But let's be honest. Even if Tim is guilty we all sympathize with him. He is one of us, whose family was massacred by a man we are beginning to despise. Let's sleep on it,' concluded an emotional Luke.

25

BUT LUKE DID NOT SLEEP. A DECISION HAD TO be made. Luke considered the purpose of his dual mission. The murders were irrelevant to Cromwell's remit. Baltimore's interests created the dilemma. He was obliged to uncover the problems affecting Robert Browne, and to provide him with assistance. If Robert Browne were a more noble character, and Tim's guilt proven, Luke would not hesitate to remove the latter. If Baltimore were aware of Browne's personality and actions, would he still expect Luke to support him? After all, Browne was flouting Baltimore's authority by trading in New Sweden, and shipping through Dutch vessels. As dawn broke Luke rose from his palliasse, and went for a long walk around the shores of South Island. The situation now appeared clear. He would inform Baltimore that Browne was now a liability in maintaining his lordship's authority. He would immediately ignore Baltimore's expectation that his unit support Browne, rendering the murders irrelevant to his mission. From now on his paramount concern must be to defend England's interests.

Over breakfast with Andrew and Harry, Luke outlined his reasoning which also justified not acting harshly against Sir Timothy Beale.

Harry agreed, 'You could monitor Tim's situation by removing him from his potential victims here, and take him with you to the Jesuit mission.'

'No, I was not impressed by Tim during our Delaware adventure. He stays here,' declared an obstinate Luke.

'In that case I could stay with him night and day as his companion gaoler. We are friends, and have similar backgrounds.'

Andrew grunted his approval, 'The trooper we assigned to that task was overawed by Tim's status and gave him too much freedom. Harry can hardly do worse.'

Luke accepted Harry's offer, and with the young man seconded to a full time gaoler, Andrew would assume command of the troop while Luke was absent delivering Renaud's message. Luke would take one trooper, and an Indian guide.

'No Indian guide,' protested Andrew.

'The natives are central to Jesuit plans. Keep the Indians out of this, until you know exactly what is going on.'

'How then do I find my way?' asked a bemused Luke.

'Ask Renaud,' Andrew replied.

Luke went immediately to Goodwin's and was received by Richard and Father Renaud. 'Richard, I need Father Renaud's assistance. I am sorry Father I did not collect your clothes from the Brownes.'

'No worry Colonel! A woman servant brought them across late last night. How can I help?' replied the priest.

'Father, Lord Baltimore and your Order have not always seen eye to eye. Part of my remit is to investigate any new missions. Can you give me directions to the new English establishment?'

Father Renaud's face radiated warmth, 'I have never been there, but my missing companions told me that you follow the Indian trail south along the upland between the eastern and western flowing rivers for a day and a half, and you could not miss it.'

'Come with me?' asked Luke, not so innocently.

Richard intervened, 'Father Renaud is not yet up to a long journey. When he recovers, my men will take him wherever he wishes to go.'

'Thank you Colonel,' replied the priest, 'but there are things I must do here before I leave. Give my regards to Father Austin, with especial greetings from Father Le Jeune.'

Richard showed surprise when Le Jeune's name was mentioned, but did not comment. Why was the French head of the Jesuit mission for Canada communicating with English Jesuits in Maryland? Perhaps this fitted well into his own plans. A French Jesuit base in Maryland could certainly assist his fur trading ventures in the interior. He had raised such ideas with people close to the French government, but he did not know what position the Jesuits had taken. Renaud had not told him anything. Luke was also tempted to ask Renaud why a French Jesuit was sending his special regards to an English missionary, but he was anxious not to alert Richard to his precise mission, which Renaud had just cleverly re-emphasised.

Next morning Luke and a trooper moved up river dressed in full uniform and equipment, including breastplates and helmets. They reached the first set of rapids and left the canoe on the bank. Following Humphrey's advice Luke informed Straight Arrow that they would be moving through Nanticoke territory. Luke explained he needed to investigate the establishment of a Jesuit mission to the south. 'Something to do with the Black Robe that was washed ashore?' asked the astute war chief.

'In part, it reminded me of Baltimore's remit. The Jesuits challenged my Lordship's authority in the past. The Black Robe is a Frenchman and a Jesuit. The mission to the south is a house of the English province of the order, and the French should not be involved. Lord Baltimore would be furious if the French have penetrated his lands,' said Luke with less than complete honesty.

'No wonder my people do not accept the god of the white man nor his servants. None of you agree as to God's nature and commands, and fight each other over these disagreements. Whether this mission is French or English is meaningless to us. Nevertheless my braves and I will come with you. There are rumours that these men of God are arming their Indians with powerful weapons. A powerful armed neighbour is not what my people want.'

'If that is true these armed mission Indians could be strong allies for you against the Susquehanna. Thanks for your offer but I prefer to visit the mission with just my trooper. I don't want the Fathers to think that this is a military expedition. It is a casual visit.'

'Let a few of my braves accompany you as guides,' suggested Straight Arrow.

'No, we will be all right. I have clear directions,' replied Luke, increasingly exasperated by Straight Arrow's persistence.

'I was thinking of you getting killed, not lost,' responded Straight Arrow.

'But the area to the south is largely uninhabited.'

'That's the problem. The area is no longer the territory of one nation. There are small groups of displaced peoples wandering the area – some dispossessed first from Virginia by the

Powhatan, and others by the Susquehanna. These people have come across the Bay from the western shore. Without clear structures there are renegade individuals and unpredictable groups. The Black Robes have not brought all of them under control. Reconsider my offer!'

Luke obstinately rejected Straight Arrow's assistance and headed down the north south Indian trail. Some time later they rounded a bend on the trail and were amazed to find White Deer coming towards them. Luke was astonished. He knew this was not a social visit, or a chance encounter. When he left the Nanticoke village earlier that day after talking to Straight Arrow, White Deer had waved him farewell. The young Indian greeted Luke warmly, and whispered in his ear. 'You are being followed by a large Susquehanna war party. They surround us as we speak.'

'How do you know all this?'

'Father asked me to follow you, although he was very annoyed at your refusal of assistance and muttered that he should leave the arrogant white Colonel to his fate. I picked up your trail and that of your stalkers. I took a wide berth, and got in front of you. Return with me! If you proceed they will kill you both, and your bodies would never be found.'

'Why would they kill me?'

'Several possibilities! They don't want you to reach your destination, or they don't like a powerful envoy of Lord Baltimore in the area as it might cut across their own plans. Turn around and come back with me! Tell your man to writhe in a bit of pain, and sit on that log wiping non-existent sweat from his brow. I will examine him and tell you he has a bad fever and cannot go on. We must do this properly. The Susquehanna are not fools and will pick up on any pretence. At the moment they will not attack you in the company of the son of Straight Arrow whose support they need.'

Luke took White Deer's advice. As the three returned along the trail Luke confided in White Deer. 'I must get to that mission. Short of taking all my troop, or accepting your father's offer of help is there any other way I can get there?'

'Take father's advice!'

'There is a malevolence slowly crushing the Brownes and I feel they need protection. I dare not withdraw my men at this time. Secondly I don't want to march into a Jesuit mission with a show of strength. This is a friendly visit to discover how reconciled the Jesuits are with Lord Baltimore.'

'There is a way, but you will need to trick the Susquehanna.' White Deer outlined his plan.

Next morning an officer and trooper paddled up river on their way to the Jesuit mission. This time they enlisted the help of the Nanticokes. It was several hours into the march before the shadowing Susquehanna realised that the officer was not Luke. In fact it was a junior trooper dressed in an officer's uniform. They soon discovered that the Nanticokes were not primarily an escort for the white men, but a normal hunting party going about its business. When they obtained their required kill the whole party turned around and headed back towards the Nanticoke village. The Susquehanna were furious.

Meanwhile Luke was well out to sea, as he, Trooper Ackroyd and four other soldiers rowed south down the Bay in a six oared shallop. White Deer had outlined the features that Luke must pass before he entered a sheltered cove, and moved up a river that the Indian claimed would lead them to the Jesuit mission. A two-man canoe trailed behind the shallop. The shallop's return journey with only four men would be helped by the prevailing winds and take it home without the need for much rowing.

The river was eventually located, but was very different to that which bisected the Browne grant. This was a slow moving waterway, surrounded for many miles by low lying marshes infested with reeds, with the forest hardly visible in any direction. Luke and Ackroyd climbed into the two man canoe, and the shallop slowly turned around and headed out to sea. Luke suddenly felt very exposed as he paddled upstream. He relieved Ackroyd of paddling duties so that the soldier could prime his musket ready for any sudden attack. Luke's failure the day before even to suspect that a large Susquehanna war party had been tracking them had broken his confidence. He could not detect the enemy before they struck.

Luke was frustrated as the river meandered through the tidal marshes, keeping parallel with the coastline, and refusing to lead him inland. Walking in a straight line would have been preferable, but completely impossible in this watery environment, where a riverbank was often indistinguishable from the expanses of flooded marshes. In places Luke was not sure that he was still on the river. The area was rich in bird life, and as the canoe moved through the water large flocks of ducks and other water birds took to the skies, breaking the eerie silence with their discordant cacophony.

It was the noise of the birds that temporarily distracted Luke from the human cries of alarm. In the distance a large number of Indians were scrambling to board their canoes from a sandbank amid the marshes. The Indians had been fishing, and alerted by the sudden rush of birds into the air were now preparing to meet the cause of that disturbance - a single two man canoe. Trooper Ackroyd's fingers tensed on his musket. Luke ordered him to place it on the floor of the canoe, and resume paddling.

The Indian canoes moved into mid river and formed a crescent shaped welcoming party as Luke and Ackroyd paddled directly towards its centre. Luke shouted the trite but useful slogan of white men whatever their real intention, 'Greetings brothers, we come in peace,' and immediately added, 'We seek guidance to the Jesuit mission.' Luke hoped his friendly demeanour and tone would convince the Indians of his peaceful intentions, even if they did not understand a word that was said. He was surprised when he received a response in fluent English.

26

'WELCOME TO OUR LANDS.' LUKE WAS ASTONISHED. THE MAN who had replied was no Indian. He wore a black cassock, and the silver cross around his neck gleamed in the sunlight. Luke's canoe reached that of the priest, and Luke introduced himself as an envoy of Lord Baltimore, and a messenger from Fathers Renaud and Le Jeune.

It was now the priest's turn to express surprise. 'I am assistant to Father Austin. We hoped everybody had forgotten us. I trust your arrival does not augur unwarranted interference from the outside world. We are doing God's work here. We protect our Indian brothers from the predators of this world, whether they are European or Indian. Follow us back to the mission!'

Eventually the river narrowed, and the woodlands with which Luke was familiar replaced the tidal marshes. After half an hour the Indians ran their canoes ashore and Luke followed them into the woods. A few minutes later they reached a large clearing, in the middle of which was a big building displaying a large wooden cross. Beside the church stood a man as tall as Luke with broad shoulders, and the weather-beaten face of a person who had spent his life outdoors. He was younger than Luke had expected, perhaps in his early thirties, and his black curly hair was not tonsured. He wore a white shirt, collarless and cuff less, and black breeches and stockings. The reason for this relative state of undress was obvious. He held in his hands a large axe, and the pile of partly split timber indicated that the returning fishermen had interrupted some vigorous chopping by this physically powerful priest.

His colleague motioned Luke to advance no further, and the two priests entered the church. Luke sensed that any attempt by him to follow would be resisted by the Indian flock that gathered in large numbers to ogle the visitors. A few minutes later the assistant emerged, and beckoned Luke to join them. Trooper Ackroyd took up a position at the door. Luke entered the building which he realised was a combination of church and manse. At the far end of the edifice were the living quarters of the priests, which Luke noted catered at the most for three men.

The tall priest, now dressed in his black cassock introduced himself as Father Peter Austin, superior of the mission. He immediately challenged Luke, 'You claim to act for Lord Baltimore, and as a messenger for senior French Jesuits. If that be true, why do you wear the uniform of the king-killing English Republic?'

Luke was surprised that Austin could identify the partial uniform he wore and replied aggressively, 'Yes, we are New Model soldiers but have been seconded to Lord Baltimore to assess the situation. He is interested in your mission. I would have come to see you eventually, but Father Renaud gave me an urgent reason to visit.'

'I saw many a brutal New Model soldier in a recent trip to my native Ireland. To have such a soldier here on my mission fuels my apprehension and suspicion,' replied Austin.

Luke handed over the letter, and Father Austin's anger and apprehension increased further, 'Sir, the seal of this letter is broken. You have read its content?'

'Yes, but I did it in good faith, and believe that is what Father Renaud wanted me to do. He was very anxious that it reached you, and suspected that others might try to prevent this happening. I memorised it in case the actual letter was taken from me.' Luke explained how Renaud had delivered the letter to him.

After he had finished reading Father Austin sighed, 'Renaud was delivering not only a message vital to our future, but bringing with him two experienced priests to help man this mission. Do you know where these men are?'

'No, Father Renaud who escaped before they were attacked has no knowledge of them. What is going on here Father?' asked Luke, deliberately changing the topic.

'Forgive me Colonel, you may represent Lord Baltimore, who never understood the aims of our order, and you have delivered me an important message from our French colleagues, but you are a soldier of the Protestant English Republic. I will not give my enemies details of our aims and operations. You know too much already that we have plans for the future, which we must develop through our own resources. Expected support has too many strings attached to it.'

'You are setting up an independent Jesuit colony! ' Luke fired back with steely intensity.

'We have learnt from bitter experience that our earlier missionary activity was undermined by the behaviour of European colonists. Our brethren in South America have shown us a different approach. Encourage the native to keep his own political structure, and as much of his culture that is compatible with the Lord's teaching. And above all protect them from contact with the European colonist. The Holy Spirit will gradually create a prosperous, free and independent Indian community under our leadership. Circumstances in Canada and here are not exactly the same as in Spanish America, but the same principles can be applied. Our simple aim is to protect the Indian nations from destruction.' It was clear that Luke would not receive any useful details from Father Austin. Luke and Ackroyd were fed, and led to a small round house in which were two palliasses. Austin made clear that he expected the soldiers to leave first thing in the morning.

And he made sure that they did. He awakened them before dawn, fed them again, and had two Indians lead them towards the north south trail. It was still dark when the Indians having reached the trail, left the two soldiers to progress north alone.

Luke was increasingly nervous. He sensed that the Indians continued to follow them. Austin certainly did not trust him.

Soon Luke had glimpses of Indians all around him, deliberately making themselves visible and then disappearing, obviously to create fear if not panic before they moved in for a final assault. These were not the mission Indians. By the way they wore their hair, Luke realised they were the dreaded Susquehanna. Moving through the forest along a trail was not a good defensive position. As soon as Luke could find a position which two men could defend at least initially, he would stop and await the attack. Soon the trail opened out into a large clearing in the centre of which were a number of large logs. It was better than nothing.

They did not have to wait long. With a lot of shouting the now visible Indians unleashed waves of arrows, cleverly flighted to drop down over the protective logs. Several of these hit branches as they descended. Then Luke sensed the worse. He got a sniff of musket powder, and almost immediately two volleys of musket fire deafened the defenders. Luke could hardly believe he had not been hit. He looked up over the logs and was amazed to find that the attacking Indians had gone. He stood up, and emerging from where the attackers had been was Father Austin and the mission Indians armed with new French muskets.

The priest explained, 'My men need training. I followed you to make sure you did not double back and spy on us. A scout reported that you were being followed, and surrounded by hostile Indians. When they unleashed their arrows I ordered my men to open fire. Sensing our superiority in terms of weapons they ran off.'

'Father, I am most impressed with your military presence. Your men acted like professional soldiers. And those muskets are the very latest. A private army?'

'Not quite, but in this colonial world which lacks institutional or community structures and values to maintain law and order, my Indians are defenceless lambs in the face of human wolves. My aim is to defend the Indian, and the best way is to meet fire with fire. My Indians will become the most effective military force on the Chesapeake,' declared the proud priest. He continued, 'Tell your Lord Baltimore that if he cannot exert his authority, he has none. He should have sent an army to enforce law and order years ago. Until he can do this he has no moral authority to claim any power in this province. Tell him that the Holy Spirit governs this part of Maryland!'

'With the aid of French arms,' added Luke pointedly.

The shouting of a scout further up the trail interrupted the developing political discourse. Luke and Father Austin ran along the trail to where the scout was assisting two Black Robes along the path. On seeing Austin the priests went down on their knees, and thanked God for their rescue. These two men where not bookish, privileged clergy like Renaud. Austin sent some his men off to catch some game, while others gathered wood to start a fire in the middle of Luke's defensive logs.

The three priests talked in French for some time. Luke failed to pick up anything meaningful. After some time Austin turned to Luke, 'Please forgive our rudeness but the Black Robes had much to report. They are glad to hear that Father Renaud is safe, and ask that you tell him about them.'

'Where have they been since the initial attack on them and Renaud?'

'Moving through the forest avoiding the Indians who attacked them, and then you?'

'How did they manage that? Indians in the forest are a formidable enemy. I can never tell that they are there.'

'These are no ordinary priests. They have spent decades living with the Huron, and have learnt how to conceal themselves, and move unobserved through the countryside as well as any Indian.'

169

'These men are from your Canadian mission. Did they come here by sea or did they walk?'

'They have been walking for weeks from the Great Lakes of Canada, across the mountains and down the Delaware to Fort Christina.'

'And that is where they met Father Renaud, who had been landed there from a French frigate?'

'No comment,' replied the politically sensitive Father Austin.

After a meal of venison and wild fowl, followed up by forest berries Austin ordered his group to return to the Mission. He provided an escort of six Indians for Luke and his trooper, until they reached the next river. He informed Luke that he had already sent a messenger to inform the Nanticokes that two soldiers were entering their territory and needed assistance. Luke thanked Austin, and with his enlarged entourage headed north.

As they moved along the trail Luke thought about how recent events had modified his bitter obsession against Catholics. In Ireland he had met a formidable priest who impressed him with his honesty and determination. Now in the person of Father Peter Austin was a man, who despite his religion and vocation appealed to Luke. He was a man's man. He would be a good friend, or a formidable enemy.

Soon a river was reached at the point of white water, and the Indians pointed out how Luke and Ackroyd could cross it rock by rock. The Indians then disappeared. Luke progressed cautiously and with some trepidation. Every rustle alerted him to potential Indian attack. A pack of wolves, a group of grazing deer and one small black bear had Luke on his toes. He even considered leaving the trail and finding his way north through the forest. He was not a Black Robe with decades of woodland experience. He would get lost. His vulnerability was highlighted by the sudden appearance beside him of White Deer and several Nanticoke braves. Again Luke had not seen them coming. If they had been the enemy he would be dead. He hated the forest. It would be the death of him. Surely it was time to return to England,

When the group reached the east west trail that led back to the Browne settlements White Deer insisted that Luke come first to his village as Straight Arrow wanted to talk to him. Luke indicated that he was tired, and wanted to return home, but White Deer made it clear that his father would brook no refusal. When they reached the village Straight Arrow was waiting for them, and beckoned Luke to join him in his round house, and waved White Deer away when he attempted to follow.

'I need your help,' pleaded the Nanticoke war chief.

27

STRAIGHT ARROW MOTIONED LUKE TO SIT CROSS LEGGED ON the layers of furs that covered the floor. Luke could hardly keep awake. Straight Arrow repeated his plea, 'Colonel I need your help. My people face two enemies. The European settlers, whatever their good intentions to start with, such as Robert Browne, in the end will take our lands. They must grow more crops, and raise more animals. They will clear our forests and push us out, if not kill us. And then there is the Susquehanna to whom we have sworn loyalty, but already they have pillaged one of our villages, and taken its inhabitants. I must defend my people against both the Europeans, and the Susquehanna.'

'Straight Arrow, I don't envy you your problems, but how can I help? I am just passing through, and I would need an army a hundred times the size of my troop to effectively deal with the Susquehanna on your behalf. I would never receive permission to use such an army to assist any Indian nation against the white settlers, whatever government ruled in England or on the Chesapeake.'

'No colonel nothing as difficult. I have a very simple request. Help me speak to Father Renaud. What are the Black Robes up to regarding the divided Susquehanna? Black Cougar wants to be chief in place of Tamuagh. My people will be safer if Tamuagh continues to rule. I must know if the priests are supporting Black Cougar?'

'You don't need my help to see Father Renaud.'

'I do. Goodwin refused to let me see him.'

'I see. You had planned to meet him before, but the Black Robes were dispersed and could not keep the appointment.'

'The failure of that meeting is part of the mystery I want to discuss. Goodwin, Black Cougar and I arranged to meet the priests on two occasions in one of my villages. They did not turn up on either the designated meeting dates.'

'We know they were too late for the first, and were attacked on their way to the second. Do you know by whom?' asked Luke.

'Yes, they were attacked by Black Cougar.'

'Why would Black Cougar want to kill them after arranging to meet them?'

'He didn't want to kill them. He simply wanted to stop Goodwin and myself meeting them. He desired access to them under his own terms. Unfortunately for Black Cougar the priests panicked, and fled. Renaud made it to the coast and finished up with Goodwin. The other two Black Robes from Canada outwitted the Susquehanna and avoided capture, and now I hear are safely at the Mission. That is why the forests have been alive with Susquehanna war parties - desperately trying to find the missing priests.'

'Straight Arrow, I understand why you want to see the priests without the Susquehanna or Goodwin looking over your shoulder. Why don't you visit the mission, and talk openly and freely with the Jesuit Fathers.'

'I am trying to save my people. One option is to place them under the protection of the priests and have them armed with the best European firearms. But most of my people oppose such a solution. Recent events around the Great Lakes do not help my case. The Huron nation placed themselves under the protection of the Black Robes, and was all but wiped out by the Iroquois. The medicine men of my tribe argue successfully to the elders that the Christian message of the priests make Indian peoples weak, and an easy prey to their enemies. That is why I cannot go openly to the Mission, nor meet openly with Father Renaud. You must arrange a secret meeting for me.'

'I will try, although Goodwin zealously protects Renaud.'

'Have you ever asked why?' asked the war chief, with a knowing smile.

A weary Luke did not answer, and ended the discussion,

'I must go. It has been an eventful day.'

'In anticipation of your help I have information regarding the murders of Lucy and James. They spent more time in this village with White Deer than they did on their own plantation.'

'I need all the help I can get,' sighed Luke.

'My braves move freely through your settlement without being seen. We have helped ourselves to the poultry and beef that roam unrestrained on your own South Island. Your troopers did not know we were there. On both the days that the Browne children were killed my men saw the same three people near the sites of the murder - the overseer Lipton, Mr Goodwin and Mr Browne's blonde serving girl.'

'All three together in a location relevant to the murder?'

'No, and yes. No, all three were not together; yes, they were in a location relevant to the murder.'

'Details, Straight Arrow?' as a reinvigorated Luke.

'In the hours before Lucy was killed my men saw the overseer, and a woman at Lovers Cove. A little time later they saw a girl with Goodwin standing on the beach just around from the Cove.'

'Are you sure the girl was the servant?'

'Well not exactly. They were a long way away. It was definitely a young white woman, and there are few of them in this area.'

'What about James's death?'

'On the morning of James's death the girl was seen with the overseer on North Island, and at the same time Goodwin was patrolling his beach opposite with a musket. Strange that the same three people were in the crucial areas at the relevant times.'

'We have the overseer under house arrest for both murders, but your information does suggest that I should look more closely at Goodwin, and the serving girl, although the woman at Lover's Cove with Tim Beale was Lucy.'

Straight Arrow expressed surprise but continued, 'Goodwin is up to something. He keeps his men isolated on his plantation. They do not fraternize with those on the other estates. Have you not thought this odd?'

'No, I assumed Goodwin's bossy nature led him to control everything on his settlement, and isolating his men made this easier.'

'He has another reason to keep his men isolated - and guarded.'

'Yes?'

'Most of his men speak the language of the Black Robes.'

Luke's interest increased, 'The workers on his plantation are French?

But why is that a reason for isolation and confinement. In the colonies peoples from all over Europe mix together.'

'True. Being French is not the issue. Why does Goodwin have armed guards watching his workers all the time?'

'It is unusual outside of slave plantations,' admitted Luke.

'One of his men, despite the guards, regularly frequents this village, seeking the friendship of one of the women here. He told her that most of his fellow workers came from a big fortress called the Bastille.'

'God's Blood! Goodwin's workers are French convicts. His guards now make sense.'

'Why is Goodwin filling our land with evil men?' asked Straight Arrow with feigned innocence.

'It is not unusual for European nations to increase their colonial population by exporting their gaols. Many of the indentured labourers on other plantations are convicted criminals. They are often given an option of death, heavy fines or migration as indentured servants. They are little better than slaves.'

'Goodwin's men are his slaves?'

Luke realised his discussion was becoming complex. It was easier to agree with Straight Arrow.

Next day Luke landed alone on Goodwin's estate. He was on his best behaviour and waited on the beach until approached by one of Richard's men. 'My man, would you inform your master that Colonel Tremayne would like to meet him and Father Renaud. The guard signalled for Luke to follow him. Luke was suddenly alert. Something was different. He thought about it until he reached Richard's abode where he was asked to wait on the fallen log near the entrance. Then it struck him. There were twice as many huts surrounding the tobacco field than there had been only a week before.

He would not to raise it with Richard. The reason was obvious. The French ship that had anchored in the inlet and then discharged a few shots across West Island as it headed south, had unloaded an unknown number of French prisoners to augment Goodwin's labour supply. Within a few minutes both Renaud and Goodwin emerged. Contrary to his normal fastidiousness Richard was dressed in an uncollared and un-cuffed white shirt and blue breeches.

'What can I do for you Colonel?' asked Richard affably.

'I have a message for Father Renaud, which will also interest you. I reached the Jesuit mission and passed on your good wishes Father Renaud.'

'Thank you my son. My English brethren are well?'

'More so than you could hope for. While I was returning home your two missing French comrades were found, and are now safely at the Mission.'

Renaud beamed, and Richard relaxed. Now that the Jesuits had reached their destination Renaud could join them. Luke took advantage of the relaxed atmosphere. 'Father, I can take you to the Mission. The quickest and easiest way is by boat, and Robert has one available. I am sure you want to be re-united with your colleagues as soon as possible.'

Renaud looked at Richard whose slight nod was sufficient for the priest to readily accept Luke's offer. 'If suitable Father, I will collect you at Richard's landing beach this time tomorrow. Now could I have a few words alone with Richard?'

The priest rose from the log, and re-entered the house. Luke was direct. 'Richard, I have just received new information regarding the murder of the Browne siblings that puts you at the relevant place at the right time.'

'Where was I supposed to be?' asked a smiling Richard.

'On the morning of Lucy's murder you were seen on a beach next to Lovers Cove talking with Abigail Hicks.'

'Yes, I was there. Most mornings I patrol my beaches with a musket in case I can bag a couple of wild ducks. I saw Beale leave Lovers Cove at least ten minutes before I saw the wench. She paddled ashore and we chatted for a few minutes. What about James's murder?'

176

'You were reported to have been in roughly the same place talking to Abigail Hicks once again.'

'True I was on the beach and I saw Abigail paddling to North Island with lunch for the workers. She diverted to my shore and after a brief conversation she returned across the river to North Island. As she came ashore I noticed Beale in the vicinity.'

Luke wandered back to his canoe with two thoughts uppermost in his mind. Goodwin had reinforced his plantation with an unknown number of French prisoners, and Tim's innocence seemed further away than ever. He sent a message to Straight Arrow to be at South Island just after dawn. He would know why.

28

LUKE AWOKE EARLY BECAUSE THE CHICKENS THAT ROAMED FREELY across South Island were unusually noisy and agitated. Luke admired an unusually reddish sunrise, and was surprised to find the tide was incredibly high. When he arrived to collect Father Renaud, Goodwin's landing was completely under water and the priest had to board well up the embankment. On returning to South Island the landing beach he had left less than half and hour earlier was now completely under water and he ran the canoe aground on a grassy embankment well above the high tide mark. Straight Arrow was waiting. The war chief and the priest wandered off into an overgrown former tobacco field, while Luke and his men readied the six oared shallop. An hour later the two men returned.

Father Renaud asked, 'Colonel, can you delay our departure for an hour or so? Straight Arrow would like his son to come with us so that he can take a message back to his father, after I have discussed what he has proposed with my brethren.'

'Of course. There is plenty of room in addition to the six oarsmen. We will trail a two man canoe so that White Deer and yourself can move upriver to the mission. There are no overland trails from the estuary to the Mission.'

An hour later White Deer arrived. He was not happy. 'Colonel, postpone your trip until tomorrow!'

'Why?'

'Look around! The seabirds are leaving the islands in the Bay, and flying deep into the interior. The chickens on this island are running around in a most excited state, and the water is rising very fast.'

'I noticed the chickens and the water. So what?'

'These signs foreshadow big rains and winds - what your people call a hurricane.'

'How long before these strong winds and heavy rain begin? Can we reach the estuary before the storm descends?'

'Maybe.'

'Then let's not waste time. We leave now, and if the weather closes in we will seek shelter along the coast.'

White Deer was still not happy. He knew that Luke had no comprehension of what a severe thunderstorm would be like, let alone a hurricane. As the shallop left Browne's estuary the sail was lowered. The breeze blowing in their faces was beginning to strengthen. The soldiers would find rowing in these conditions heavy going. Luke could see the sky covered with rooster tailed light cirrus clouds emerging from a central point on the horizon. As they rowed south Luke began to regret his decision The white cirrus clouds were replaced by an over all dark grey sky, overlaid by swirling spirals of the blackest clouds Luke had ever seen.

In no time the low cloud obliterated his vision, as steady rain began to fall. It was so heavy that White Deer and Father Renaud were kept busy bailing out the rainwater that threatened to sink the shallop. Waves, which were hardly visible when they left the Brownes, were progressively bigger, and a swell that developed meant that many oar strokes ploughed through the air, missing the turbulent water entirely. Luke was worried that his calculation for reaching the mission river, based on his previous trip, was way out. When the storm hit with its full force they could be forced ashore on the most dangerous part of the coast.

The heavy rain alternated with lighter showers, and eventually Luke reached the estuary of the mission river without serious mishap. He was amazed. What a several days earlier had been a sluggish river meandering through the marshes after it left higher ground, had completely disappeared. In its place was a large bay. The rising water had completely inundated the marshes. It was so deep that Luke did not hesitate to turn the shallop towards where he remembered the river flowed down from higher ground. He raised the shallop's sail and he and his men sat back as the heavy boat skipped across the surface. In no time the boat was well up the river.

White Deer was alarmed. He shouted at Luke, 'Beach the boat and move inland fast ! A surge of water as high as I am tall often comes with rain and wind of this type. It strikes without warning and will drown us all.'

A concerned Luke immediately followed White Deer's advice as the winds increased in ferocity. The party watched in amazement as trees around them cracked, and in some cases were uprooted. White Deer screamed through the noise of wind and breaking trees. 'Get to the largest clearing we can find, or we will die.' It was not as easy as Luke expected. The wind was of such intensity that he could hardly move against it. He was being driven inland by the gale.

Eventually a large area of cleared forest was found, and White Deer signalled the drenched and wind swept party to lie on the ground behind a large tree trunk that lay at right angles to the prevailing wind. There they lay for hours. The rain continued to pour down, but the winds momentarily dropped away. They took advantage of the temporary respite to make their way towards the Mission as fast as they could.

They trekked over a drenched forest floor, made very difficult by the need to leave the trail to move around dozens of trees that had been uprooted. The forest floor was elevated several inches by the branches and leaves that had been stripped from the forest canopy. Luke was appalled when he reached the Mission clearing. Utter devastation! The large church and the surrounding huts were all gone. Not only had they been demolished by the winds but also the components of these buildings had been carried away from the site. Only a few heavy items remained - a stack of muskets lay where the storage hut had stood. Father Renaud was in tears.

Luke tried to fire his musket to announce their presence but the continuous rain had wet his powder. Shouting into the raging wind was useless. Luke placed his party in the centre of the clearing where they could do nothing but wait out the storm. There was no shortage of water, but the only food they carried was cold corn and chicken fritters which Luke ordered to be broken in four, and only a quarter consumed. Sleep did not come as the rain soaked group huddled together.

By dawn the rain had eased to a heavy drizzle. Mid morning Indians began to emerge from the forest, and eventually Father Austin and three other priests appeared, and were delighted to greet Father Renaud. The priests gathered their Indians around them and prayed, thanking God for their salvation. Immediately after, the priests organised their congregation to regather as much of the building material that they could find.

White Deer whispered to Luke, 'Don't let them rebuild. The storm will come back as strong as ever within the hour.'

Luke spoke to Austin. The priest responded, 'I agree. I have lived through several of these great storms. We will simply re-gather our building materials and will not try to rebuild our village until the second part of the storm passes by. As if on cue the wind took up, and rain began to fall heavily. There was little to be done except for all to sit in the centre of the clearing and hope that the wind did not force massive tree branches crashing into the vulnerable massed body of humanity.

Ten days later, with the rubble cleared, and new huts built around the edge of the clearing the Jesuit mission was almost back to normal. Unfortunately the storm, which the Black Robes doubted was a full scale hurricane had nevertheless destroyed the tobacco crop, and devastated most of the corn. The Indians were now deployed hunting and fishing to build up sufficient supplies to last for the next twelve months. Two larger buildings were begun – a new church and a separate manse for the four priests who would remain at the mission.

Luke's party left the Mission, and searched for their aban-doned shallop. It was not where they had left it. Eventually it was found stuck in the mud on the far side of the river. The men backtracked on their side until they reached some white water where the rocks, despite the rise in water levels, enabled them to cross. Finally reaching their shallop they were amazed for find it intact except that the mast and sail had gone and only one of the oars remained, high in a tall tree.

Luke returned to the Mission where he would use its man-power, materials and implements to make a new oar and mast. It took several days but in the end the soldiers returned down river not only with a well crafted oar and a new mast, but also through the generosity of the priests, with sufficient material to serve as a sail. Once aboard the shallop the fast flowing river hurtled Luke and his men towards its mouth at incredible speed. This torrent appeared to have carved a new route for

181

itself directly across the marshlands to the Bay. The wind, still a stiff breeze was blowing from the southwest so Luke hoisted his makeshift sail on an untested mast. Two men were fully occupied ensuing the mast remained secure. The sail picked up enough wind to send the boat northwards faster than the men could have rowed.

This luxury did not last long as the sail shredded, and the mast broke free from its base. Rowing had to be resumed, but the currents appeared to be favourable and it was much easier work that the southward voyage. The rowers tried to stay just far enough out to sea to avoid rowing in and out of coves and bays. Towards midday Luke saw on the shoreline a sole European figure waving his shirt. Along the beach there were bits and pieces of what must have been a fairly large sloop, whose hulk lay partly submerged just off shore. Luke with one trooper left the shallop and waded through the water to the stranded man. The other oarsmen readied their muskets.

Luke's caution was unnecessary. The man was the sole survivor of the shipwreck. Luke asked why he boarded a ship in such a dangerous weather. The man replied, 'I had arranged to come north on a ship of a Captain Murchison's to reach the Browne Plantation. Captain Murchison refused to sail, and declared he would not take to the Bay for at least three days. Just at the time a Virginian sloop anchored at St Mary's and was anxious to leave immediately for Kent Island. Its captain believed he could outrun the storm, which he anticipated would cross from west to east, and not proceed on a northerly course. He was partly right. It did turn towards the east but not before it caught up with us. The rest is obvious.'

'Why were you in such a hurry to get to Browne's plantation, which is also our destination?'

'What luck! I am a servant of Mr Charles Browne, and my master sent me with a message for his brother Mr Robert.'

'You have that message?'

'No, when I hit the water it ripped off my outer clothing and the pouch which contained the letter. I scoured the beach from headland to headland, but it was not washed ashore.'

'Do you have any idea what you master wanted to tell his brother?'

'Yes. It was to warn him not to trust anyone. Someone very close to him was determined to kill him and his whole family.'

'Sadly, sir, that lethal enterprise is well advanced.'

29

As they neared the Browne plantation Luke realised that the storm had missed this more northerly coastline. The castaway was Willie Green, a lifelong servant of the Brownes. He served Robert and Charles's father, and had grown up with the brothers. He was now in his fifties with long grey hair that still had streaks of its original reddish brown. All he had were the clothes he was rescued in - a torn white shirt and olive grey breeches with darker olive grey stockings. His shoes had been swept away by the elements. Luke chatted, hoping to pick up information relevant to his enquiries. 'Willie, why did a man of your age and seniority in the Browne household volunteer to travel across the world?'

'Last year my wife and adult daughter died after catching a fever. I had no other family, being sent to Mr Browne's household decades ago as an orphan of six or seven. When Mr Charles Browne asked a few of his senior servants who would like a new life in America, and in the process take an urgent message to his brother, I stepped forward. The letter also recommended me for service with Mr Robert.'

'Do you remember any visitors, or strange happenings around Mr Charles's manor house just before your master sent you here?'

'Master has hundreds of visitors, but seeing your uniform Colonel reminds me of one unusual event. The Brownes are devoted Royalists, and most of them Catholic. They have no contact with the Parliamentarians, or any agents of the current republican Government. Yet a few days before my master requested a volunteer, a detachment of Government soldiers arrived at the manor house. This was no local detachment. My master addressed its leader as General.'

'General Cromwell?' asked a surprised Luke.

'No, I have seen enough drawings of Noll Cromwell circulating in Royalist households to know it was not that devil.'

'So, a New Model general visits your master, and soon after you are sent here with an urgent message?'

'The events may not be related,' commented Willie.

'Any other developments?' asked a now very interested Luke.

'Yes, and it is related to the first. When Mr Robert's troop was disbanded early in the war in unworthy circumstances, the men fell on hard times. Mr Charles gave them positions on the family estate. After this visit from your high ranking officer Mr Charles called together a meeting of the remaining former troopers.'

'Jesu! The plot thickens! What did the general tell your master that led him to call a meeting of Robert's old troop and send you here? When Charles employed Robert's troopers did any of them come to Maryland to work with Robert?'

'Yes, two or three.'

Luke thought aloud, 'So there are local witnesses to what happened at Beale Hall. It also increases the number of possible suspects.'

As the boat came in sight of West Island Luke let off a few volleys of musket fire to alert the inhabitants of his return. As he did so he noticed that Willie was shaking - the man was in shock.

Andrew was delighted to see his commander. He was preparing to mount a search and rescue operation as a two day trip had taken almost two weeks. Andrew heard from Straight Arrow that his hunting parties had reported massive devastation in the south. Robert was genuinely moved to see Willie Green whom he recognized immediately. He asked Humphrey to find an empty hut for Willie, and recognising his fragile condition made sure he went straight to bed. He asked Abigail to feed him and check on him at regular intervals.

Robert turned to Luke, 'A sorry business, but at least Willie is alive. He told me about the questions you asked, and his responses. Do you think all this stems back to the early years of the Civil War? Is there someone other than Beale who wants to punish me and my men, for something allegedly done eight or nine years ago?'

'That is still the question. Do present troubles stem from the immediate situation, or from the distant past? Willie mentioned your brother employed some of your old troopers, and that others came here to you. Could I talk to these men?'

'You can talk to the three of them whenever you like, but they will not answer. They are buried in the cemetery on the south west bluff of this island. Malaria affected them badly and they did not survive the third or fourth recurrence.'

'Did they leave behind any family?'

'No, Charles looked after all the married men with families, only the bachelors came to the Americas.'

Robert was appalled at the damage done to the shallop. His carpenters could repair the stricken boat, but he would import a larger vessel from England. Luke rested for the remainder of the day. He dozed in a hammock whose gentle swaying created a cooling breeze as the temperature rose. He anxiously watched the horizon as black clouds gathered as a harbinger of another storm. He didn't like storms. They were another aspect of colonial life that he could not control. Fortunately for Luke's peace of mind this storm stayed out in the Bay, and provided a magnificent display of lightning and ear splitting thunder.

Next morning Luke went to see Willie. As he passed the cookhouse en route to Willie's hut Abigail came to the door and commented, 'He is still asleep. I left him some food and drink last night, which has been consumed, but he now appears in a deep sleep. She ran her tongue invitingly over her lips which she formed into a mock kiss – overtly repetitive but still effective. 'Luke, have you recovered from your journey? I am free for an hour if you need me.'

This sensuous wench rekindled his lust. He would fill in time most happily until Willie awoke. Humphrey saw them disappear into Abigail's hut. Sometime later Humphrey knowing that Abigail was otherwise engaged looked in on Willie. Luke, even amid the noise of his embraces heard Humphrey's cry, 'My God!' Before Luke could react Humphrey burst through the door, 'Forgive me, come quickly both of you. Willie is dead.'

Luke examined the body. There were no wounds other than those suffered in the shipwreck, and no tell tale bruises around the neck. It appeared that Willie had died peacefully in his sleep. Later Dr Sherman agreed with such a verdict. Robert concluded that a man who had spent his whole life in the comparative luxury of in house service to a wealthy family had found the turmoil of travel to the Americas, and the shock of the shipwreck, as well as the guilt of having failed to deliver his master's message, just too much. Sherman recorded it as death by natural causes provoked by the trauma of recent days.

Luke relayed the consensus to Andrew. The sergeant was not impressed, 'Too convenient! A man arrives with important information about someone on the plantation, and dies within a day of his arrival. He is another victim – this time the murderer isn't punishing Browne, but protecting his identity until his mission is completed.'

'But Willie brought no meaningful message. How could his presence upset the murderer?'

'He could recognize someone on the plantation who is not whom as he purports to be. Are all of Browne's former troopers really dead? Is Beale Beale? There are many other possible false identities that Willie could have exposed. Question everybody as to their whereabouts during Willie's brief sojourn on the island! This is murder.'

Luke saw merit in Andrew's outburst, and a thorough investigation could do no harm. The enquiries proved straight forward. Only two persons had entered Willie's hut from the beginning to the end of his residence - Abigail and Humphrey.

Luke questioned Abigail again. 'How many times did you visited Willie?'

'I helped Humphrey put him to bed. After I had finished here for the night I took some cold chicken and a mug of beer to his hut, and placed it beside him. In the middle of the night after my visitor left, I looked in again. The food and drink had been consumed. This morning on my way to light the fires I checked him out. He appeared peaceful, but in hindsight he may have already been dead.'

Humphrey confirmed the picture Abigail had given. After his initial visit he looked in on Willie mid evening and saw that Abigail had left some food and drink. He heard Abigail pass his hut about midnight and assumed she was checking on Willie. This morning before Abigail had risen he looked in and saw that the food had been consumed. His next visit was mid morning when he realised that Willie was dead.

'Could he have been dead on your earlier visits?' asked Luke.

'Yes. My early morning visit was rather casual. He may have been dead at that point. I did not go right up to the bed, but simply poked my head through the entrance.'

'Was there any one else in the vicinity of Willie's hut, other than you and Abigail?'

Luke was surprised by Humphrey's answer. 'Yes.'

'Who?'

'Mr Timothy.'

'Where did you see him?'

'I didn't see him. I heard him.'

Abigail had told the truth. She had had a visitor. It was Tim. Luke was furious. Not with Abigail, but with Harry who was supposed to have been with Tim day and night. He turned to Humphrey, 'Would the path from Tim's bed to Abigail's have led him close to Willie's hut?'

'Right past the door. He could have easily slipped in without us knowing.'

Luke was perplexed. What he hoped would be a routine enquiry had now put Tim back into the frame as the prime suspect for a third death, a death that everybody had assumed was natural. Luke stormed into the house, and confronted Harry.

'Zooks, you puny pottle-deep puttock. You are a fine watchdog, boy. Remember your childhood? Pretending to be asleep until your parents had gone to bed and then sneaking out for adventures.'

'Relevance, sir?' asked a bemused Harry.

'Well, while you were peacefully sleeping Sir Timothy was out gallivanting. We know he spent time with a woman, but he also had the opportunity to murder yet another victim.'

'Tim was asleep when I went to bed, and asleep in the same bed when I awoke. If you want him watched throughout the sleeping hours then assign a guard to the bedroom door.'

'Exactly what I will have to do? Where is he now?'

'In the hall having breakfast.'

'Or that is where you think he is. Not good enough Harry.'

Luke found Tim and questioned him. He was forthcoming. Yes, he sneaked out most nights to enjoy the company of the sensuous Abigail. It was not only lust, but she consoled him, understanding how much the loss of Lucy had affected him. Harry was no obstacle. He slept like a log. Once asleep nothing could wake him. Luke finally asked, 'Did you look in on the castaway we picked up?'

'No, I did not know he was there until Abigail told me she would look in on him after I left.'

'You left alone? Abigail did not walk with you part of your journey back to your own bed?'

'No.'

A perplexed Luke paddled leisurely toward South Island. If Tim had killed Willie what was his motive? Everybody knew his real identity – the man employed by Robert Browne as Tim Lipton the overseer, was in reality Sir Timothy Beale. He was the sole survivor of a family massacred by a troop under Browne's command. What more could Tim have to hide? He stopped paddling, and was unaware that the current was sweeping him into the Bay. It suddenly dawned on him that Andrew might have had a point. The only evidence that Lipton was in fact Beale came from Harry Lloyd who claimed to have served with him. What if these two young soldiers were in a conspiracy to destroy Browne? They were both Puritans to whom the vengeance of the Lord was a personal and ever present concept. Lloyd had gone out of his way to come to Browne's plantation, and was over eager to serve Luke. It was a very bad move to have Lloyd guard the suspect Lipton, or Beale or whoever he really was. Luke eventually realised his immediate plight, and with extreme effort redirected the canoe back towards South Island, as another thunderstorm rolled up on the Bay.

189

30

THE FOLLOWING DAY THE SETTLEMENT WAS HIT BY A series of recurring thunderstorms. They were so prolonged that Luke spent the whole day isolated in his hut, overindulging in West Indian rum, and catching up involuntarily on much overdue sleep. Towards evening the weather improved, and Humphrey arrived with a request from Robert. Captain Murchison was expected around the midday following. Robert thought Luke should give him the details of the shipwreck and the deceased castaway, for the information of the Governor.

Next day aboard the *Mary Jane* Luke delivered his written statement to Murchison. After much verbal elaboration, and several drafts of Dutch spirits Luke disembarked along a thick plank. He was half way along it when he was suddenly pushed from behind. He felt sick as he extended his arms into thin air in a vain attempt to find support. Luke would have toppled into the water, or more dangerously onto the rocks if strong arms had not enveloped him at the last second.

Angry at being pushed, but thankful for the assistance Luke was even more surprised to realise that both had been the work of the same man. Standing behind him, grinning from ear to ear was John Halliwell.

'My God, John! You should be halfway across the Atlantic with urgent letters for the General. I will have you court martialled if you do not have convincing reasons for disobeying my direct orders.'

'Let's return to South Island and I will tell only you and Andrew. You may wish to keep the details from others.'

The three men settled down to a meal of chicken stew with fresh bread that Abigail had baked especially for Luke. John began his story. 'I reported to the Governor of Virginia and presented the coin he had given you as proof of my credentials. He asked whether I was happy to leave before our mission was completed. I explained that you needed to report to Baltimore, and I drew the short straw. He then beckoned to his equerry to admit another officer. I was surprised. It was your former deputy from our days in Ireland, Captain Cobb. Cobb had letters for you from Baltimore, and also I later discovered from Cromwell. They were to be delivered as a matter of urgency. It suited Cobb to return to England on the ship he had just left. I offered to deliver his urgent mail to you, and Cobb was happy to take your reports straight to Cromwell and Baltimore. So we exchanged our letters, and both returned the way we had come.'

'And how is our old comrade Simon Cobb?' Luke asked warmly.

'Still very intense. He resented his voyage to the Americas. It distracted him from his mission to find his evil brother. He sends his regards, and reiterates his promise to exact vengeance on your behalf.'

Luke preferred not to dwell on the painful past. He changed the subject, 'I have been very patient John. Where are the letters?'

John was enjoying the moment. He withdrew two sealed letters from inside his doublet. Luke broke Lord Baltimore's seal, and after a casual perusal put it aside. 'His Lordship is asking for a report, which is already on its way to him.' He then turned to a letter bearing the seal of Lieutenant General Oliver Cromwell. It was an extensive letter and a long read. Luke whistled from time to time while Andrew and John finished up the last of the chicken stew. He finally turned towards his men.

'This letter gives us a new suspect.'

The sergeants nearly choked on their last mouthfuls. Luke continued, 'We know that someone here is wiping out the Brownes. Our English friends do not yet know how far that has gone. I will read the relevant parts of General Cromwell's letter:

From Hampshire came reports that former Royalist soldiers and their families were being murdered. One of the local magistrates put two and two together and realised that the parties being murdered were all involved in the massacre at Beale Hall – an issue the county refuses to forget. Quite separately one of my generals, a former Royalist captain, was in Hampshire on army business. He heard of these developments and was most interested and concerned. He had not only been a member of the Royalist court martial that condemned Captain Goodes for the massacres, but was the officer designated to carry out the execution. He told me that Goodes just prior to execution reiterated his innocence, and called on his children, twins, to avenge their father on Browne and those troopers who had lied at his court martial. Goodes went further and called on his children to take vengeance against not only the alleged lying soldiers, but their families as well. I sent my general to inform Mr Charles Browne, who still employs several of the surviving troop and their families. He has probably already warned his brother that any threat to him may come from the family of Captain Goodes.'

The astounded soldiers immediately took the news to Robert. He received the information calmly and commented, 'Then young Tim is innocent. You concentrated on the Parliamentary family that had been murdered, when you should have concentrated on the family of the Royalist officer convicted of their murder. I'm glad I did not indict Tim.'

'No Robert, this changes nothing. Tim could be one of the twins pretending to be Sir Timothy Beale. We only have Harry Lloyd's word that your overseer is Sir Timothy Beale. But whoever he is, Lipton, Beale or Goodes, all the evidence points to him as the murderer. He remains the prime suspect,' Luke declared emphatically.

Robert seemed lost in thought and his trembles became more pronounced. He finally spoke, 'You may have stumbled on something there. If Tim is a Goodes then I know who his twin brother is – that new man of yours, and the source of the false information, Harry Lloyd. They look quite similar.'

Robert's remark took Luke by surprise. He had never seen any similarity, but Robert's comments had thrown his view of events into disarray. Tim and Harry working in concert to destroy the Brownes. Maybe the settlers on the Severn, and Dr Sherman were also involved. This would fit the facts. He immediately reviewed the situation with his sergeants.

Their discussion was fruitless and frustrating. The soldiers could not progress beyond the view that Thomas had accidentally killed himself, and that Tim had shot James and strangled Lucy, despite a few loose ends. But that was the problem. There were still too many loose ends.

As for the political situation they agreed on the obvious. Everybody in the area was building up potential troop numbers. The planters on the Severn had a fort, and a well disciplined and regularly trained militia of settlers, Richard Goodwin was increasing his manpower with an army of French convicts, and the Jesuits were training dislocated Indians to defend themselves with a cache of the most modern weapons. The Susquehanna were always on the warpath, and the Nanticokes could put a large force into the field. The only problem for Luke and his men was why? For Maryland's future he feared the truth of the maxim that, 'All can start a war but few can finish it.'

Luke's concern intensified two days later when Captain Murchison on his return journey south unloaded a dozen men who impressed Luke as soldiers rather than settlers. They were replacement workers for Dr Sherman from the Puritan settlement on the Severn. Everybody was preparing for conflict but over what? Why did Sherman need more men? Were Sherman and Goodwin amassing troops for a final showdown over Browne's grant when Robert was removed? Perhaps Sherman or Goodwin or both were behind the murders?

Luke was frustrated, and increasingly disinterested. He could do no more. He wanted out. He completely reversed his position on Beale. Tim should be formally indicted for murder although Luke expected Browne to refer the matter to Governor Stone as the accused was an English gentleman, and the victims had been Browne's children. On the political side of his mission, Luke's report could say little more than the province was in chaos, and several parties were arming for some future conflict. Both Baltimore and the English government would have little prospect of restoring order. Although he hated to admit it, the one authority capable of bringing a semblance of order was the Governor of Virginia. He would recommend to Cromwell that if Baltimore lost his authority, Maryland should become part of Virginia which by then should be under republican control.

The depressed soldiers agreed to leave the Americas as soon as possible. That night they drank many healths to their imminent return home.

Next day Luke formally asked Robert to indict Sir Timothy Beale. The two men argued strongly over the issue – Robert was still reluctant. Rachel O'Brien entered the chamber and spoke to Robert quietly but with a sense of urgency. Robert left, but returned after a few minutes. 'Please follow me to my wife's bedroom. She is dead.'

Luke entered the room where Mistress Elizabeth lay peacefully upon the bed. She was indeed dead. Rachel comforted a weeping Priscilla, but Luke casting aside any sensitivities immediately questioned the distraught daughter, 'When did you last see your mother alive?'

'Last evening. I gave her the potions as prescribed by Dr Sherman, and made sure she drank them before I retired for the night. This morning she appeared asleep, so I did not disturb her. However when it was well past her normal breakfast time I decided to wake her.' The rest of the sentence was lost in increasingly louder sobbing. Luke beckoned Rachel to him.

'Did you look in on your mistress last night, or this morning?'

'No, since Mistress Elizabeth's decline Miss Priscilla has taken over the nursing of her mother. I simply fetch and carry as ordered by Miss Priscilla.'

'So nobody other than Miss Priscilla entered your mistress's room?'

'Nobody, except for Abigail.'

'Why Abigail? I thought her duties were limited to cooking.'

'They are. Every night before she retires Abigail places a jug of fresh water on the mistress's bed table. Every morning Abigail, after she had lit the fires in the cookhouse, wakes me, and I in turn wake Miss Priscilla. Abigail would pass Mistress Elizabeth's room each morning. Sometimes she looks in to check on the water.'

'Did the master not visit his wife?' Luke asked tentatively

'Colonel, you have been here long enough to know they hated each other. I have never seen the two of them together, other than when the master comes close enough to beat her. See the lump on the side of my head! I received that from the master when I stepped in front of my mistress to prevent her being battered.'

'When did this happen?'

'Yesterday.'

'Did the master land any blows on his wife before you intervened?'

'Several. It was Mistress Elizabeth's screams that brought me, and Miss Priscilla to her aid.'

'Could those blows have killed her?'

'I hope so. Master is a fiend. He deserves to die for his treatment of the mistress. Men do not see him for what he is.'

Sherman arrived and inspected the body. After he had completed the formalities he approached Luke, 'A nasty business, but she died of a broken heart. She lived in a private world of terror and fear.'

'So your potions did not poison her?' Luke asked bluntly.

Matthew looked appalled, and Luke responded, 'Let me put that a different way. If she overdosed on your potions could they have killed her.'

'Yes, it's possible. They induce sleep. After her previous attempts to take too much medication, and in the light of her deteriorating mental condition all my medicines were kept by Miss Priscilla, well away from her mother.'

'If Priscilla accidentally gave Elizabeth a double dose of the medicine would that prove fatal?'

'No, it would need the patient to drink a whole bottle in one session for it to kill her.'

'Did you notice any thing unusual about the body?'

'It was badly bruised around the chest and ribs. A few bones were broken. There is so little flesh on the body that bruising was difficult to assess, but the broken bones suggest a recent beating.'

'Matthew, you must have noticed such treatment in the past. Did you not confront Robert about them?'

31

'YES, I HAVE KNOWN OF THE PHYSICAL ABUSE FROM the day I arrived. I reproached Robert on each occasion. He apologises, puts it down to his temper, and promises it will never happen again. But it does. Increasingly so. It happens whenever Robert enters one of his moods, which is set off by trifling events or comments.'

'Not related to him being drunk?'

'No, he gets drunk after he has abused his victims.'

'So it is not only his wife who suffered from these assaults?'

'No, Priscilla and Thomas in particular were regularly attacked. Once he even attacked me, and appeared to be in a trance.'

'Servants?'

'Many a time. There were one or two extreme cases where he suddenly went berserk while inspecting the tobacco fields, and lashed into the men with his ever present cane. On one occasion Tim had to forcibly remove the cane from him. When he settles down he does not seem to remember what he has done. He never exhibits any remorse, because in his mind he has committed no assault.'

'What's wrong with him?'

'Many things. He has a violent temper that flares from nowhere, during which he can be extremely violent and after which he has no memory of the outburst. He has spasms of violent shaking and trembling with an uncontrolled jerking of the head. Less obvious but more worrying is that he talks to, and sees demons that he claims are persecuting him. Sometimes I wonder whether the man may have been bewitched. Perhaps his brother got him out of England before he became an embarrassment.'

'Is there a common cause for these disabilities?'

'I can only guess, but I suggest they all stem from unresolved guilt.'

'The massacre of Beale Hall?'

'Maybe. I think he needs a priest rather than a physician.'

Luke was uneasy with such ideas and changed his focus, 'Would the recent beating of Mistress Elizabeth have contributed to her death?'

'Not directly, but the pain from the broken bones may have intensified Elizabeth's desire to be rid of her earthly travail.'

'Is it possible that with her mother's consent Priscilla overdosed Elizabeth to free her from these unhappy circumstances? She was devoted to her mother, and appalled at her treatment.'

'If she did, then I hope you will find it in your heart to recommend a verdict of suicide against Elizabeth, and not murder against Priscilla.'

'Matthew, what happens to Browne's grant from Lord Baltimore should he not be able to exercise his authority over it?'

'It depends. Should he die, it is governed by his will.'

'And who benefits from that?'

'He has two options that the law would uphold. He could leave it to his only surviving child Priscilla, who would hold it in trust until she married. It would then become the real property of her husband. Or it could be left to the nearest male heir, which would be his brother Charles or any of Charles's male children.'

'What if Robert lived, but was unable temporarily to exercise his responsibilities through illness or prolonged absence?'

'In that case the estate would be administered by his tenant in chief until such time as Lord Baltimore restored it to Browne, or reallocated it to someone else.'

'You are the tenant in chief?'

'No, I am a relative newcomer. Richard Goodwin is the senior tenant by at least three years.'

'Fascinating! If Robert dies, and you marry Priscilla you take the whole grant; if Robert disappears or becomes too ill, too mad to function then Goodwin gets the lot, at least temporarily. In this environment once anyone has control it would be very difficult to dislodge him. Is that why both of you are increasing your labour force, your potential militia? Are you preparing to fight Goodwin over Robert's grant?'

'Fanciful Luke. This is a busy time on any tobacco plantation. I simply needed more labourers to keep my crop advancing efficiently.'

'I should have realised this earlier. Both you and Goodwin have an interest in the fate of the Browne family. The series of fatalities affecting them could stem from neighbourly plotting in Maryland, rather than an alleged massacre in England. To whom has Robert bequeathed his lands?'

'His original will left it to James. I doubt that he has made a new will.'

Luke thanked Matthew, and went in search of Robert whom he found sitting pensively in his entrance hall. Luke expressed his condolences as a matter of form, recognising that Robert probably felt relieved to be rid of his hated wife. He then said, 'Robert, there may be a conspiracy between your neighbours to gain control of your grant. The conspirators can achieve their end by your death, or disappearance. Should you not be a position to administer your estates Richard as tenant in chief takes over until Lord Baltimore determines the future? Is that so?'

'Yes, the senior tenant takes over the administration of a grant assuming legal and military authority.'

'The second possibility is your death. Have you brought your will up to date?'

'No. But I can see the urgency in the circumstances you outline. Give me an hour. I will write a new will and you and Sir Timothy, as gentlemen, will witness it.'

Luke withdrew, and hoped to fill in the hour with Abigail who he needed to question about Elizabeth. Abigail was in the cookhouse chopping parsnips and carrots into small pieces, after which she began to dice a slab of beef. To the side there were peeled apples awaiting a similar fate, Abigail was making a double pasty. One half of the pasty was meat and vegetables and the other half apples and berries. The thick pastry acted as a trencher, and was not usually eaten. Luke pined for good old English food of this ilk. The Maryland diet was a monotony of corn, squashes, chicken and pork. Luke returned to reality, 'You are obviously too busy for a quick walk to your hut so I will question you while you work. Did you see Mistress Elizabeth last night?'

'Yes, and again this morning.'

'Why?'

Last night I took her a jug of water, freshly gathered from the spring. She had an obsession that water went bad if left lying around. This morning as usual I went to waken Rachel, and passing the Mistress's door I noticed it was wide open. It is usually shut tight – another of the mistress's obsessions. I peered inside to see if anything was wrong. It didn't appear to be, so I shut the door.'

'Thanks Abigail. Do you know where Mr Timothy and Mr Harry are?'

'They went across to North Island just after dawn. The plants need special attention after the thunderstorms of the last few days. They started as early as they could. That is why I am making special pasties, for what will be a long day in the field for everybody.' Luke made his way across to North Island, informed the men of Elizabeth's death, and asked Tim to return with him. On the way he explained that they were to witness Robert's new will - as gentry they were the most appropriate witnesses. He also told Tim that he was about to be indicted for murder, but as the evidence was very circumstantial he stood every chance of being acquitted.

Robert was waiting for them, 'Gentlemen, this task has presented me with a dilemma. My brother Charles has no interest in this estate and always made clear that if it was left to him he would sell. Priscilla is also unhappy with life here, but if she married Sherman she would stay. With the original grant, less Goodwin's tenancy, Sherman and Priscilla should have a prosperous future on this land. Subsequently I have left everything to Priscilla and if she predeceases me, to a string of nephews one of whom may be more inclined to migrate than their father Charles. It would set the youngest one up quite well. Should Priscilla not be married, or fail to marry within twelve months of my death the estate passes to one of these nephews.'

The two men witnessed Robert's signature after which he invited them to eat. To Luke's delight they were served the pasties that he had seen being prepared. After the meal Robert decided to visit Richard and discuss the issues that Luke had raised with him, and to indicate the contents of his will. Robert asked Tim to help Priscilla organize his wife's funeral.

Later Luke discussed the day's events with his sergeants. Andrew speculated, 'This could easily be another murder. Anybody could have done it. Elizabeth was so heavily sedated with Dr Sherman's medicines anybody could have put a pillow over her mouth. There would have been no struggle. The woman was so small and weak. A child could have smothered Mistress Elizabeth.'

'So we have a serial killer who has removed Thomas, Lucy, James, Willie and Elizabeth?' Luke commented sarcastically. 'You can't believe that?'

John responded, 'Why not? There is as much evidence for that as there is for indicting Tim. Everything is circumstantial. The real villain on this plantation is Robert Browne. All the problems stem from his actions and personality. The man is vicious. He ordered the massacre of the innocents at Beale Hall. If Tim is the murderer I don't blame him, although attacking the women and children is going a bit too far. Let's return to Ireland now. I feel very uncomfortable protecting a wife beating madman.'

It was noon the next day and the soldiers were about to eat when Humphrey arrived. The retainer was agitated and appealed to Luke, 'Colonel we need your help. The master has disappeared.'

'How do you know he has disappeared? He may have sought solace in the woods given everything that has happened.'

'He told Mr Timothy that he would be back yesterday afternoon to confirm the arrangements Tim was making for the funeral. He did not return. His bed was not slept in, and he is nowhere on our plantation, or that of Dr Sherman. His canoe, which was a special gift from Straight Arrow, was on our shore having been run aground in its usual place. It suggests he returned from Goodwin's, and went missing on West Island between the beach and the house.'

'Have you contacted Mr Goodwin? Robert may have stayed overnight, probably having consumed too much of Richard's hospitality.'

'No, that is why I am here. Goodwin does not encourage visitors. You are the only one with the status and authority to visit him unannounced.'

'Right, I'll go at once,' Luke replied.

Richard's men did not to impede Luke's passage. He was soon being ushered into Richard's study and had placed before him a draft of Dutch spirits. Luke went straight to the point. 'Richard, have you seen Robert in the last twenty four hours?'

'I certainly have. He came across yesterday afternoon to tell me about his wife's death, and to discuss the future of his grant in case he was no longer able to exercise his jurisdiction. He also kindly made me aware of his will, so that I would know the position should he die.'

'When did he leave here?'

'Why do you ask?'

'He has disappeared.'

'Oh, I am not altogether surprised. He was a strange mixture of elation and depression. We both drank heavily through the afternoon, and well into the night. He stayed for the evening meal but his main sustenance continued to be these Dutch spirits. It was very late when he decided he must return home. I offered him a place here for the night, but he refused. I personally walked him to my landing beach, and made sure he knew where he was and I suggested he keep his paddling in line with a clump of trees that were silhouetted in the moon light.'

'His canoe was found just where you suggested he should paddle. Perhaps he is sleeping it off in the woods. Did he often seek solace with the natives as his children tended to do?'

'No, never! Robert hated the forest. Perhaps he re-entered the water again in another canoe. He was very drunk. Maybe he fell asleep, and the canoe drifted off. Luckily the tide was coming in so he would have been taken upstream. If he was not washed ashore on North Island, he may be on my lands in the vicinity of Lovers Cove. I will have my men search the area.'

32

RICHARD'S SEARCH WAS NEGATIVE, AND AS ROBERT DID NOT appear Priscilla agreed to postpone her mother's funeral in hope that he would soon be found. Twenty four hours later the funeral had to be held. Dr Sherman and Luke officiated. Luke in his eulogy deliberately spoke of Lady Elizabeth. He was determined that she be buried with the dignity and honours her husband denied her. Given the circumstances there was no wake, and Luke returned to South Island where he discussed the situation with his sergeants. Andrew again was full of speculation, 'Robert is either dead by accident, his own hand or by that of our serial killer; or he has been detained against his will, or yet again he might have just wandered off until his wife is buried. More likely, given his personality and their relationship, he may have deliberately missed the funeral.'

'Thanks Andrew, as usual there are more questions than answers in your comments,' replied Luke with a touch of sarcasm.

'Lets start with the basics. Who gains by Robert's disappearance?' asked John

'In the short term it is Richard Goodwin. He takes over Robert's judicial powers.'

'What does that mean?' interrupted Andrew.

'I will now have to take my evidence to indict Timothy to Richard, and my remit from Robert to investigate all these deaths becomes void. However I will use my overriding authority from Baltimore to continue the enquiry. The indentured servants on the plantation are legally transferred to Richard, as are the current crops.'

'When does this transfer take effect?"

'Richard can act as the trustee of the grant immediately.'

Andrew interposed, 'So it suits Richard for us not to find a body. A dead body hands everything to Priscilla.'

'That could help us. Richard may keep him alive for some time. It gives us a chance to rescue him,' declared an optimistic Luke.

John was pessimistic, 'No, Browne is dead. His body would never be found in this wilderness.'

Luke returned to Robert's house, and met Matthew at the entrance. His men were removing boxes of possessions from within the house. 'Glad to see you Luke. We need to talk urgently,' announced the gaunt doctor.

'About what? And why are you ransacking your neighbour's house?'

'These are Priscilla's possessions. She is moving to my house, and bringing Rachel O'Brien with her. With the new workers I can provide a constant guard to protect the women. Abigail wants to remain behind to feed Tim, Humphrey and the single men who work the tobacco fields. With Robert's house virtually deserted, you should move your soldiers here without delay, to protect Browne's workers and possessions.

'A good idea Matthew, but you speak as if we are about to undergo immediate attack. Do you know something that I don't?'

'Yes, the men who recently arrived from the Severn plantation carried a message from Commandant Lloyd. An attack on Browne by his enemies was imminent. Robert's disappearance is possibly the start of the offensive.'

'Why did you not mention this before? We could have been preparing for a such an assault for the last week or so.'

'I thought it was yet another of the many rumours that circulate along the Chesapeake but with Robert's disappearance I think we must give it some credence.'

'Did the Commandant name the attackers?'

'Not exactly. The attack would be launched from close to Robert's plantation and would include both European and Indian insurgents. Independently he has heard that the French have landed troops in the area, and Captain Murchison had seen an armed French merchantman lurking about the upper Bay.'

'A mish mash of half truths and rumours. The French story has some basis. An armed merchantman landed an unknown number of men on Goodwin's plantation. Most of the men speak French, and I suspect are the outpourings of French prisons indentured to Goodwin. He may be training them into an effective militia, but that will take time. How is it that Richard, our friendly neighbour, has suddenly become the enemy? Have I missed his dastardly deeds?' asked Luke somewhat bemused by the sudden change of outlook by Matthew.

'Commandant Lloyd long suspected that Goodwin is the centre of support for those who want to overthrow Baltimore's authority, and create a direct Royal colony in allegiance to Charles II. He probably persuaded the King to revoke the charter and appoint a royal governor, who has never appeared. But there have been no rumours of any links between Goodwin and the French.'

John interrupted, 'What if the latest influx of labour for Goodwin were not convict dregs, but trained French soldiers? Not only would they provide a significant counter balance to us, but a group of them could very quickly train Goodwin's convicts into a ruthless force.'

'What is behind all this? Why would the French help Goodwin?' asked Luke.

'The French have always wanted a colony, or at the least a secure trading post on the coast in this part of America. Goodwin could provide the nucleus for that colony especially if he held Browne's grant whose eastern border is the Atlantic Ocean. Goodwin is helping the French, not the reverse. The Jesuits also may be involved. Why are they equipping their Indians with the most modern French muskets? Richard's men who exercise up and down the riverbank have the same weapons. An army of French regulars and mission Indians would be an irresistible force,' lectured Matthew.

'What are you up to Matthew? You are not the innocent doctor settler that you pretend?' Luke asked.

'I am here to protect the interests of Protestant England. My brethren on the Severn are ready to move against any Royalist, French or Papist activity. I am on this plantation to delay such mischief until Commandant Lloyd can bring his forces into play.'

'Matthew you could be right. Richard may be preparing to act. He has built a large number of new huts. That merchant-man was a large vessel, and could have unloaded hundreds of men for all we know. My twenty men could not hold out for long, and I guess you would not have many more to add to our small army?'

'Between us and Mr Browne's servants we could raise fifty men at the most.'

'If Commandant Lloyd is right, why is Richard waiting?'

'Either he has not received sufficient support as yet to enable him to act; or he hopes to achieve his ends without using force,' answered Matthew.

'Maybe he expected aid from the Jesuits, or at least their help in obtaining more support. A letter I saw suggests that the Jesuits don't want a bar of what Goodwin may be up to. I suspect he is the unnamed X in that document. I must find Robert.'

Matthew led his men with their boxes to the landing beach, while Luke pondered the situation. Given a possible attack by Goodwin, Tim's situation troubled him. It was more important to protect England's interests, than restrict the activities of a man whose political allegiances were well known, whatever his criminal activities. Luke needed more men, and here were two experienced officers devoting their time to tobacco plants. He caught up with Tim and Harry. Luke put them in the picture regarding an imminent attack by Goodwin, who might be assisted by French regulars. 'Harry you no longer need to guard Tim. Tim, I am conscripting you into the army of the parliament of England, as a Lieutenant of infantry. Both of you will assume full time military duties, and report to our new headquarters in Mr Browne's house.'

Later Luke informed his sergeants that they now had two junior officers, and that they should immediately move the unit to Browne's manor house. The men were jubilant, as the thunderstorm season had revealed numerous leaks in their amateurish attempts to build huts. Luke took Andrew aside. 'Tonight you and I are visiting Goodwin's estate. We need to know how many armed men he can bring into play, and how many of them, if any, are French soldiers.'

It was a dark overcast night, although the moon broke through from time to time. Luke and Andrew set out to row across the river. Disaster struck. The tide was running out at such a speed that any silent gliding to Goodwin's shoreline was out of the question. They went with the tide and were swept out beyond the Northern Arm into the Bay itself. Luke accepted his fate. They would approach Goodwin's cultivated fields overland from the heavily forested northern boundary. They would paddle to the inlet that had concealed the armed French merchantman. Luke knew that there were no guards on this northern perimeter, none until you reached the cleared portions of Richard's land along the river. Richard expected visitors to approach his property from the river on his southern boundary.

Hiding their canoe in the undergrowth the two men headed for Goodwin's fields. After half and hour of brisk walking the forest became thicker. Luke and Andrew stopped and listened. There were no human sounds. The howl of wolves, and the constant rustle in the undergrowth was increasingly disconcerting. Luke was lost.

He gambled. He took a full right angle turn and hoped to return to the coast, not far from Goodwin's fields. Three quarters of an hour later Luke motioned Andrew to stop. They heard human voices. And the language they heard was French. Soon the flicker of fires in front of numerous huts could be seen through the trees. The soldiers crawled closer to the encampment and began to count. Luke froze. Just in front of him a man burst through the undergrowth and began to urinate, just where Luke had taken a dive. There was no way Luke would not be seen, but God was on his side. Another soldier called out, and the man turned to answer, directing his flow of urine in a new direction. At the same time clouds obscured the moon, and the forest returned to darkness.

Eventually Luke and Andrew collated their information. There were ten new huts in each of two rows. By the muskets stacked outside the entrance of each they contained three men. And they were French troops. They all wore a navy blue doublet and breeches and white stockings. To Andrew that uniform was vaguely familiar. Luke concluded there were sixty troops, in addition to Richard's convict work force – already sufficient to easily overwhelm the Browne and Sherman plantations.

The two men made hard work of the return trip. They paddled well out to sea to avoid rocks and shoals that they could not see when the moon was hidden, and the tides and currents were against them. Eventually they found the North Arm, and headed for the landing on West Island. As they approached it Luke held up his hand to stop paddling and listen. Both men heard another paddler very close to them. A canoe swept passed them in the darkness, but just after that moment the moon re emerged. The paddler who had beaten them ashore was Abigail Hicks. Luke called softly to her, 'Abigail where have you been at such a late hour?'

If Abigail was disconcerted by being apprehended she did not show it, 'Colonel you well know I have a sweetheart on Mr Richard's estate. I cannot visit him during the day. I am just returning. Where have you two been?'

'Fishing,' lied Andrew.

'Don't believe you sergeant. No one fishes at night.'

'No, Abigail. We have just moved into the house and set up guards around the estate, and it was reported that lights were seen. We decided to circumnavigate the Island to see if there were any intruders coming in from the water.'

The girl appeared to accept Luke's lie. 'All this talk of strangers worries me. I don't know if I can trust your men. Luke stay with me tonight?' Abigail took Luke's hand and was rubbing it through her flowing hair. Andrew sighed to himself and moved ahead. On reaching Abigail's hut after an initial passionate series of hugs and kisses Abigail and Luke's sensual evening suddenly ceased. Luke fell fast asleep, and within minutes was snoring loudly.

33

LUKE AND ABIGAIL HALF AWOKE AS THE SUN WAS rising, and mutual lust transported them into a state between reality and dream. As the rays of the sun strengthened, the ever practical Abigail dressed and headed to the cookhouse to light the fires. Luke followed her, and after a few hugs and kisses headed for the main house. He was half way through the door when he heard a firm and business like voice - not Abigail's usual sensuous and languid tone, 'Come back Luke! I have something important to tell you.'

'It must be serious. I thought there was someone else in the cookhouse calling me,' mocked Luke.

'I am about to betray a trust, but as he has betrayed me, I feel released from my promise.'

Luke was expecting that because of a lover's tiff Abigail was about to reveal some minor secret about a worker on Goodwin's estate. Maybe that many of them spoke French. He was shocked by her revelation, 'Richard Goodwin abducted the master, and has sent him away.'

'Where to?'

'The new men in dark blue uniforms took him into the forest just after breakfast the day after he disappeared.'

'Did they kill him? Have they returned?'

'No – to both questions. His captors were prepared for a long trip so you may have time to find Mr Robert alive.'

Luke kissed Abigail on the lips, and then awakened his sergeants with the loud banging of pots he had taken from the cookhouse. One of his men unearthed a cornet that had not been sounded since they landed in the colony. Within half an hour his complete unit was assembled in the entrance hall. Luke addressed them, 'Good and bad news. The bad news is that Goodwin kidnapped Robert Browne, and is poised to attack this island at any time. The good news is that Robert maybe still alive, and has been moved into the forest on his way to an unknown destination. I will take Humphrey, Andrew and three troopers and search for Robert. The rest of you will stay here under Lieutenants Lloyd and Beale and Sergeant Halliwell, and construct defences against the expected attack. Harry you will be in command as the senior lieutenant.' Moral was high. Luke's men were elated to be once again soldiers preparing for battle.

Humphrey's skill as a woodsman proved immediately beneficial. After paddling half a mile upriver the party landed on Mr Browne's yet to be utilised lands east of Goodwin's clearings. Humphrey hoped to find evidence of a group of men moving through the undergrowth as there were no Indian trails or settler pathways in that undeveloped area. He did, but it was subtle. He commented to Luke, 'The French have either an Indian guide, or one of their number is an experienced woodsman. They are deliberately covering their tracks. There are no unwieldy cuts from large knives or swords. All I can see is the occasional footprint, and foliage regularly broken by hand. Maybe the master is leaving us a clue.'

'Some of Richard's new men could be old Canada hands. Are we far from Straight Arrow's village?' asked an anxious Luke.

'No, the path of the kidnappers is parallel to the river and will cross the trail we usually take from it to the Indian village in about half an hour.'

When they reached this north-south trail Luke ordered his men to rest, while Humphrey and he continued to Straight Arrow's village. The Indian chief was alarmed at the news. 'Bad! It was what I feared, and warned the Black Robes about. Goodwin is planning a major insurrection, and trying to involve the priests. The Susquehanna war parties that have been wandering around beyond the ridge, and down to the Ocean coast, are part of the plan. My scouts have reported a large fort being constructed near the mouth of one of the small eastern flowing streams.'

'Who is building the fort?'

'The Susquehanna under Black Cougar, and a few Europeans.'

'Did your braves report any detail about these Europeans?'

'They all wore very dark blue jackets.'

'As in an army uniform?'

'Yes.'

'Maybe Robert is being taken to this new fort. It is well away from his plantation, and probably well defended. Can your men find it?'

'Yes, White Deer is still with the priests so I, with a few braves, will come with you.'

Luke noted that the six Indians were well armed. In addition to the bow and quiver of arrows slung over their shoulder, each man carried a spear, and what appeared to be a combination of axe and club hung from his waist. Straight Arrow expected trouble. The group met up with Luke's remaining men. Straight Arrow told Luke, 'Do not follow the French. Move north and cross the peninsula along another of our trails, which reaches the sea some miles north of the new outpost. This will avoid any sentinels the Susquehanna may have posted deep in the forest, or rear guards the French have protecting their progress.'

With Straight Arrow available to guide the party, Humphrey returned to the Browne settlement to supervise the tobacco cultivation. For the others progress was steady and easy as they followed an east west trail towards the Ocean. Into the afternoon one of Straight Arrow's scouts returned highly agitated. The Indian war chief quickly informed Luke, 'A large Susquehanna war party is moving along the trail heading straight for us. Their advance scouts will soon be upon us.'

'Do we ambush them, or hide? asked Luke tentatively, somewhat fearful of forest conflict.

'We don't have a choice. There are too many to confront, and we do not want anyone to know we are here. Withdraw off the path as far as you can. Their outrunners will find us if we stay at the side of the trail. Follow me!'

The whole party moved rapidly through the forest, and away from the trail, except Straight Arrow who returned to monitor the progress of the Susquehanna. To avoid detection he climbed into the branches of a giant tree. Luke waited with the soldiers and braves. Two hours later Straight Arrow reported to Luke, 'This is the whole Susquehanna party that my braves saw at the fort. They must have finished their task, and left the new fort completely to the Europeans. I was delayed because the whole party stopped just under the tree I had climbed. I overheard much of their conversation. They are eventually headed for Browne's plantation.'

'Did you recognize their leader?'

'Oh yes, it was Black Cougar.'

'Did you pick up any other aspects of their conversation?'

'Yes, one clear statement was being made. Every time I heard the word Tamuagh mentioned, the group scowled and spat. If Browne's plantation is their eventual destination somewhere in their plans is the overthrow of their high chieftain Tamuagh.'

Back on track Luke's party eventually reached the coast. Luke's jaw dropped. Well to the south, and well out to sea lay a large merchantman. They moved south along the forest edge of the beach to conceal themselves from anybody aboard ship who may have a spyglass. As they came closer they could see the French flag fluttering in the wind. This was probably the same French merchantman that had fired on the Browne plantation. Even closer inspection revealed pinnaces from the ship laden with blue uniformed men being transported to the shore.

Luke took his men further inland and moved slowly through the undergrowth as they approached the fort from the landward side. It was lucky that the Susquehanna had departed because the Europeans had not placed sentinels or lookouts in the forest. The group halted. Straight Arrow, Luke and Andrew moved through to the edge of the clearing. Luke was shocked. A large palisaded fort had been built and sentries moved about its perimeter, and others manned four towers that made up each corner of the edifice. In the centre an even taller tower was still under construction. Straight Arrow spoke, 'If Mr Browne is a prisoner here there is no way we can rescue him. We have too few men to successfully assault the fort. We are outnumbered by about eight to one.'

'And look at the quality of their weapons,' exclaimed Andrew in admiration, 'If we wait until dark we may be able to infiltrate the fort, and find Robert,' countered the optimistic Luke.

'You are dreaming Colonel,' replied the war chief. 'I am sending one of my braves back to raise a war party double the size of the defenders of the fort. While we wait for superior numbers you can play your games.'

Luke spoke to his own men, 'Straight Arrow has sent for reinforcements. In the meanwhile we will try to enter the fort. Keep an eye out for any soldier who leaves its precincts to move into the forest. We may be able to replace him.'

Hours of fruitless watching went by, then Andrew suddenly gesticulated wildly. The gate of the fort had been opened and a group of four men wheeled a cart out in direction of the forest. Luke acted quickly. The English troopers followed him through the forest in the direction of the French soldiers while the Indians remained with Straight Arrow watching the fort. It was not long before Luke heard the ring of axes cutting into solid tree trunks. The French were felling trees.

The English soldiers removed their outer garments, and equipped only with daggers approached their hard working enemy. As one of the Frenchmen wandered off in search of the next suitable tree Andrew dispatched him with one blow. He quickly dressed in the dead Frenchman's uniform. A few minutes later another of the woodcutters came in search of his friend, and suffered the same fate. Meanwhile the troopers cut the throats of the remaining Frenchmen. Andrew complained that they should have allowed the French to fell, cut and load more logs before they had been killed. After considerable effort the four English soldiers, all now dressed in French uniforms loaded the cart, and began to take it back towards the fort. Luke who was not one of the impostors halted their progress. 'Wait an hour or so until it is dark. You are less likely to be recognized.'

Two hours later the cart pulled by two men, and pushed by the other two approached the gate of the fort. What followed was a cascade of abuse by the soldier manning the nearest tower as to the time it had taken to chop down a few trees. Eventually the gate opened and Andrew with three troopers entered the enemy's sanctum. Andrew's French was minimal, but he hoped that as in all armies many of the troops were foreign mercenaries with a range of languages.

Once through the gate they were approached by an officer who reprimanded them for their delay, but then directed them towards a half finished large building next to the incomplete central tower. Andrew noted that around the edge of the palisade there were many small huts undoubtedly constructed by the Susquehanna to house the troops. The central building was probably to be a large hall for administration and eating. Robert was most likely in one of the huts that stood around the perimeter wall. They all looked alike, and none had guards. They would have to wait. But first they must find an empty hut in which to hide.

The last pinnace had returned to the ship, but a senior naval officer remained, and was clearly visible eating in front of a large fire that had been lit in the centre of the building under construction. Andrew was concerned that the large armed merchantman had been seconded to the French King and was in fact a ship of the line. Normally French merchantmen were not commanded by French naval officers. This one was. Andrew suddenly remembered where he had seen the dark blue uniform, with the incongruous white stockings before. When he fought for the Swedes against Spain and the Austrian Hapsburgs, his unit, besieged on an island in the Baltic, was rescued by French sea borne soldiers. The men assisting Goodwin, and who manned the fort were French marines.

34

Andrew reconnoitred the camp. The occupied huts had two or three muskets stacked against them. The officers inhabited a large tent. On the far side of the fort were a couple of half finished huts into which Andrew and his men temporarily concealed themselves. In the centre of the fort, beside the building under construction, were boxes of muskets, containers of shot, and barrels of gunpowder. If he could get a lighted taper into those barrels he could cause a lot of damage. He could see the officers drinking in front of the blazing fire. There were at least four marine officers. They were distinguished from their men by the red waistcoats they wore under their dark blue topcoats. And there was a senior naval captain whose more azure blue uniform, with its concentration of silver braid distinguished him from the marines.

Andrew was in luck. The fort had been stood down for the day, and apart from the sentinels in each of the four towers the men were free to sleep, play cards, drink or simply gossip. The disguised English soldiers wandered around the fort hoping to gain news of Robert Browne. When they regrouped the consensus was that Robert was not there. Andrew feared that he had been killed during the march from Goodwin's to the new fort. If they had followed the French instead of taking an Indian trail to the north they may have found the body.

The Englishmen tried to sleep. As the sun rose the silence was broken by a long series of whistles, which Andrew assumed was the marine equivalent of the cavalry's cornet. He saw the marines were lining up to receive a meal from two large cooking pots near the main gate of the fort. Andrew decided it was best for his men to avoid breakfast. After the meal had finished another series of whistles indicated roll call – a muster of the troops within the fort. Andrew considered their best chance was to take advantage of this orderly procedure and make a run for it through the main gate, which had just been opened. Andrew marched his men as close to the gate as he could, but before he gave the order to sprint for the forest the sentries on the two northerly corner towers opened fire, and the smell and swirl of smoke enveloped the area. The shots had not been fired at the escaping Englishmen, who quickly disappeared back into the general confusion as the marines scrambled to deal with the situation. The Nanticokes had set the northerly palisade alight. The gate was quickly shut and the whole fort ordered to mount the raised ground behind the wooden defences, and to repel whoever was attacking the fort. Musket fire, arrows and spears bombarded the special detachment sent to put out the fires along the northern wall.

The marine commander realised the nature of the attack, and took the initiative. He ordered his men from the makeshift ramparts into battle order, and marched out of the fort to confront their attackers. This was not the battle Straight

Arrow had wanted. The marines were drawn up in rows and took it in turns to fire at the advancing Indians whose spears did little damage. Unless something changed dramatically the Nanticokes, and Luke would have to withdraw.

Andrew and his men ignored the order to assemble in battle formation and returned to their huts. Andrew re-emerged and moved quickly to the barrels of gunpowder. He broke them open and then rolled them in several directions. Taking an ember from last evening's fire he fanned it, and when it burst into flame, threw it into a heap of the gunpowder.

He was about to return to his men when he was stopped by the naval captain who had obviously had a heavy evening, and had only been raised from a deep sleep by the gunfire and general tumult. Andrew raised his hands in surrender as one of his men crept up behind the captain, smashed the pistol from his hand and placed a dagger to his throat. The exploding gunpowder and the fires that broke out all over the compound as a result of these explosions disoriented the defending marines. The appearance of the naval captain with a dagger to his throat created further dismay.

At that moment Luke emerged from the forest to which the allies had withdrawn, overwhelmed by the superior firepower of the marines. Having removed his shirt Luke was waving it as a white flag. Ever rising to the dramatic he announced he was Colonel Tremayne commander of a large English cavalry unit. He claimed he and his Indian allies had no desire to destroy the fort, but simply wanted an Englishmen who had been kidnapped, and taken to the fort. A marine officer stepped forward, 'I am Jean de Liette, commandant of this fort, and commanding officer of two marine companies. Colonel we do not have this man, and you as a cavalryman do not appear to have any horses.' An annoyed Luke ignored the French sense of humour.

'Your men brought an Englishman against his will from the other side of this peninsula a day or so ago?' reiterated a pompous Luke.

'Yes, they did, but the prisoner is not in the fort. He was transferred to the *Notre Dame des Carmes*, the ship you can see riding at anchor beyond the shoals. He is to be sold into slavery in the West Indies, the ship's next port of call.'

Andrew with the naval captain reached Luke and Liette, 'He speaks the truth Colonel. Browne is not within the fort.'

Luke turned towards the French officers, 'I have no desire to continue this conflict. If you return your men to the fort there will be no further attack from this side. If any of your men leave the fort or attempt to impede our recovery of Mr Browne our Indian friends will attack. As for you Captain, we will trade you for your captive.'

Liette agreed, on condition that the naval captain was returned to his ship unharmed. The marines returned to the fort and Andrew and the troopers rejoined Luke. He asked the naval captain what arrangements had been made for him to contact his ship. He was to fire a pistol shot from the beach, and a pinnace would be launched to collect him. Luke asked, 'Can you signal your ship to vary instructions?'

'Ship to ship, yes; but not from shore to ship.'

'Alright fire your pistol!'

Luke was delighted when he saw the pinnace approach the shore with only six oarsmen and no superfluous marines. The oarsmen were unarmed. The pinnace ran aground, and Luke accompanied the captain to the boat. With a dagger overtly placed across his throat, the Captain ordered his men to return to the ship, and bring the captured Englishman back with them. If they returned without the prisoner, or with any armed men he would be killed. Luke hoped he would not be forced to break his word to Liette.

Within half and hour two pinnaces set out from the ship. Luke had been double crossed. Straight Arrow acted quickly.

He lined his men along the beach with their spears waving aggressively. The second pinnace turned around. Luke was delighted to see Robert sitting in the bow of the boat that continued shoreward. Robert hobbled ashore, and Luke motioned the captain to take his place. The pinnace then pulled away as quickly as possible.

Luke and Straight Arrow moved their men back into the forest, and anxiously awaited Robert's story. Robert appeared more composed than Luke had seen him. Perhaps the adventure had brought out the basic character, that had long been hidden, of the former brilliant cavalry officer. Robert recounted his adventure. 'After having lunch with Luke and Matthew I went to inform Richard of my wife's death, my new will and the situation should I be incapacitated. I thought Richard, as my tenant in chief should be fully informed. We had a very pleasant afternoon. I drank too much. I stayed on for the evening meal, but felt very sleepy. The next morning I awoke on a rough palliasse on the floor of a hut with the door guarded by an armed man in a dark navy blue uniform and white trimmings. I have no idea where I was. After a breakfast of a cold quarter chicken with these soldiers, they told me I was to accompany them to the Ocean. When I protested about such treatment their ensign cheerfully suggested that I was better off with them than remaining where I was.'

'So Richard didn't arrest you, or threaten you in any way?'

'No, Richard was the genial host. All this could have been done by the French without his knowledge. Richard might be a prisoner as well,' Robert innocently suggested.

'Sorry Robert, Richard is a French agent, determined to turn your grant into a French colony or trading post. French marines have been landed both at Goodwin's and here. Matthew and I have your estates on alert, as we expect an attack at any time. My informant told me categorically that Richard ordered your detention. Did you pick up any information while you were a prisoner that might help explain what has been happening to you in recent weeks?'

'A little. One of Richard's old retainers who had originally worked for me guided the French marines until they reached some sort of recognizable path. He kept apologising for what was happening. I asked him whether Richard knew who was responsible for what had happened to my family. He denied that his master had anything to do with the deaths that have plagued my household, but admitted that Richard was somehow involved in the attack on Matthew.'

'That fits the emerging pattern. Matthew is more than he appears, and has recently received an intake of men who are more soldiers than settlers. He is being strengthened by the Severn settlers to prevent any part of your land being taken over by the French. Goodwin is arming to forcibly seize your grant, and Sherman is determined to prevent him.'

'Are we on the brink of a local civil war?' asked an unusually alert Robert.

'At least armed insurrection - and none of the parties are rising in support of Lord Baltimore or yourself. Were you well treated by the French?'

'Very well. I explained I was a wealthy English gentleman, and I could see the thought of a healthy ransom enter their thinking. Were they really going to sell me into slavery?'

'That was the intention, but I am sure you could have convinced them you would have brought more through ransom than sale,' half joked Luke.

'What now?' asked Robert, almost enjoying the situation.

Luke explained that Priscilla was staying with Matthew, and that the English soldiers had moved into Robert's house, and that all the men on both plantations were building defences. Robert asked, 'What happened to the Indians that were here when I first arrived? They were Susquehanna led by Black Cougar.'

'They moved out early yesterday either headed for your plantation to assist Richard, or to some other destination to overthrow their chieftain Tamuagh.'

'Will the Nanticokes help us?' Robert asked.

'Straight Arrow has no time for Black Cougar, and I am not sure how loyal he is to Tamuagh. He certainly does not want the French in the area, and he raised a large war party to rescue you.'

The group headed home. After some hours Straight Arrow put up his hand to indicate silence. He moved quickly beside Luke. There is a vast body of men moving up the intersecting trail from the south.'

'With our large army we do not need to leave the trail. We would outnumber any other parties in the area now that the Susquehanna have moved north.'

Luke and Straight Arrow waited in the middle of the trail, while the Nanticoke braves stretched out along the track but well away from it. Straight Arrow was delighted. The new party were Indians from the Jesuit mission led by Father Austin and White Deer. After an exchange of pleasantries White Deer explained that the mission Indians were hunting well north of their mission when they heard that much of the Nanticoke nation had been called to arms. 'We came as fast as we could to offer our assistance.'

Luke spoke briefly to Father Austin whom he asked to inform the French priests of developments. Austin replied, 'That is what they feared. They believe that the French connection, especially the presence of French troops will provoke a Protestant reprisal including the English, the Dutch and the Swedes. They fear that Protestant fanatics will associate us with the ambitions of Goodwin and the French, and will crush our mission in retaliation. The French government obviously rejected Le Jeune's advice to abort this enterprise.'

35

Luke's party headed home, but avoided the river in case Richard's marksmen shot at them as they paddled down stream. They took a longer route to the south through the forests and into Matthew's plantation, where he was brought up to date. Matthew immediately sent a message to the Severn to inform Commandant Lloyd of the size of French involvement, and to seek urgent reinforcements.

Matthew, Luke and Robert reviewed the situation. Luke, after much discussion summed up, 'We need to protect Robert, and obtain help. We can do both, Robert, if you catch Captain Murchison's ship on his next visit south. You can inform Governor Stone and Governor Berkeley of what is afoot. Berkeley can commandeer enough armed ships to deal with the new French fort on the Atlantic coast. Stone should inform Baltimore, and the English Government, and may need to raise his militia from around St Mary's. After all Baltimore needs support. At the moment my small force and your workers, Robert, are the only group dedicated to maintaining Baltimore's authority. Even Matthew here is waiting his opportunity to overthrow it.' Matthew did not respond.

After a halfhearted protest Robert agreed, noting that the supply ship was due the next day. He gave Priscilla a cursory farewell, and with Luke returned to West Island, where Luke informed his men of immediate plans. Robert would leave next morning to alert the authorities, seek assistance, and in the process remove his presence from immediate danger.

Around midday the *Mary Jane* could be seen out on the Bay beginning to change course to take advantage of wind and tide, and gently drift towards Robert's quay. The conditions pushed the ship closer to Richard's estate than normal. Luke was horrified as Goodwin's men raked the berthing ship.

Murchison did not hesitate. He immediately increased sail and headed out to sea. Luke saw a potential problem, and ordered John to launch the nearest available shallop from the South Arm, and take Robert out to the receding ship. Luke rang the warning bell in a haphazard manner to attract Murchison's attention to the little shallop trying to catch him.

Out to sea Murchison surveyed the damage. A prize pig destined for a planter on the Potomac was dead, and one of his men had a flesh wound across his cheek. The Captain's first reaction was to take leave of the area as quickly as he could, but he heard the bell and saw a shallop trying to reach him. He called for his spyglass and recognised Robert Browne in the shallop. He reduced sail. The shallop eventually pulled alongside, and Robert came aboard. Some of the more easily handled goods that Murchison intended to unload at Browne's were lowered into the shallop.

Meanwhile soldiers manning the shore of West Island along the North Arm alerted Luke to a large body of men drawn up along Goodwin's riverfront. They were his convict workers. Not a dark blue uniform could be seen. Richard waving a white flag left his landing beach, and was paddling towards West Island. Luke saw an answer to one of his problems. Richard was a sitting duck. Any one of Luke's musketeers could dispatch him. This was unacceptable conduct for gentlemen, but when drums beat, laws are silent. Luke resisted the temptation. Richard was already disembarking when Luke reached the beach to greet him. The two men sat on a low rocky edge that bordered the sandy beach.

Richard began, 'I won't waste time, Colonel. I have come to negotiate your withdrawal. In the absence of Robert, who I just saw skulking away, I assume you are acting for him?'

'Don't try to claim any legal rights. Given the authority I have from Lord Baltimore I have withdrawn the grant from Robert, and leaving it to his Lordship to relocate in due course. As the province is under threat from a foreign force I am invoking all the powers of a state at war.'

'Luke, I do not underestimate your ability as a soldier, nor the loyalty of your men aided by those Protestant heretics under Sherman. But as you have prematurely discovered, I will soon have two companies of French marines to assist their advance guard, and the disciplined ruthless convict militia they have trained. My Indian allies, which I expect any day, will add hundreds to my already superior force.'

'But you are still not game to attack us until you receive all these reinforcements?' mocked Luke.

'Don't rely on that! My delay is to give you time to withdraw, and in particular to remove all the women and children from the plantations. Once the battle begins I will not be able to control the heathen – and I am not going to risk French lives to do so.'

'Richard, you have a fine record as a soldier. Why are you acting for the French?'

'I fought in an English Catholic regiment within the French army most of my life. If a civil war had not occurred in England, I would have stayed in France. The French government gave me a title, and small estate. In that world I am the Chevalier d'Anglais. Not a very original or ancient title I admit. I have spent much time at the French court, and am a friend to several powerful nobles.'

'Is this French effort the work of the young King and his wily cardinal adviser, or of the rebellious princes and Parisians, some of whom still work within the government?'

'Astute, Tremayne, but wrong! Various arms of the French government have different, but not contradictory aims. My political friends see the future of France in her colonies and navy. Others have convinced the child king that he will become the greatest general in history, and are relocating resources to the army, and plan a great extension of French borders at the expense of the Dutch, Germans and Spaniards. The French troops sent to help me are not soldiers. They are marines controlled by the navy, and the group that desperately believe France must challenge the Protestant powers along the mid Atlantic coast. At the moment France has a few islands in the West Indies, and Canada, which unfortunately is isolated by ice for more than six months of year. To develop a trading post and permanent colony, and to receive goods from the inland as the French move down the Ohio and Mississippi Rivers the French need a coastal location with a temperate climate, and ports open all the year. We must act now before the boy king embarks on his European adventures and deprives us of much needed resources.'

'These plantations are a very poor choice Richard. How can a French colony survive long on the Chesapeake? English ships, excluding ships of the line could blockade the Hampton Roads easily and cheaply, and prevent any assistance from reaching here.'

'That is why the French have built a base on the other side of the peninsula.'

'Yes, but there are no decent ports along that coastline.'

'Enough of high politics. Will you withdraw?'

'No.'

'Inform Sherman of what I have said, and get Miss Priscilla out of the area immediately. I would hate her to fall into the hands of Black Cougar. He likes white women.'

'One last question. Did you kill any of the Brownes?'

'No, but the murders have suited my purpose to destroy morale. I was involved in a number of disruptive incidents including the kidnapping of James, the musket fire across West Island, and the attack on Sherman, but I played no part in the deaths of the four Brownes.'

Luke suddenly changed his focus, 'Why keep a spy in Robert's household?'

'No comment.'

'Your spy is Abigail Hicks. She never had a sweetheart among your men at all. It was an excuse to report to you. But about what?'

'If it were once true, it is no longer so. Abigail betrayed me. You have incredible charm, Tremayne. Abigail has fallen for you. I can think of no other reason for her treachery. She was very well paid. As you have no intention of withdrawing, and handing over Browne's plantation to me, I will not waste any further time.'

With that Richard left, and was paddled across the river. Luke immediately called a conference of the defenders. He reported Richard's demands and intentions. Humphrey responded, 'Colonel the worst part of Goodwin's statement is that he will unleash an Indian attack. I have seen the ferociousness of Indian battles. Nobody is spared, and death is often tortuously slow, and horrendous. All women and children must be removed immediately.'

'His Indian allies are Black Cougar's renegade Susquehannas?' queried Andrew.

'Yes. Do we know where Black Cougar is at the moment?' replied Luke.

Andrew summed up, 'It will not help if we do. Correct strategy would be to wipe out the Susquehanna renegades before they reach Richard, and ideally do the same to the French marines on the other side of the peninsula. But we can't. We could only do that if we took every able bodied man away from here, thereby handing the plantations over to Goodwin.'

There was general agreement. They were on the horns of a dilemma. They needed to stop reinforcements and allies reaching Richard, but they did not have the manpower to do that, and at the same time defend the plantations.

'All is not lost,' said Humphrey warmly.

'Trying to cheer us up old man,' said Harry Lloyd somewhat rudely.

'Look around you. In this colony there are a few hundred settlers at the most spread across the land in isolated settlements. There are many times more Indians organized into efficient fighting machines – the Piscataway, the Nanticokes, the Lenapes and above all the main group of the Susquehanna under Tamuagh.'

'And the Jesuit trained mission Indians with their superior fire power!' added Harry obsessively.

'There is only one problem. Why would they help us? The Catholic French have a much more sympathetic attitude to the heathen than the English, Dutch and Swedish Protestants,' Andrew observed.

'You have not been in the Americas long enough. You see things from a European point of view. As far as the Indians are concerned we Europeans are about as important as a mosquito bite. The Indian nations have their own power structures and alliances. They will not intervene to help one European side against another. They will intervene, if it affects their own interests in terms of other Indian nations,' advised Humphrey.

'Is it in any of their interests to assist us?' asked Luke.

'You could not expect the papists to aid us against their co-religionists, the French. So expect no help from the mission Indians. The Nanticokes and Piscataway are unhappy under Susquehanna suzerainty, and might see a chance to get back at the Susquehanna, but as this is not the mainstream Susquehanna itself but a renegade group they may desist,' Humphrey answered.

Andrew interjected, 'From what we know the first priority of Black Cougar was to take over the Susquehanna. If we can prevent that, it would help.'

'We are dead without the help of one group of Indians or another. Governor Stone, if he decides to act might be able to raise the Piscataway. Realistically our only possible ally is the Nanticoke. I must see Straight Arrow immediately,' concluded Luke.

He decided to go alone, rather than deplete the defences of the plantations. He arrived at Straight Arrow's village at an inconvenient time. Straight Arrow was sitting in a circle with elders and other Nanticoke chieftains and medicine men - the high council of the Nanticoke nation. Straight Arrow acknowledged Luke's arrival and signalled for him to wait in his hut. Sometime later a young girl brought him a bark platter covered in berry fruits and nuts.

As he waited he could hear the voices of the high council becoming louder and argumentative. It was some hours before Straight Arrow who looked tired but elated, joined Luke.

36

'Important meeting?' asked Luke.

Straight Arrow nodded, 'The future of my people rests on the decision we have just taken. The invading Mohawks have defeated the Susquehanna under Tamuagh.'

'That should suit you. You have never willingly accepted Susquehanna sovereignty.'

'Normally it would be to our advantage, but the Mohawks instead of moving on to wipe out the Susquehanna villages have changed direction, and forced the remnants of Tamuagh's war party southwards into our territory, and away from their own villages. Tamuagh cannot get home.'

'And that is important?'

'Yes, because Black Cougar is taking advantage of the disaster, and is moving home to replace Tamuagh, and have himself proclaimed paramount chief of his nation.'

'A civil war within the Susquehanna would also suit you?'

'Not if Black Cougar wins. He will crush us. Our high council has a request from Tamuagh to go to his assistance, break the Mohawk blockade, and assist him to get home to deal with Black Cougar. Black Cougar has demanded that we remain neutral, or he would destroy us, after he has dealt with Tamuagh.'

'Who is the Council supporting, Tamuagh or Black Cougar?'

'At first it was divided. Black Cougar had strong support from several of our northern villages, but in the end the elders re-appointed me as war chief of all the Nanticokes, and ordered me to assist Tamuagh without delay. Now, Colonel, what did you want of me? I have little time.'

Luke explained the situation. Straight Arrow responded, 'If the Susquehanna join with the French to attack Browne's plantation, you will be annihilated. A united Susquehanna nation on the warpath is awesome. A few hundred Englishmen would have no chance. I cannot help. My instructions from the council are clear. All our resources are to be moved north to help Tamuagh.'

'Are there other Indians who might help us?'

'Why should they? They have their own interests, and are not going to get engaged in your petty European quarrels, unless it is in their interests. Most local tribes are indifferent to your plight, or scared of the Susquehanna. While some may assist the Governor, or larger settlements, Browne's grant is too small to risk involvement.'

'Is there no way of diverting the Susquehanna renegades?' Luke asked.

'Colonel, there is one military force that could effectively deal with Black Cougar, if it strikes now before he can draw on the full resources of the Susquehanna nation.'

'And which force is that?'

'The hard men on the Severn who believe their God will make them victorious against all heathen. Unknown to you or the Governor, that settlement is constantly being reinforced by experienced settlers from Virginia, and a few from New England. They train as soldiers every day.'

'Sherman has already asked them to send him aid.'

'Even these Puritans may not waste their resources to save an outlying plantation, which is not part of their plan for a godly settlement. You need to convince them that if Black Cougar gains the full resources of the Susquehanna nation, he poses a major threat to their very existence, let alone expansion. They must wipe him out now, while he remains a poorly supported renegade. Tomorrow will be too late.'

'But it is already too late. Black Cougar was moving towards his home villages days ago, immediately he left the new French fort,' Luke pessimistically surmised.

'Not so. Black Cougar is superstitious. He does not act without the approval of the spirits, and guidance from his dreams. My scouts have reported that he has camped on the edge of a river well to the north of Kent Island awaiting a favourable sign before he crosses it.'

'How long will he wait?'

'The spirits are free agents. They may have already given him a sign to advance, or he could have to wait days, even weeks.'

'English luck will have to prevail against the Susquehanna spirits, if I am to get a message to the Severn settlers in time to redirect them against Black Cougar.'

'I will give you a guide to lead you there by the quickest route.'

'I will return to Browne's plantation, and brief one of my men.'

'No! Your return to Browne's and your man's trip back here will cost you a day. You don't have time. And the Severn settlers may not listen to a trooper. You must go yourself, and use your authority and charm to persuade those Puritans to attack the renegade Susquehanna. After all, are you not a Colonel in their God's army?'

Straight Arrow was right. Although Luke was reluctant to leave the defence of the plantation in the hands of two young, newly appointed officers, he was confident that the experience of his sergeants, and Humphrey's advice would make up for any shortcomings. The Indian brave who followed Straight Arrow towards Luke looked vaguely familiar, despite his ferocious scowl. The war chief spoke, 'This is one of my sons, a half brother to White Deer. He is not happy to miss the oncoming battle with the Mohawks in which he could achieve his manhood. I have explained that in destroying Black Cougar, he is doing more for his people than achievements in one battle.'

Luke looked quizzically at the lad, because in addition to his bow and quiver of arrows over one shoulder, he had a light flimsy canoe strapped across the other shoulder. Straight Arrow noted Luke's interest. 'The quickest way to reach your settlers is to move as the wild geese fly. You must cross many streams and rivers where they are deep and wide. You will not have the time to move up and down the banks looking for a convenient place to cross by foot. This canoe will be useless in the Bay, but most landing places along the coast have larger and heavier canoes lying around. Now, catch some sleep. I will send a message to Humphrey to let him know what you are up to.'

It was still dark when Luke and his guide left the village. They had gradually moved closer to the Bay as the morning progressed. The tall trees and widely spaced undergrowth gave way to grasslands, and around noon Luke found himself ploughing through water covered marshes. He was increasingly uneasy. He knew how the tides rapidly covered these flats, and his experience of rising water and tidal surges made him distinctly uncomfortable. By mid afternoon discomfort changed to alarm as gathering black clouds erupted into another thunderstorm with its continuous display of lightning and thunder. As the rain poured down Luke looked anxiously around him. His guide signalled in the direction of tree covered higher ground, and both waded successfully to reach the shelter of a forested ridge.

The two men rested under an ancient tree, which diverted most of the rain. All of a sudden a bolt of lightning struck the tree, followed by the loudest of thunderclaps. Deafened by the thunder the men did not hear the noise of breaking branches which crashed towards the ground, hitting both men and pinning them to the forest floor.

Luke did not recover consciousness for several hours. He only knew this as darkness had already begun to fall. Blood had been streaming from his head although this had long ceased, and dry clots hung from his face. He struggled to lift a smaller branch that had pinned him to the ground. He eventually succeeded, and assessed the situation. The Indian lad had taken the full force of the thickest branch. His body lay mutilated, and unmoveable under its weight. He was dead.

Luke had no idea of the burial customs of the Nanticokes, but he felt a sense of honour towards Straight Arrow. He could not move the body, and contented himself with covering the corpse with other branches that the wind and lightning had stripped from the tree. The death of his guide was not his only problem. The falling branches had smashed his musket, and bent his sword. He could not recover any of the weapons of his Indian companion, and the canoe had completely disintegrated. Luke armed only with a small dagger had to progress alone. It was now dark. Luke would not risk a fire, even if he were capable of lighting one in the damp conditions. He covered himself in branches, and slept fitfully until dawn.

At first light Luke moved on, and crossed several small streams whose volume of water had been dramatically increased by the storm of the previous day. As the sun rose higher Luke became aware of agitated birds. He had learnt enough of forest lore to know that disturbed birds often indicated human presence. He advanced with increased caution, and soon heard voices, and then through the trees he glimpsed an Indian - a Susquehanna in his tell tale coiffure of half a head shaven and the other half with hair to the knees. It was the edge of Black Cougar's camp. In minutes Luke reached a large river which he guessed was Black Cougar's psychological barrier. Luke moved up river away from the camp and flung himself into the raging torrent. It was a mistake. Luke could not swim, but ever the optimist he expected to walk across, or at worst be carried to the far shore by the torrent.

Instead he was drawn down into the depths of the river, and unable to breathe. He swallowed a lot of muddy water. The torrent then fortuitously thrust his head above water. He drew a big breath and took himself under as he vaguely grasped that he was being swept passed Black Cougar's camp. The second time he surfaced with his lungs bursting, the camp had been left far behind and he was being driven to the northern shore of the river. Without warning his feet hit the riverbed. Looking back along the river he realised that the Indian camp remained relaxed. There was no sign of imminent departure. He might still have time to rally the Puritans. He followed the river to its mouth.

The estuary was littered with canoes - most of them destroyed. Upon one of the banks he found a heavy two man dugout which might withstand the vagaries of the Bay. He wasted considerable time looking among the debris for a suitable undamaged paddle. He took in the natural features around the mouth of the river so that he could give clear instructions to the settlers. Just out to sea there were three islands arranged in a triangle which would be a reliable reference point.

37

LUKE GUESSED HE WAS SOME MILES NORTH OF THE Severn settlement as he could see out in the Bay in the distance the northern shore of Kent Island. He paddled with difficulty across to the western shore of the Bay, and moved more easily down the coastline. Luckily unfavourable winds and tides dissipated, and Luke was soon approaching the estuary of the Severn, where he saw five large shallops carrying ten to twelve men each leaving the fort. Ten minutes later and he would have missed them. He rose precariously in his canoe with every chance of falling out, took off his jerkin and waved it wildly. He had almost given up hope when the leading shallop changed direction, and headed for the waving canoeist.

Luke was delighted. Edward Lloyd was in the bow of the boat. Luke was assisted aboard and he brought the Commandant up to date with developments, and put to him the alternative of wiping out the Susquehanna renegades, rather than waiting at Browne's plantation to repel what by then could be a superior force. Lloyd did not answer directly, but barked instructions to his men and the boats turned around – not towards the eastern shore, but back to Fort Providence. Luke was crestfallen. The Commandant had failed to appreciate the urgency of his request.

Luke was wrong. Back at the fort Lloyd explained, 'If I were to attack the Susquehanna renegades successfully I need many more troops than were in the shallops. My officers are scouring the settlement as we speak. By midday I should be ready to move once more.'

On schedule the Commandant set forth with all the boats he could muster. A few older settlers remained to man the fort. Luke returned to Brownes in Matthew's shallop that had brought the message of Goodwin's imminent attack. It carried eight additional men who would only marginally improve the defence of the Browne and Sherman estates. Lloyd's main flotilla headed north, and then turned east to skirt the coastline of Kent Island, while Luke turned south into yet another thunderstorm.

His return was welcome, although Matthew was heavily disappointed at the number of men he brought with him. Luke explained what had happened. He would immediately visit Straight Arrow, and inform him of his son's death. Humphrey put an end to this intention. Straight Arrow and his warriors were in the far north assisting Tamuagh against the Mohawk – days away. Humphrey would inform the boy's mother.

Harry Lloyd's leadership and organizing abilities had blossomed during Luke's absence. He had planned a thorough defensive perimeter that included West, North and South Island and Sherman's coastline along the South Arm of the river. He had developed a system in which the fields could be maintained, yet the labourers ready to take up arms and be in designated positions within minutes. Andrew and John gave glowing assessments of the young officer.

Matthew remained agitated, 'We remain seriously outnumbered. When is Edward Lloyd sending more men?'

'If the Commandant destroys Black Cougar he will be here within days with at least sixty men. The others have to return to their crops. No one can afford to be away from their fields at this time of the year, as Harry's excellent arrangements here underline,' replied Luke.

'If the worst comes to the worst, and Black Cougar with enlarged numbers comes to Goodwin's aid then we will be massacred. We must send all the women and children to the safety of St Mary's or Jamestown immediately. There is Priscilla, two female servants, twelve married women and six children. I think we should send them south in two of the shallops,' pleaded Matthew, whom Andrew assessed as in a state of panic.

'No, we will not deplete our forces by twelve to sixteen men. The women and children will wait until Murchison visits in a few days time,' declared Luke.

'There is no guarantee that Murchison will keep to his usual schedule after the reception he got on his last visit.' Harry unhelpfully contributed.

Andrew suggested, 'Send them to the protection of the Jesuit mission.'

Harry violently disagreed, 'Would you put English women at the mercy of Catholic priests with a highly armed Indian force that could turn on their masters at any time? You cannot trust the barbarian.'

Luke turned to Tim who was responsible for defences beyond the settlement, 'Do you have outposts in the forest to monitor the movement of the French marines? I am sure that Richard won't attack until he has reinforcements from the fort.'

Tim replied, 'Humphrey has recruited the Nanticoke boys who were too young to go north with Straight Arrow, to report regularly to him.'

'I should go away more often. Apart from evacuating the women and children, all that can be done has been accomplished,' concluded a satisfied Luke.

The warning bell interrupted the group's leisurely dispersal. The loud continuous peel indicated trouble, and the men quickly moved to their designated position in case of attack.

Luke ran to the bell tower, and the trooper manning it pointed out to sea, to the south. In the distance and heading for them was a large schooner. It was too far away to distinguish the colours that it flew. If this was a French ship loaded with marines they were doomed. Luke and Tim climbed the tower, and with the aid of a rather inadequate spyglass focussed on the ship's identity.

Luke was perplexed; 'She flies strange colours – a quartered standard with yellow and black in one set of diagonals and red and white in the other.'

Tim beamed, 'Relax Colonel, they are the colours of Maryland. The Governor must be aboard.'

On a second look Luke saw that it also flew the Cross of St George. It was an English ship carrying Baltimore's governor William Stone. Rather than risk Robert's quay, which could be raked by Richards's troops, the schooner anchored just beyond the South Arm of the river and immediately launched its pinnaces filled with men. The first ashore was Governor Stone. Luke was delighted, 'Your response has been remarkably quick. Many thanks. How many men have you brought?'

'Not many. You cannot recruit around St Mary's at this time of the year. I have brought with me a dozen men who form my personal guard. Most are Royalist veterans of the Civil War. However what I have done is bring supplies - food and ammunition – which should enable you to defend the plantation for some time. My men are about to unload two small cannons which might come in handy. Robert Browne went on to Jamestown, and Sir William Berkeley will undoubtedly raise a large force to eject the French. He will also redirect armed English ships from the Caribbean, which regularly stop at Jamestown, to attack the French fort you reported south of the Delaware. I have also sent messages to the Dutch and Swedish governors in the area. Neither would appreciate a French colony on their doorstep. I expect Dutch and Swedish forces to move south, and ensure the utter annihilation of the new base if our ships fail to accomplish it.'

Luke and the Governor adjourned to Robert's study at the end of the hall. Luke asked, 'Sir, as Governor do you wish to assume command of all the forces here?'

'No. Colonel. You are the soldier. I will formally place you in command of all troops here, including my own. I return to St Mary's in the morning.'

'Governor, will you take the women and children of this settlement to St Mary's? The men fear a Susquehanna massacre, and want their wives and offspring safely out of the way. Dr Sherman who is currently looking after Miss Priscilla Browne also fears that as the last Browne on the island our serial killer will take advantage of the circumstances to kill her.'

'I heard that you had someone under arrest for those crimes - a relative of the family that Browne's troop was alleged to have murdered during the War,' probed the Governor.

'Yes, all the evidence points in his direction, but I do not believe he is guilty, and in these extraordinary circumstances I have released him from supervision. He is now one of my junior officers defending the plantation. A man who wants to wipe out the Brownes is not likely to risk his life defending his enemy's property,' explained Luke, as he rationalised his controversial decision.

Mid morning of the following day the women and children gathered on a small beach on the south side of West Island to await the pinnaces that were to take them to the armed English schooner. Luke, at Humphrey's suggestion, had mugs of drinks lined up on a few trestle tables. It was basically fruit cordial enhanced with Dutch spirits and a few drops of Humphrey's tonic. He believed it would relax the women, and prepare them for an uncertain immediate future.

Priscilla, as the only gentlewoman, took the first mug at random, and sipped it slowly, if at all. The other women gathered around as Abigail topped up the mugs, joking that Rachel had only half filled them. Some of the women gulped down their drink and farewelled their husbands - often both parties in tears. Others ignored their male partners, and stared intently into the ground. Abigail refused to go. She, with the help of allocated troopers would cook for what had become a beleaguered garrison. She argued to Luke that if the men were not fed properly their health and loyalty might suffer. Luke agreed. Although he knew that she had been Richard's agent within the Browne household his lust overruled his caution - but it was becoming more than lust. Luke had found that in over a decade of fighting the company of a woman just before conflict began, was the best preparation. He increasingly needed Abigail as a companion and friend.

Priscilla was the first to board the pinnace. She gulped down her drink and gave Matthew a lingering kiss. He eventually released her, and as a sailor assisted her into the pinnace she collapsed. Matthew had her carried to the house, but it was too late. She was dead. Matthew was distraught, and as the only woman left on the island Abigail was left to wash and prepare the body. Humphrey warned Luke, 'Don't bury Miss Priscilla immediately. Her death is similar to Thomas's. She has been poisoned. It looks as if she is dead, but she might recover like her brother.'

'You supervised the drinks, old man. You must be my first suspect,' Luke commented half seriously.

'If I poisoned the drinks before Rachel and Abigail brought them to the tables, why was Priscilla the only one affected? There are another thirteen women who drank heartily; some came back for a refill and none were affected. You face the same problem as you did with Thomas. How could the poisoner know that the designated victim would choose the one poisoned offering?'

38

Luke discussed Priscilla's death with Matthew later that evening. Matthew was angry, 'That old fool Humphrey! His tonic killed her.'

' Maybe, but why were none of the other women affected. Priscilla had the choice of some twenty mugs and she chose the only one containing poison.'

'How was she alone poisoned?' asked Matthew soulfully.

'It had to be in the drink. She only sipped hers until she was about to leave. Then she gulped it down in one hit – and died. Is there a substance that if you drink it slowly does you no harm, but in a large amount all at once, could kill you?' questioned Luke.

Matthew replied cautiously, 'There may be, but how would the killer know that Priscilla would gulp rather than sip? With her upbringing he should have presupposed genteel sipping.'

'Perhaps it was an accident. I'll ask Humphrey what exactly he put into the drinks, and question Abigail as to its preparation.'

Abigail was in the cookhouse with her two soldier assistants, whose presence forced Luke to show some discretion. He beckoned Abigail to follow him outside. He led her towards her hut. She followed - half angry at being dragged away from her work to satisfy Luke's lust, yet at the same time pleased that he still had designs towards her. She was disappointed. Luke gathered up her few possessions. 'As the only woman on the island, and with so many new and unknown characters seconded here, you are moving into the manor house. Take Rachel's old room!'

'Very convenient Luke – for you. You are in the next room.'

'All the better to protect you,' teased Luke.

Luke moved Abigail into the manor house. Once settled she wanted to return to the cookhouse, but Luke motioned her to sit on the bed. Again the expected dalliance did not occur. Luke was focussed on his questions. 'What do you know about the drinks that were provided for the departing women?'

'Twenty mugs were set out on a table in the cookhouse. Humphrey poured a small amount of his tonic into each. The mugs were then taken to the outside trestles where Rachel filled them from the jugs of fruit juice, strengthened by a fair amount of Dutch spirits. She half filled each cup because she was not sure how much we had left. She had just finished her task when the women arrived, and Miss Priscilla took a mug. I noticed they were half full and we still had a full jug left so I asked the other women to wait until I had filled all the cups to the brim – which I did.'

'How many jugs were prepared?'

'Two jugs, prepared by me, at the same time, in the cookhouse.'

Luke could not resist a big hug, but for Abigail the mood had passed. She broke free and returned to her chores. Luke was chastened, and went in search of Humphrey who was finally located at the far end of North Island, supervising the workers topping plants and removing the suckers. It was a warm day and Humphrey was happy to sit awhile under a bushy shrub. Luke began his questioning. 'One difference, that witnesses have mentioned between Priscilla and the rest of the women, is that the other women drained their mugs progressively. Priscilla hardly touched hers until the last minute before departure, and then gulped it down in one effort. Were there any ingredients in your potion that could have had a bad effort on the drinker, if swallowed quickly?'

'There was nothing in my tonic that could have harmed people. It was a herb that induces relaxation, and in big doses – which I did not use – sleep.'

'Can you explain what happened?'

'No, but the evidence is simple and straightforward. We have missed the obvious,' mused Humphrey.

'How did Priscilla's behaviour differ from the other women?' Luke asked, as much to himself as to the old retainer.

The two men sat in silence for several minutes, then Humphrey jumped to his feet and exclaimed, 'God's Blood! It's obvious. Priscilla was the only person who drank from a mug that had not been topped up by Abigail.'

'How does that help our probe?' asked a confused Luke.

'That's the vital clue. Whatever was in the jug that Abigail used to top up the mugs prevented the other women from dying. This reminds me so much of Thomas's death. We know that One Ear gave Thomas a poison, and also an antidote. The original draft was poisoned. The top up contained the antidote.'

'Jehu! I did miss the obvious. I must requestion Abigail immediately,' replied Luke with a sinking heart.

Before Luke could follow up this vital lead a young Indian boy came running through the field, having beached his canoe on the eastern end of North Island. The boy spoke to Humphrey who immediately translated, 'The French marines, sixty to eighty have crossed the ridge, and are heading for Goodwin's.

The warning bell rang long and loud. Men stopped work, and took up their allotted positions. The allied leaders met on West Island. Harry opened the discussion, 'Colonel, we should attack the marines before they reach us. As regular soldiers they probably have no experience of guerrilla warfare. Remember how the Irish, usually heavily outnumbered could tie down companies of our troops when they used this approach.'

'Do we have time?' Luke asked.

'Yes, we could delay them, and hopefully demoralise the more recent conscripts. A small party could launch a series of hit and run raids. We ambush them, killing as many as we can in bursts of initial musket fire, then fade back into the woods. We move ahead of them, and attack them again and again,' outlined an enthusiastic Harry.

'Good idea Harry! Take twenty men including Andrew but I want you all back here ahead of the marines who survive your attacks.'

Harry and his men departed, and Luke thought aloud. 'Richard will not attack until the additional marines reach him. Before that the odds would not be overwhelmingly in his favour, and he does not know how many extra men Governor Stone brought with him. The visit of such a large schooner may have misled him into thinking that it unloaded hundreds of men. He may even wait until he gets his Susquehanna reinforcements.'

Tim disagreed completely, 'He can't wait. He must know that we have sent for help from across two colonies. He can't afford to wait for his Indians, because with the help of our reinforcements from Virginia he will be outnumbered. His current advantage is his vast superiority in trained professional soldiers. He has over a hundred French marines, we have twenty five Parliamentary troopers and ten Royalist veterans from Stone's bodyguard.'

' I don't think that matters. The majority of all the militias are former soldiers from both sides of our civil war,' replied Luke.

The conversation ceased as six heavily manned shallops rounded the headland at the estuary of the North Arm. To Luke's surprise they moved out to sea, and made landfall well south of the South Arm. They were going to attack Matthew from the southwest moving overland towards his house and fields. The North Island sentries noted dozens of canoes that crossed the river from Richard's, but paddled down the South Arm, passed the eastern edge of North and South Island and landed on the mainland where Sherman's plantation began.

They would make their way along the river line and attack Sherman from the northeast.

Luke was disconcerted. Harry's planning had been based on defending North and West Island and then if necessary withdrawing to Sherman's mainland. He had not expected the initial attack would be a pincer movement against Matthew, or that it would be launched at this time. Luke now faced a dilemma - deplete the main force on West and North Island to aid Matthew, or ask Matthew to immediately withdraw as quickly as he could to West Island?

Matthew solved the problem. 'Luke, I have no defences against an attack from the landside. We would have to face the French in the open fields where professional soldiers shine. It is too late to stop the western attack in the forests. I will move my people here before the two arms of the attackers meet.' Matthew ran to his canoe, and within fifteen minutes his people were streaming across the South Arm of the river. This gave Luke another problem. Would he defend South Island? After discussion with Tim, John and Matthew, who had rejoined them, it was decided to consolidate the defence to West and North Island. Tim and John were soon barking orders as men were relocated to different locations. The southern coastline of both these islands would be reinforced.

Later in the day Trooper Ackroyd who had remained on the southern edge of South island to spy on the enemy reported that the two wings of the invaders had met, and they had redeployed themselves along the South Arm of the river. The shallops that had disembarked the troops further down the coast had reappeared on Dr Sherman's landing bay. Simultaneously Luke's lookouts on the eastern edge of North Island reported canoeists pulling four or five empty canoes behind them moving towards the same location. With the arrival of the canoeists and the shallops the enemy had sufficient transport to cross the river in great numbers and assault West Island from the south.

Luke hoped that Richard would await the arrival of his additional marines before launching from the north a frontal attack on West and North Island. Luke expected that when this occurred the marines and convict militia now entrenched along the South Arm of the river would simultaneously attack from the south. Night fell, and Luke was appalled to find that it was an overcast sky, and no early moon. It was pitch black – the perfect conditions for Richard to strike. Luke ordered his men to gather as much wood as they could find, and light fires around the perimeter of their defences. This would enable Richard's men to see where they were going, but it also afforded the defenders at least some warning of attack.

Later that evening Harry and Andrew returned. Harry was ashen faced. 'Sorry Luke, we did not slow them down, and they took very few, if any, casualties. We were out manoeuvred. There were one hundred and fifty men, twice what we expected, and after our first attack a small detachment of marines came after us, and instead of being the attacker, we became the hunted. I was wrong. At least some of the marines were experienced woodland fighters, no doubt trained in the wilds of Canada. The main body of troops marched relentlessly on, and would have reached Goodwin's well before now. We had to take diversions to avoid the pursuing marines. Then coming in through Sherman's land we discovered it infested with enemy troops. We had to backtrack, and came across through North Island. Have we missed much of the action?'

Luke brought Harry and Andrew up to date. Given the large addition to Richard's forces, and the imminence of the attack at first light, Luke cut his losses. He recalled all his men from North Island. He would concentrate his defences on West Island, and in the last resort, about the house. He left a couple of men on South and North Island to create the impression that they were occupied, which might delay the attack on West Island.

246

39

Luke's delaying plan worked – but only briefly. At dawn Richard's frontal attack began. His troops fired across the river at Luke's defences on West Island, while the shallops unloaded marines on South Island. These shallops immediately headed into the Bay and north to beyond the estuary of the North Arm. It was clear that they would return loaded with the recently arrived marines. Constant musket fire on both sides of the river was just a skirmish, and serving no purpose. Luke ordered his men to stop firing, and conserve their ammunition until Richard's forces invaded West Island.

After some delay the shallops returned around the headland but instead of sailing directly for the northern edge of the island where Luke had concentrated his defences they landed their troops on the southwest edge of West Island. As soon as they had unloaded the marines the boats moved to the northern edge of South Island to pick up the troops who had moved through South Island unmolested. Simultaneously with the appearance of the shallops around the headland, a hundred canoes were launched across the river containing a few marines but mainly Richard's convict militia. Both the French marines and convict militia were equipped with the same modern muskets as those that the Jesuit fathers had made available to their Indian charges.

Within the hour Luke's men were forced back on all fronts, although luckily with little loss of life. He pined for his horses. A good cavalry charge would have sent the marines flying. Instead his men were now concentrated behind a hastily erected low fence around the manor house. The cannons were proving almost useless. The attackers remained spread out, and refused to present a viable target to the artillery. The only success was a lucky shot that shattered and sank a loaded shallop, although most of its passengers escaped unharmed.

Luke's defensive fence consisted of large logs on top of each other giving a height of roughly a yard behind which the English felt reasonably secure. Behind these Luke had raised a number of low towers from which the defenders could look down on the attackers and beyond this again, a number of men were located on the roof of the house – a most dangerous position, as they had no protection.

The French marines were a highly efficient force. This was no hastily collected contingent for some wild adventure in the Americas. The French had committed one of its better fighting units to a cause it obviously considered important. This was not a local skirmish between Goodwin and Browne, but a battle for colonial possessions between France and England. Luke must hold out, not for the pitiful Browne, but for the sake of his country.

It was not long before the marines breached the outer defences, forcing Luke and his men back to the house. Luke noticed Abigail armed with a musket at one of the upper windows. A marine lieutenant scaled the defensive logs and headed for the house. Luke saw Abigail fire. The officer went down. Luke could only surmise it was a direct hit to the head or heart. He had little time to ponder on Abigail's marksmanship as several marines came running towards his position, and engaged in a deadly sword fight with the defenders. The English repelled the first onslaught, but injuries were multiplying rapidly. A second onslaught was harder to repel. At a crucial stage of a duel with a young marine lieutenant Luke slipped and the officer drew back his sword to deliver the fatal blow. Luke heard an explosion, and blood spurted from the young man's chest. Luke looked around and there was Abigail with a big smile of her face, her musket still smoking. He was beginning to love that woman.

Suddenly the firing ceased. From the midst of the French attackers Richard emerged with Jean de Liette carrying a white flag. 'Come to surrender have we Richard?' Luke asked with scarcely any humour.

'I have come once more to negotiate. None of us want this needless loss of life, nor delay from tending the tobacco fields. You are clearly outnumbered, and it is only a matter of time before we take the house. Surrender now, and your people can leave by the next available ship. In fact my new shallops will ferry your people to the Severn, or St Mary's. I will assume the lordship of this grant as a vassal of His Christian Majesty King Louis XIV of France. I will also take over the indentures of all servants who will be forced to continue to work the plantations.'

Luke was outnumbered. To risk the lives of the settler militias against a superior foe was stupid. Nevertheless he stalled for time. 'You make an overwhelming case, but as my defenders are made up of various groups I will need to talk to their leaders.'

'Half an hour,' declared an imperious Richard.

Right on time Richard and Liette returned. Luke was preparing to hand his sword to the marine officer as a token of his formal surrender when one of the men on the roof called out, 'Three large ships sailing directly for us from the south west.'

All parties froze, awaiting identification. The wait was excruciating. Finally the lookout shouted with enthusiasm, 'They are English.' Unrestrained cheering broke out among the defenders.

Luke replaced his sword in his scabbard, 'Richard, the wheel has turned. These are trained Virginia militia with Indian auxiliaries – probably four or five hundred men. We have been relieved.'

Richard coolly moved away. Liette assessed the situation and within minutes withdrew his troops with military precision. Before the English ships had unloaded any men, the

French had returned to Richard's plantation. Luke waited outside Robert's house to receive his rescuers. At their head, was the charismatic Governor of Virginia, Sir William Berkeley. Luke was right. Most of the men were experienced Indian fighters from the frontiers of Virginia. Luke was surprised to find a smattering of uniformed troops. Sir William explained that they were Royalist troops who had fled Ireland and were seeking service in the West Indies. A ship carrying them had just landed at Jamestown as he was raising men for his emergency expedition. He conscripted them.

In the next group of people approaching the house was Robert Browne. Luke moved to greet him and thank him for persuading Berkeley to send help so quickly. A few minutes later and the result would have been a humiliating defeat. The two men stretched their hands towards each other, and for the second time that day, Luke felt a whoosh pass his ear, and witnessed the man opposite him slump to the ground with a musket shot to the heart. He swung around in time to see a puff of smoke spiralling away from a window in the house - the same window that Abigail had used earlier in the day.

Berkeley's officers hustled him out of the way, initially concerned that the Governor might be the next target. Luke ordered John to go to the window and secure the scene, and Andrew to find Abigail, and confine her to her room, with a trooper on guard. Luke met with Governor Berkeley. The task was only half completed. West Island had been saved from French attack, but a large French force occupied the mainland north of the river and had a major base on the other side of the peninsula. Both had to be removed. Sir William spoke first, 'This is an awkward legal situation. I have no authority here. I represent the Royalist government and have full authority only within the borders of Virginia.'

Luke cut through the legalities, 'Let's avoid any contention between the government of Charles II and that of the English Republic. This land as bestowed by the King's father is the property of Lord Baltimore. I currently represent Lord Baltimore, and have authority to suspend existing jurisdictions until Baltimore can decide the situation. Under that power, I formally give you authority to operate within Baltimore's grant to restore law and order, and to eject the French.'

'Thank you Tremayne. Stone has given me similar authority. Where do we go now?'

'Governor, you are now in charge of this military operation. I suggest you negotiate with Richard Goodwin and the French marines for their immediate withdrawal.' The meeting was almost immediately interrupted by one of Berkeley's orderlies who reported that a French marine officer carrying a white flag was being rowed across the river in a small shallop. Sir William asked his orderly to immediately escort the French officer to them.

Liette was blunt. With the English alerted to their plans the French must cut their losses, and leave the area. The initial negotiations were simple and to the point. The French would withdraw to their fort and wait there for two English ships that would take them to the French island of Guadeloupe. Luke suggested that the English should monitor this withdrawal. Both leaders rounded on him. Sir William was direct, 'This tiny settlement may be important in your world, but our prime interest is the total withdrawal of the French from these colonies. Most of the men in all the groups now under my command need to return to their fields, or they will be ruined financially.'

Liette also responded, 'A French captain of marines has given his word. We will quietly withdraw to Guadeloupe with the aid of English ships, who undoubtedly will charge a fortune for our passage, and there await further orders.'

'No, captain you will be transported free of charge in return for all your muskets, powder, shot and artillery which you have here, or at your fort,' smiled Berkeley as he added an additional condition.

'You drive a hard bargain Sir William,' muttered Liette as he nodded a reluctant acceptance of the terms.

Luke was not satisfied, but he changed the topic,' I thought Mr Goodwin, or should I say the Chevalier D'Anglais, would be part of this meeting.'

Liette replied with a hint of disgust, 'So did I. But he has disappeared.'

'Do you know where he is?' asked Luke.

'No,' answered the Frenchman coldly.

Sir William ended the meeting, and called for drinks. The three men chatted for some time until Liette excused himself to organize the withdrawal. The Englishmen continued drinking when an orderly again interrupted, 'Sir William, Commandant Lloyd has landed, and wishes to speak to you and Colonel Tremayne.'

Edward Lloyd was warmly greeted by Luke, and less so by Sir William. Lloyd immediately congratulated the victors.

Luke asked, 'And what about your attack on Black Cougar? How did it go?'

'God gave us a brilliant victory. Black Cougar is dead, and the few braves that survived have sneaked home to their villages ready to applaud their successful war chief Tamuagh, who with the Nanticoke's help have finally turned back the Mohawks.'

Sir William brought Edward Lloyd up to date. Lloyd fully agreed with the Governor that the priorities were to get the French out, and to return the various English militias to their fields. Lloyd was not as happy about the disappearance of Richard Goodwin, and suggested that the French marines knew exactly where he was. 'The man is disguised as one of the marines. You need to interview every marine to find him.'

Luke saw some hope, 'Why don't we do that?'

Sir William replied, 'Colonel you have not been in the Americas long enough. As soon as we lined up the marines Richard would quietly slip away into the forest. He may already be on his way to the fort ahead of the main detachment. Even if we had the time and the manpower to examine the marines again at the fort, Richard's ability to disappear would be equally possible. Finding needles in haystacks is easy compared to finding a particular individual in this American wilderness.'

It was Lloyd who changed the subject, 'What happens to Browne's grant?'

Sir William turned to Luke, 'Have you had time to determine the immediate future of this settlement?'

'I will appoint Matthew Sherman as the temporary holder of the grant to ensure that the tobacco crops on all three plantations are harvested. I understand that with the death of Priscilla, Matthew wishes eventually to return to the Severn. By Robert's will it has been left to one of his nephews who will probably take over the grant in time for next season. Sir William, I will temporarily leave my men under your control for the next few days, but will withdraw myself from the mechanics of the French withdrawal and the return of the English militias to their various homes, and concentrate on solving the death of Robert Browne.'

'A bad business, a whole family murdered by an unknown killer. Isn't this the family you were sent to protect?' teased the Royalist Governor with eyes atwinkling.

40

Luke withdrew, smarting from Berkeley's friendly gibe, and made his way to Abigail's room. He could not bring himself to question her. He signalled for the trooper on guard to stay in place, and he withdrew to his own room. Emotionally he was a mess. His feelings for Abigail were deeper than he had suspected. Thoughts that she was involved in the death of Priscilla and Robert completely devastated him.

It was twenty four hours before he brought himself to visit Abigail, who sensuously asked, 'Am I locked up for the pleasure of the victor?'

'Abigail, thank you for saving my life. I have been near death many times, but never as close as that. How you missed me, and hit the marine officer in the chest from the angle you were at, required the skills of an experienced marksman. The cookhouse does not train you in such skills.'

'No, but having a father who was an expert marksman, and who brought us up on a chateau in France with daily hunting expeditions, when he was not on campaigns, is excellent training.'

'That information bears on the other matter, the shooting of Robert Browne. The shot came from the same window where you spent the day.'

'Yes, it did. I was firing to celebrate our victory and a shot went astray,' Abigail said with a teasing smile. Luke was momentarily distracted. He wanted to grasp at this fanciful explanation to free Abigail from suspicion of murder. But common sense prevailed.

'But Abigail it hit Robert right through the heart.'

'Yes, my father would have been delighted with me,' she proudly announced.

'What do you mean?'

There was a long silence. Abigail drew in a deep breath and exhaled slowly and noisily, and confessed, 'It is over. Father can rest in peace. Mother of God forgive me.'

There was another long pause as tears welled up in her eyes. She held both of Luke's hands, and looked him directly in the eyes. 'Luke, I have avenged my father's death. I am ready to face the consequences. I killed all the Brownes as planned, and Willie Green to buy me time to complete the mission.'

Luke was staggered. He suspected that Abigail was involved in the deaths of Priscilla and Robert, but to be responsible for all was beyond his comprehension. He took Abigail in his arms and whispered, 'Why, why? Why destroy a whole family?'

'Because Robert Browne destroyed mine. I am not Abigail Hicks. I am Abigail Goodes, daughter of Robert Browne's deputy who was executed for the massacre at Beale Hall. My twin brother and I saw father the night before he died. On the Blood of Christ he swore that he had spoken the truth. Browne had ordered the massacre, and that at the court martial four of the troopers who knew the truth had lied to protect their Colonel. Father believed that as Browne had destroyed a whole family, justice would only be achieved if the families of Browne, and the lying troopers were annihilated. My brother and I promised father that we would avenge his wrongful death in the manner he desired.'

'What did you do after your father's death?'

'Our mother died within months of father during an influenza epidemic. I knew that Robert Browne had left the country, but I approached his brother Mr Charles, a kindly man. I explained who we were and implied that Mr Robert Browne had a duty to look after us. Charles took us in as servants. At the same time he began to employ former troopers of Robert's disbanded unit. Three of these were men father had named. My brother killed two of them and their families, but in attempting to ambush a third he was killed in a fight that ensued. It was then I decided to come to Maryland, and complete my sacred mission. I had to kill Willie Green. He knew me as Abigail Goodes and my mission was not completed.'

'How did you kill Thomas? I was convinced that I had proved that as an accidental death.'

'You were absolutely right Colonel. Thomas accidentally killed himself, but I could have saved him – and did not. He gave me the antidote to the poison he had used, and asked that when James, who was his intended victim slumped forward apparently dead, I should give him a glass of water which contained the antidote.'

'Why did Thomas trust you with this. He was not a friendly type, and he clearly was not your sort of man.'

'You are an insensitive blackguard Tremayne. No man can resist me. That strange boy only wanted a female hand to run over his privy parts, and he was forever grateful. I also showed a great interest in his poisons and antidotes, and he taught me much. That is how I killed Priscilla. The half empty mugs that I cleverly let Rachel fill contained the poison. After Priscilla chose her mug I quickly filled the others with the antidote. It was so easy,' gloated a satisfied Abigail.

'You poisoned these two, and you shot two others. I was misled because James would have had to been shot by an excellent marksman. At the time I was ignorant of your ability.'

'Shooting James was opportunistic. I was on North Island and had just made love to that beautiful Sir Timothy. After he left I looked out of the hut, waiting till it was appropriate to leave, when I saw James talking to Humphrey and about to row in this direction. I had seen the muskets in the hut and the supplies of ammunition. I took a musket and moved onto the headland. I waited till James had turned his body at an acute angle and shot him. I thought that that might confuse you as to the location of the shot. I returned to the hut, replaced the musket, and waited until most people had disappeared from sight. To the casual observer I was just returning from delivering the food for the plantation workers.'

'And Willie Green and Mistress Elizabeth did not die in their sleep of natural causes?'

'No, but they had peaceful deaths. I mixed a sleeping draft into their drinks. While they slept I smothered them in their beds. My hut was next to Willie's, and when I went to wake Rachel in the morning, I entered Mistress Elizabeth's room first.'

'And Lucy?'

'I was on the river and I noticed Tim leave Lover's Cove. I suspected that his lover would have been Lucy because apart from myself there are not many available women. I ran my canoe ashore, one of the many that lie about West Island, and in no way recognizable as being mine or used by me. Lucy was dressing and asked me to help lace her bodice. I moved behind her, ran my hands down her face and strangled her. Because my left hand hurt I folded my fingers and allowed my knuckles to eat into her neck.'

'That is why I suspected Black Cougar of the murder. With fingers missing strangulation by pressing the knuckles into the neck seemed a possibility. Where did Goodwin fit into your murderous scheme? What was your link with him?'

'What is my link with any man on this settlement, including you?'

'So Richard was your secret sweetheart on his plantation?'

'Not recently. At the beginning, yes. He was infatuated with me. I expressed some negative views about Robert Browne, especially the way he treated servants and family. I told Richard that Browne was a violent and evil man. Richard indicated that he too had his problems with Robert. He offered me a position with him. For obvious reasons I rejected it, but promised to pass on any information that might help him at a price. It was only when he kidnapped Robert that I turned against him. He was removing my opportunity to kill Robert. That is why I told you what had happened. My only regret is that Robert did not die a slow and painful death. Unfortunately I knew time was running out, especially after I left myself a suspect after Priscilla's death. I guessed Humphrey would put two and two together. I had to take the first opportunity which arose, and this unfortunately gave the monster a clean exit. All this talking has made me thirsty. Could you ask your trooper to get me some water?'

Luke obliged.

'What will happen to me now?' asked Abigail

'You will be tried for murder, and hanged,' Luke solemnly announced.

'Can you do one last thing for me?'

Luke turned to Abigail, 'What is your final request?'

'Make love to me.'

Luke did not answer. Such an act was inconceivable in the circumstances. On the other hand she had saved his life, and to refuse her last request would be mean. The trooper returned with a large container of water. Luke spoke to her gently, 'Abigail, I will come back shortly.' Luke needed to think. He climbed aboard a canoe and refusing to paddle let the tide take him out into the Bay. As he drifted he made his decision. He would express his love for Abigail, and promise to stand by her through her trial, and to the moment of her hanging. He would love and comfort her, but eschew any sexual activity.

Half an hour later Luke returned. He let himself quietly into the room. Abigail lay on her back completely naked except for a small silver cross she wore as a necklace. She was indeed very beautiful. Then a cold chill ran down Luke's spine. He saw her vacant stare, and then noticed a pouch of dried herbs that had spilt onto the bedside table.

Abigail was dead by her own hand.

Luke partly dressed the girl, and sent his trooper to bring Dr Sherman who confirmed that the girl died by the same poison that had killed Priscilla and Thomas. Luke threw himself on his bed and sobbed. It was so unfair. Luke fantasised that Abigail was a beautiful avenging angel, and the dysfunctional collection of individuals, the demonic Brownes, deserved their fate. The pressures of the last days caught up with Luke who did not awake until after midday the next day. He missed Captain Murchison's latest visit, which brought good news for Tim. The courts had decided in his favour, and he would return home as soon as possible as Sir Timothy Beale and with authority to repossess his family estates. After a short service early that afternoon conducted by Berkeley's chaplain, Abigail and Robert were buried.

Luke took one last trip up river with Humphrey to visit Straight Arrow. Luke explained in detail how his son had died, and the two men hugged, and then departed with tears in their eyes. On the way downstream Humphrey told Luke that Sir Timothy had offered him a position on his English estates, but he had decided to see out his days on the Chesapeake.

The two men had almost reached West Island when they heard shouting from upriver, and could see Straight Arrow and several his braves paddling furiously after them. Luke and Humphrey pulled into the bank and allowed the Indians to overtake them. Luke commented, 'Jehu! Straight Arrow, what's the hurry? There hasn't been another murder?'

After a significant pause Straight Arrow replied, 'Yes, there has.'

The Nanticoke chieftain pulled a half empty canoe beside that of the Englishmen. Lying in it was the dead body of Richard Goodwin. Luke gasped, 'Do you know what happened?'

'Yes, one of the young boys you had spying on the French saw Goodwin moving quickly through the undergrowth as soon as the battle ended. He was followed by two of his convict labourers who without warning fired their beautiful muskets into his back. His harsh treatment of these men returned to kill him.'

The following day Luke asked Governor Berkeley to take his men to Jamestown, so that they could return to England. Their mission was over. It had been a total failure. The family that they had been sent to help were wiped out under their very noses. Lord Baltimore's province was nearly taken over by the French, and had to be rescued by the Severn Puritans and the Royalists from Virginia – neither of them natural friends of his Lordship's authority.

Chaos, not Lord Baltimore, ruled on the upper Chesapeake.

Other Luke Tremayne Adventures

THE SPANISH RELATION

A gripping murder mystery set in 1655 against the potential collapse of the Cromwellian regime. Luke Tremayne is sent by Cromwell as his special envoy to investigate the murder of an obscure Somerset squire. Tremayne discovers that the squire's family and village are deeply divided, revealing a multitude of suspects – feuding relatives, corrupt politicians, a secret Royalist society, clandestine militias, Spanish agents, religious fanatics and wanton witches. Luke stumbles on a plot to alter the government, and in the process, experiences the suspicion, violence, bawdiness and superstitions of village life; enjoys the attention of several lusty women; and is perplexed by a mystery man wearing a golden cape. (Trafford 2007)

THE IRISH FIASCO

In 1648 Cromwell sent Luke to Ireland to investigate the murder of a fellow officer and the disappearance of a fortune in Spanish silver. Disaster strikes before he leaves England and an obsessed deputy creates additional tension. Luke is thwarted by the mysterious Arabella and confronted by several fanatics. Lust leads him to near death deep in the Wicklows where he discovers a secret refuge and a sensual witch. In completing his mission he uncovers a traitor at the heart of the English government and contributes to a military victory that paves the way for Cromwell's reduction of Ireland. In a final twist Luke's world is turned upside down (Trafford 2008)

COMING SOON

THE BLACK THISTLE

*In 1651 over a decade of Scottish independence was under
threat from the armies of the English republic, and a resurgence of
Royalist support for Charles II who wanted to restore the English
dominated monarchy. As Scottish political leaders wavered as to
whom they would support some of them plotted and murdered their
way to a solution. Luke finds himself in a castle in the Western
Highlands, the location of several kidnapped victims and their
possible abductors, and the alleged source of a conspiracy to murder
the Scottish political elite and the English military high command -
a murder mystery, high adventure and political intrique*